Also by R.G. Armstrong:
Silicon Valley Affair

Hollywood Heyday

R. G. Armstrong

HOLLYWOOD HEYDAY

iUniverse books may be ordered through booksellers or by contacting:

iUniverse
1663 Liberty Drive
Bloomington, IN 47403
www.iuniverse.com
1-800-Authors (1-800-288-4677)

*Because of the dynamic nature of the Internet, any web addresses or links contained in
this book may have changed since publication and may no longer be valid. The views
expressed in this work are solely those of the author and do not necessarily reflect the
views of the publisher, and the publisher hereby disclaims any responsibility for them.*

*Any people depicted in stock imagery provided by Thinkstock are models,
and such images are being used for illustrative purposes only.
Certain stock imagery © Thinkstock.*

ISBN: 978-1-5320-1250-1 (sc)
ISBN: 978-1-5320-1252-5 (hc)
ISBN: 978-1-5320-1251-8 (e)

Library of Congress Control Number: 2016920065

Print information available on the last page.

iUniverse rev. date: 02/02/2017

This book is dedicated to Russ and Rusty, upon whose Hollywood days the story is based; and, to Lynn and John, each of whom believed in my writing ability before I did.

Hollywood 1928

Hollywood has now become America's fashion harbinger. Hollywood Boulevard between Vine Street and the Hotel Roosevelt is lined with exclusive specialty shops. These stores can now be considered the most chic in America. They contain stunning, modern and elegant fashions, in the finest of fabrics. The styles are a year ahead of the rest of America.

All the world is intrigued by the sartorial splendor of the Hollywood film stars who obtain their wardrobes from this magic mile. A leisurely stroll along this boulevard of movie dreams confirms to the educated eye that the fashion center of America and perhaps the world has now shifted from New York's 5th Avenue to Hollywood, California.

Mencken, H.L., ed. "Strolling Along The Boulevard." *The American Mercury*, Vol. 14, No. 55 (July 1928), 312.

PART I

TEXAS 1928

CHAPTER ONE

HOUSTON, TEXAS 1928

"The moon belongs to ev'ryone. The best things in life are free ..." Edna Mae abruptly stopped skipping and singing as she approached the front porch. Her auburn hair continued bouncing as she danced up the steps. Opening the front door she was surprised to see Aunt Lillie and Uncle Justin sitting on the parlor sofa. *Oh, oh. Trouble.* Aunt Lillie was ignoring her own dictum that the antimacassars must be kept pristine for company.

"Edna Mae, sit down," Aunt Lillie ordered as she pointed to the uncomfortable mahogany chair directly across from the sofa.

Oh, oh, thought Edna, *she usually calls me 'Sugar.'* Edna sat down and looked towards Uncle Justin who shifted his head down and averted her glance. Edna's blue eyes then focused on the lace pattern in the antimacassar showing behind Aunt Lillie's left shoulder.

"We need to talk to you," Aunt Lillie continued. Then forcefully, "I want you to look at me when I talk to you."

Edna moved her gaze from the white lace pattern and directed her attention towards the general vicinity of her aunt's face.

"Your Uncle Justin and I attended the First Baptist Church near Laurabeth's house today. We thought we would see you there with her family. Her mom and dad asked us where you girls were. Laurabeth had told them that you two were spending last night here. Where were you?"

Edna knew whatever she said would not curb her Aunt's anger but she took some time to formulate an acceptable response.

"Edna Mae, answer me. Where were you this weekend?"

Edna looked over at Uncle Justin again, attempting to gain his usual sympathy and alliance. He was still avoiding her.

"Justin, tell her to speak up," Aunt Lillie commanded.

"Edna, honey," Uncle Justin complied, "you'd better answer your aunt." He now looked at Edna and shrugged his shoulders.

Edna knew Aunt Lillie's dogged nature, and determined that only the truth could expedite this discussion. But Edna was of an equally resolute nature. She defiantly raised her chin up, focused directly on Aunt Lillie and calmly stated, "Laurabeth and I went to a party in Dallas with a couple of friends. We didn't do anything bad. Jimmy Griffin was at the party and he drove me back to Houston. Nothing happened. We're all fine. I'm 16 years old and I should be able to live my own life, Aunt Lillie. I didn't go to Dallas to defy you or hurt you. We just wanted to have some fun."

As she was talking, Edna noticed her aunt's face turning a reddish color. Uncle Justin looked surprised, but then a glint in his eyes also revealed some amusement. Edna had that strong-willed, determined spirit from her daddy, while Justin didn't share his brother's nature.

"Edna Mae," Aunt Lillie said shrilly, "you lied. That's sinful. You told us you were spending the night at Laurabeth's. I've been worried about your behavior for some time now. You have too many male callers. Why would they all be stopping by to see you unless you were doing something you shouldn't?"

Uncle Justin remained silent.

Edna was suddenly disgusted by Uncle Justin's passivity. *I sure wish my daddy was alive. He'd stick up for me.*

"Answer me, Edna. You've been having sex; haven't you? You're just a little hussy. God punishes hussies and whores."

Edna was stunned by the direction this was taking. No polite words arose to answer Aunt Lillie's absurd accusation. Edna stared at her intensely.

"Edna Mae, you answer me this second," Aunt Lillie shouted as she stood up and started walking towards Edna.

Now the situation was escalating to a matter of self-preservation.

"Okay, Aunt Lillie. I'll answer you."

Aunt Lillie stopped moving towards her.

Against Edna's flicker of better judgment she spewed,

"I think you have a dirty mind, and despite all your so-called religion, you don't know how to act with compassion and love like *The Bible* teaches. I told you nothing happened and we're all fine, but you won't believe me. Yes, I was wrong to lie, but you're wrong when you condemn everyone who doesn't think like you do. Your judgment of everyone and everything is so hateful--"

Aunt Lillie again moved towards Edna.

"--and, you've never even adjusted to modern times. You won't let me listen to the radio, or dance. You don't like make-up or movies or fashion. You are--"

Aunt Lillie abruptly slapped Edna's left cheek hard.

Edna fell silent again. *I shouldn't have spoken.* Remembering a Sunday School lesson, she turned her right cheek towards her aunt and defiantly dared Aunt Lillie to hit her again.

Aunt Lillie turned around, walked back and sat down next to Uncle Justin where for a moment she calmly acted as if nothing had occurred. Edna and her aunt then began staring at one another, each trying to outdo the other's gaze, while Uncle Justin shifted uncomfortably on the sofa.

After a full half minute that felt to Edna like five, Aunt Lillie was the first to speak. "I'm taking you to the doctor this week. He'll check you out and we'll see if you're still a nice girl. Forget any plans you might have had for your day off from the slaughterhouse. Now go to your room. No supper. You're out of control. I'm sure your mama and daddy are turning over in their graves."

Edna calmly stood up and walked towards her room. *How dare Aunt Lillie say that my parents are turning over in their graves. Aunt Lillie can't begin to understand my parents' good natures, and the brightness of life around them. Aunt Lillie's perpetually tied up in knots within her own self-righteous, judgmental, so-called "Christian" behavior.*

Edna was careful to not slam her door shut. She kept to her usual routine of laying out her clothes for the slaughterhouse the next day. *I'm grateful I have a job, and this room in Uncle Justin's house. Even though Aunt Lillie doesn't treat me with respect, I respect myself, and no one, not even Aunt Lillie, can take that away from me.*

Thursday afternoon, Aunt Lillie and Edna rode the streetcar to Dr. Hodges' office. Edna felt uneasy seated next to Aunt Lillie, but was thankful that at least the window seat was hers. Since Sunday evening, Edna's mind had worked overtime arbitrarily ascribing malicious motives to Aunt Lillie's every inconsequential word or act.

During most of the ride, Edna stared out the window. *Slower than molasses in January.* The hot Houston streets were quiet this afternoon and quivering air ripples rose from the sidewalks. Little of interest captured her attention as the streetcar ambled towards the doctor's office. It was too late to observe the office lunch crowd dressed-up in their fancy clothes, and too early for the after-work parade. Edna usually loved to study the ladies in their dresses with their varying styles of accompanying hats and gloves, and the men in their business suits with their panamas, homburgs and derbies. Left without any such distractions, she fretted about the doctor's appointment. *What will he do?* kept repeating in Edna's mind like a scratched Victrola record, the phrase keeping time with the clickety-clack of the streetcar.

Immediately upon entering the physician's office, Aunt Lillie loudly announced to the receptionist: "I'm going in with Edna Mae. I don't believe she'll tell Dr. Hodges the truth." Aunt Lillie emphasized her pronouncement with her straight arm and index finger pointing directly at Edna. Edna fought a strong urge to say something. A number of people were seated in the waiting area.

Her aunt then grabbed her wrist and pulled her towards the two nearest empty chairs where they both sat down. Silence awkwardly marked the minutes until they were eventually called.

The nurse led them into the examining room then left them to sit awaiting Dr. Hodges.

"Now let me do the talkin', Missy."

"Yes, Ma'am." *When do you ever listen to anyone but yourself,* thought Edna. Edna knew when she was licked. She wouldn't be sitting here if it was not for Uncle Justin. He had insisted that she mind Aunt Lillie if she wanted to stay under their roof.

"Why, hello, Lillian. Hi, Edna. How are you two doing today?" Doctor Hodges entered, with the nurse right behind him.

"Dr. Hodges, Edna has been staying out late many nights, and this past weekend we found out that she had gone all the way to Dallas in mixed company. We're afraid she might not be marriage material anymore and I want you to find that out."

Dr. Hodges politely answered, "Okay, Lillian. We need you then to go sit in the waiting room. Edna will be finished in a few minutes and I'll let you know what we find."

Aunt Lillie semi-begrudgingly left the room. Edna could see she really wanted to stay. "Now you mind the doctor," were her parting words.

"Edna, this might be somewhat uncomfortable, but it will be over soon. I am only doing my job. Now, why don't you lie down here." Dr. Hodges patted the examining table.

Edna complied, and the nurse then covered her with a light sheet.

"Good. Now, Edna, please put your knees up, pull your skirt up to your waist, and pull down your panties."

Edna could not believe what she was hearing. Adrenalin started to course through her body. *What is this doctor going to do to me? Why does he want me to take down my panties?*

Dr. Hodges went over to a drawer and took out first a head band that had a light at the end of it. It looked like what a miner would wear to light his way through the dark tunnels. He placed the band around his head and turned on the light now positioned in the middle of his forehead. Then Edna watched as Dr. Hodges went to another drawer and took out a large silver-rimmed magnifying glass. He then sat the magnifier down on a table, took some rubber gloves from the drawer and pulled them onto his hands.

"Nurse, would you please pull down Edna's panties."

No, it couldn't be. What was he going to-- He wouldn't --

"No, No," Edna said loudly, pushing the nurse's hands away from her. "I'll pull them down myself." Edna complied.

"Now, now, Edna. Calm down," said Dr. Hodges. "Hold her down," he ordered the nurse as his head leaned in closer to the lower portion of Edna's torso.

Edna squirmed like a frightened, wild animal to evade the nurse's grip.

"Now, young lady, the sooner you cooperate, the sooner we'll get this done," Dr. Hodges insisted.

Edna decided the only way to get through this was to suffer the indignity. *I'm trapped.* She stopped moving and permitted the doctor to do what he wanted to do. His face got close to her lower body, he pulled her legs apart, and looked into her private area. He inserted his gloved finger part way into her.

"Ow. That hurts," Edna said loudly.

"That's fine. You're doing well," Dr. Hodges calmly replied. "That's all there is to it. Now you can pull up your panties and sit up."

Dr. Hodges began to remove the gloves. "Nurse, go get Lillian, please."

As the nurse left to get Aunt Lillie, Edna quickly pulled herself together physically and emotionally. *I will not give Aunt Lillie the satisfaction of knowing how humiliating this was.*

When the nurse brought Aunt Lillie back into the examination room, Dr. Hodges told her, "Lillian, Edna is still chaste. She's a good girl. You have nothing to be concerned about."

Edna watched as Aunt Lillie's face clearly registered surprise. "Well, thank you, Dr. Hodges. We just wanted to make sure. There are so many nice men that would like to have a decent Christian wife these days, and we want to make certain that Edna follows the Lord's ways so she can marry one of those young men."

"I understand, Lillian," said Dr. Hodges in a tone all too compliant for Edna's liking. "Now, you say hello to Justin for me."

"I'll do that, Doctor," said Aunt Lillie. She then turned to Edna. "Uncle Justin's supper will be late if we don't hurry home real quick."

Throughout the ride home, Aunt Lillie showed no remorse, no signs of apology, and in fact appeared quite cheerful. Edna maintained her own pretense of unruffled composure. At least she had the diversion of watching the after-work crowd displaying their millinery wear and other finery.

At supper, Aunt Lillie's entire conversation about that afternoon consisted of, "Justin, Dr. Hodges said to tell you 'hello.'"

Before Edna could stop herself, she heard the words come out of her mouth, "And, Uncle Justin, he said I'm a 'good girl.' Aunt Lillie, remember that?" Edna felt compelled to set the record straight with her uncle since who knew what Aunt Lillie might tell him later.

"That's good, Edna," Uncle Justin replied with a tired tone.

Aunt Lillie's response was to give Edna a hard stare.

Lying in bed that night, Edna's mind churned. She replayed the day's events and resolved that she would save every spare cent she could from her future paychecks. She determined to move out as soon as she saved enough money. *I must take responsibility for my own life. I can no longer be at the mercy of others.*

Edna looked over in the dark room towards the dresser top, trying to see her mama's ruby red, cut glass souvenir creamer. She could make out its outline if she concentrated and squeezed her eyes. Her daddy had bought it for her mama at the fair. It was engraved in white script with her mother's name, "Katherine King." Just discerning the creamer's form in the dark somehow made her feel better.

Edna resolved that one day she would have a husband and children who would love her as much as her mama and daddy had loved her. Inspired by her plans, Edna vowed, *I will never again, as long as I live, be treated with such disregard. The doctor was doing what Aunt Lillie insisted he do. But Aunt Lillie. …*

"Never, ever again, dear God, will I allow another human being to treat me with such disrespect," Edna whispered at the ending to her bedtime prayers. "And, God bless mama and daddy, and brother boy who are all up there with you, waiting for me, and watching over me. Amen."

CHAPTER TWO

GALVESTON

Edna had Sundays and Thursdays off from the slaughterhouse. She had started dating Jimmy Griffin regularly. She felt comfortable with him. They had grown up on the same block and played together as kids. Edna liked the fact that Jimmy had known and respected her parents. That made her feel closer to him.

Each time she went out with him, Edna told Aunt Lillie that she was with Laurabeth or other girlfriends. Edna hated to lie -- her parents had taught her that the truth works best -- however, self-preservation commanded she avoid this particular truth with Aunt Lillie.

Jimmy worked as a host at *Hotsie-Totsie's*, a popular downtown Houston restaurant. As they saw more of each other, Jimmy arranged his work schedule so the two of them could spend most of their days off together.

One Wednesday, Jimmy stopped by the slaughterhouse as Edna was getting off from work. "Let's go down to Galveston tomorrow and have some fun. We can go dancing."

"Sounds great." Edna was ready for a diversion.

The sun was still hot and bright in the afternoon when Edna and Jimmy arrived in Galveston. They changed into their swimsuits in the public restroom and settled in upon the beach blanket Jimmy had brought. Edna loved the feel of the sun against her skin. The only downside was that she knew her freckles would soon start appearing. But the sunlight and the warm Galveston sea air were so relaxing, like a balmy massage. It was well worth a few freckles.

Jimmy grabbed Edna's hand and dragged her up onto her feet. "Let's go cool off."

They both ran into the warm water. The small gulf waves felt like caressing bath water as they stood thigh high in the water and enjoyed the gentle lapping. The fresh sea air carried only the slightest breeze. It was peaceful, and a delightful reprieve from the hot Houston streets and the messy, bloody slaughterhouse.

"This is wonderful, Jimmy."

"Sure feels good," Jimmy said as he scooped up water and threw it in Edna's direction.

"Jimmy, don't. My hair." Edna splashed Jimmy back as hard as she could, started laughing and ran out of the water back towards their blanket.

He followed her, raced her to the blanket and pulled her down next to him. Edna was laughing as Jimmy tried to kiss her on the mouth, but got her cheek instead.

"Why, Jimmy Griffin. You're fresh. Cut that out. What will people think."

"They'll think you're my girl."

They whiled away the afternoon leisurely sunbathing and talking, their pleasure only punctured occasionally by people walking on the beach close enough to inadvertently kick a little sand their way.

"Edna, let's go get changed, and get over to the Pavilion. I've saved up for tonight. You can order anything you want."

"Sure, Jimmy. Sounds good."

While walking to the car to get their clothing for the evening, Jimmy noticed the boardwalk photography shop.

"Wait. Let's get our picture taken in our swimsuits."

"Jimmy, like this?"

"Just like this. I dare you. We can show the prudes how modern people live. You look great in that bathing suit."

"But my legs show."

"You have beautiful legs. C'mon. Let's get a souvenir photo so we can always remember today."

"Well, we could take a look," Edna cautiously agreed. She knew Aunt Lillie wouldn't approve of her wearing this short-legged bathing suit at the beach, much less photographing such wanton behavior.

They walked into the photo shop and saw a number of hats and props. On hooks covering a wall, there were hanging Civil War Confederate and Union hats; flapper and Panama straw hats; cowboy hats and Indian full-feather headdresses.

The proprietor walked up to them.

"Which hat would y'all like to wear, pretty lady?" The man asked as his eyes admired Edna from head to toe.

"Hey, quit ogling my girlfriend."

"No harm meant, Bubba. Sorry. How about my taking y'all's photograph in a couple of these hats?"

"Well, my gal here is a fun-lovin' Texan with a swelled head," said Jimmy, "so that 10-gallon might just about fit her, but it could be too small."

Edna couldn't let Jimmy get away with that comment. "Wait a minute, buster. A big heart, maybe but my head isn't any bigger than yours. You wear the 10-gallon, cowboy."

The proprietor heard the makings of a possible sale. "Yeah, the 10-gallon might be a good-lookin' hat for you, Bubba, or what about this Indian headdress? You two could be Indian Chief and cowgirl."

"No hat for me. My gal's the dramatic one," Jimmy offered.

"Jimmy, this was your idea. Unless you choose a hat, I'm not getting my picture taken."

"Why don't y'all try on some hats, choose your props, and I'll get the camera ready," offered the photographer.

Left to experiment with all the millinery, Edna could not resist. She first tried on a close-fitting flapper hat, but saw when she looked into the wall mirror, that it didn't add the appropriate flare. As she removed it and hung it up, Jimmy popped the 10-gallon on her head.

"That does suit you," said Jimmy smiling.

Edna looked in the mirror and smiled. She tilted it backwards and liked the look. The big hat was distinctive. Different. Edna now liked the idea of getting their photo taken, and decided she wouldn't insist that Jimmy wear a hat. She knew he was proud of his thick brown hair. He probably wanted it to show in the photo.

"Take a seat there, little lady," directed the photographer. "The big one."

Two large fabricated rocks sat on the floor in front of a backdrop of painted ocean with blue sky and a faraway pier. Edna sat on the big boulder and Jimmy sat down next to her.

"No, you sit on the other rock, Bubba, the smaller one." Then the photographer went over to the prop area, picked out a toy pistol and handed it to Edna. "Here, little lady. This'll spice it up."

"It's not loaded, is it?" teased Jimmy.

Edna laughed and pointed the gun directly at Jimmy as he raised his hands above his head in mock surrender. They
were both looking directly into each other's eyes.

"Hold it." The camera made a loud clicking sound. The precise moment in time was captured.

Dining was romantic. Edna loved the table Jimmy persuaded the host to give them. It was next to the railing of the dance Pavilion. They overlooked the gulf as the sunlight diminished, and the Galveston Bay turned dark. The boardwalk stores and Pavilion lights came on in an intermittent pattern. The evening scene glistened and glowed in the humid night air. A quartet's background music added to the mood. Gulf shrimp they ordered were fresh from the day's catch, the salad greens were crisp, and Edna was enjoying Jimmy's company.

When the dance band started, Edna and Jimmy were among the first on the dance floor. The orchestration was of the Paul Whiteman variety. And the band's crooner had a silky smooth voice. The quick numbers mixed with the occasional slow dances provided music to suit everyone's taste. Edna loved dancing with Jimmy and tonight Edna gladly followed as Jimmy led her with assurance through the various dance steps.

Part way through their foxtrot to "I Want to be Loved by You," Edna was surprised when Jimmy abruptly took her hand and dragged her back to their table.

"Are you winking at men behind my back?"

"What are you talking about?" Edna asked, surprised by Jimmy's brusque tone.

"Men are staring at you."

"They're probably looking at how well we're dancing together. That's all. You're such a good dancer. You lead me around that floor like I'm your puppet. They're probably trying to pick up some pointers."

"Edna, they aren't watching me. Their eyes are glued on you."

"Honey, don't let's get into something now. We're having too much fun," but Edna was concerned.

"Well, you better not be giving them any reason to stare at you. You're my girl and I don't like them looking at you that way."

"There's no reason to be jealous. You know I'm only interested in you. I can't help it if people are looking at us."

"Well, I can't help it if it bothers me."

Edna suddenly felt quite tired.

"Jimmy, it's getting late. How about if we call it quits and start the drive home?"

"I'm not going to let my girl tell me what I should or should not do. I'm going to the restroom." Jimmy took her back to their table then abruptly left.

Edna's eyes followed him walking across the restaurant, striding with energy fueled by lingering anger. She noticed how some of the women in the room smiled as he walked towards them or by them. He was good-looking and he projected virility and self-confidence.

The band began playing one of Edna's favorite songs, "Keep Your Sunny Side Up." *I love that song.* She couldn't help smiling as she listened to the tempo and lyrics.

"Would you like to dance?" Looking up she saw a pleasant looking young man wearing a white linen suit holding out his hand to her. Edna knew full well that Jimmy might not like it, but she hadn't appreciated his childishness, and this song was not a slow dance.

Edna took the gentleman's extended hand, accepting his invitation. She grabbed her small purse to carry with her. The gentleman escorted her to the dance floor and began to lead her around with a clever and quick two-step creative maneuver. He was a formidable dancer, even better than Jimmy. *Of course I'd never tell Jimmy that.* They made small talk as they danced. "Is that your husband you're with?" the gentleman politely inquired.

"No. My boyfriend, but I hope to marry him some day." Edna did not want to encourage her dancing partner beyond the single dance.

"Well, he's the luckiest man here as far as I'm concerned."

"Thank you. I believe I'm just as lucky to have him," Edna responded.

Suddenly Edna saw Jimmy bolting towards them. Jimmy grabbed the man's arm away from Edna's waist. He turned the man towards him and hit him with a hard right hook to the jaw. The man fell backwards onto the floor. Edna's dance partner just lay there for a moment with his eyes closed. Jimmy took Edna by the arm and said, "Let's go. We're leaving." He pulled her by the arm, and they headed across the Pavilion towards the exit door. Edna turned her head to see if the gentleman was alright. She was relieved to see him get up and start brushing off his clothes.

Jimmy had earlier paid for the tab and tip. There was no reason to stay and every reason not to. Edna was disgusted that Jimmy seemed determined to turn this beautiful day and evening into a disaster.

When they reached the car, Jimmy stood outside the car yelling at her. "Why did you dance with that guy? He's just a swell. How dare you embarrass me in front of all those people. You're acting like a hussy."

Edna stayed silent until she heard the last word. She suddenly became livid. The strong emotion and rage that came over her scared her and she started running away from Jimmy towards the highway. Not hearing him follow her, she momentarily stopped and took off her high heels to run faster. She held them in one hand, her purse in the other. As she reached the highway, a large Packard slowed to a crawl next to her.

"Do you need a ride?" a grey-haired gentleman asked through his open window. Edna saw that a white-haired woman was seated beside him. They were well-dressed and looked conservative.

"Yes. My boyfriend has lost his sense."

"We heard him yelling," the gentleman said as Edna climbed into the couple's rear seat. "We're headed to Houston."

"Me, too. Great." Edna accepted a ride home.

Jimmy was slow to register that Edna was actually leaving him. He had started after her too late and then was not fast enough to catch up. Edna turned her head and looked out the back window to see Jimmy standing in the middle of the road, mouthing some words she couldn't hear.

Did Jimmy really think I would put up with that kind of treatment? Who does Mr. James Griffin think he is? Edna Mae King does not need to take that kind of behavior from anyone, not even -- in fact, especially not from my boyfriend.

Sitting in back of the Packard with the nice couple, after the normal introductory pleasantries and conversation about what happened died down, Edna started thinking seriously. *No matter what I do or how I act others have their own perceptions. I can't control what anyone else thinks or does. Maybe I was careless to have danced with that man, but Jimmy plainly crossed the line when he hit him and shouted at me. I deserve to be treated with more respect.*

CHAPTER THREE

THE JAZZ SINGER

For the next two weeks, Edna's stomach churned each time she thought about Jimmy. He came by the slaughterhouse to see her a number of times, but she refused to talk with him.

She was striving to keep Jimmy out of her life because of his juvenile jealousy and temper, but as the days passed and he persisted, Edna's will weakened. Her temper, although one that flared quickly, could as easily dissipate.

She had never told him about what had happened with Aunt Lillie after the Dallas trip, so he had no idea of why his use of that word "hussy" had enraged her. Not only had his behavior been childish but he probably didn't even understand why his words had stung. *I still care about him. Maybe I owe him an explanation. He could change.*

She was getting off of work the sixth time he appeared at the slaughterhouse. Her co-worker let her know he was outside and she decided to not avoid him. He was carrying a big bouquet of multi-colored fresh flowers with a red velveteen bow around their stems.

"Hey, doll face, here's some beauty for my beauty." Edna restrained a smile as he stood there holding out the bouquet. Jimmy's charm could be schmaltzy but today it somehow worked. Edna saw the silly, guilty-looking grin on his face and her resolve to break with him dissolved. She shook her head while taking the bouquet from Jimmy's hand.

"How about letting me take you to see Al Jolson in *The Jazz Singer* Thursday afternoon? It was sold out in New York for months. I've got a couple tickets for Thursday's 2:30 performance."

Edna wanted to see *The Jazz Singer.* For years she had heard about Jolson's exciting minstrel style of singing and dancing but had never seen him perform.

"Well, okay. But you have to behave, Jimmy. No more shenanigans."

"Sure, sure. I've learned my lesson." Jimmy was too quick to respond.

Edna's nature was one of tremendous loyalty once she trusted someONE. And she and Jimmy had a common history. Edna remembered the time in grammar school when he had dipped her braids into his ink well. When the teacher saw what he had done, Jimmy was suspended for a week. Edna had to cut three inches of ink stain off of her long hair. But she felt so badly about his suspension that she took his homework to him each afternoon and helped him do his lessons.

Then there was the time when Edna's mama was taking her and Jimmy to The Soda Shoppe. When Edna heard Charleston music being played by a banjo player on the street corner she started doing the Charleston. Edna had grabbed Jimmy's hand and he tried to copy her steps. The two kids drew a crowd as they danced together to the jazzy music.

Their lives had intertwined for too long. She could not stay angry at him forever.

Thursday afternoon, Edna met Jimmy at the Houston movie house where *The Jazz Singer* was playing. She spotted him standing in front of the poster display which portrayed Al Jolson in black face playing the piano.

"There you are. Let's go in." Jimmy took her gently by the elbow and escorted her towards the door usher who wore a spiffy brass-buttoned red jacket and black pill-box hat.

They followed a second uniformed usher to aisle seats about half-way down in the right orchestra section.

"Jimmy, everyone who has seen it loves this movie."

"I know. It's remarkable that we'll actually hear sound as part of the movie. Our Baptist minister last week preached about the sin of moving pictures, but, heck, a lot of America goes every week. And who would want to miss Jolson in the first ever synchronized sound feature?"

"Yes. And I always think, why would God not want people to be happy and enjoy themselves?"

"You got that right. Say, want some popcorn?"

"Sure."

Jimmy went to buy them snacks.

Edna looked around at the people. It was a full house. A buzzing sound filled the room, the fast conversation of those anticipating an important event. Edna had always loved going to the moving picture show but could rarely do so without violating Aunt Lillie's rules, or being fearful someone might see her and tell her Aunt. No matter the consequences, this movie experience was clearly different. History in the making. *I don't care if Aunt Lillie does punish me.*

Jimmy was gone a long time getting their snacks but it was thrilling just sitting in the midst of the crowd's vibrancy, waiting. Five people asked if

Jimmy's seat was vacant. Finally, after the dimming warning lights, Jimmy arrived with his hands full.

"Excuse me, Miss. Is that seat saved?"

"Just for you," Edna smiled as she took a Coca-Cola from Jimmy's hand. He had also brought one large popcorn to share.

"It was chaos out there. The snack bar was ten people deep."

"Hush. It's about to start." The lights were now dimming and the red velvet curtains were being slowly opened, while a serious yet jazzy musical prelude began to play. Edna did not want to miss one single second. She became immediately engrossed in the total movie experience. Even reading the title and credits was vitally important to her.

She was thrilled from the very beginning. The young Jakie Rabinowitz sang "My Gal Sal" and "Waiting For the Robert E. Lee," as he danced his own unique choreography. When Al Jolson first appeared on the screen she found his obvious presence and vitality impressive.

Edna loved the Coffee Dan's scene where the now grown-up Jakie, with the stage name "Jack Robin," couldn't help moving to music as he sat eating his eggs. Then when Jolson got up and sang "Dirty Hands, Dirty Feet," he milked the song, emoting with everything in him. On screen the Coffee Dan's audience pounded their tables after Jolson's first song, but the noise was even louder inside the movie theater where the audience stomped their feet and clapped and whistled.

Edna could barely hear the words when Jolson actually spoke: "Wait a minute. Wait a minute. You ain't heard nothin' yet. You want to hear 'Toot, Toot, Tootsie, Goo' Bye?'" The Houston theater audience went crazy: yelping, shouting, clapping and stomping. *What a tremendous reaction.* Some audience members whistled along with Jolson during the song. Edna studied Jolson's dancing. She tried to understand how he achieved the wonderful fluidity of his unique combination of apparent black bottom and Charleston dance steps. *He really has his own type of movement. So graceful. He's wonderful.* Jimmy reached over to take Edna's hand, but she pulled away. She was enjoying moving to the movie music in her chair as were many members of the theatre audience.

Edna noticed that when Jolson danced he glided across the floor in such a way that his feet didn't appear to always be touching the ground. She made a mental note to focus on being lighter on her feet when she danced.

At the end of "Toot, Toot, Tootsie," most of the audience, including Edna and Jimmy, sprang to their feet with a standing ovation. *How wonderful. What a feeling.* The audience loved both synchronized sound and Al Jolson.

Later in the movie, when Jack Robin returned after years away, to see his mother again, the title cards again were transformed to actual talking. The movie audience went wild when Jack's mother said "That I should live to see my baby again." *Oh, it's so moving.* The scene tugged at so many levels of emotions.

And when Jack Robin told his father, "I'll live my life as I see fit," the audience erupted again. Some of the audience shouted "Yes," and "You tell him."

As the movie was near its ending, in the Winter Garden scene, Al Jolson donned his black face to sing in his jazzed-up minstrel way, like Edna had heard and read about for years.

The grand finale was Jolson singing *Mammy*. "I'd walk a million miles for one of your smiles, my mammy." As the last note ascends then ends, Jack Robin's mother smiles at him lovingly. Too soon, the theater curtain began slowly closing.

Edna, thinking of her own mother, struggled to contain her tears. But when she heard some of the audience sniffling, then turned to find Jimmy's tear-filled eyes, she started crying loudly.

As the exit music played and the lights went up in the movie house, the theatre audience remained motionless in their seats, stunned. Then someone ended the silence with a slow clapping, which spread louder and louder until there was a pounding sound throughout the entire audience. People began whooping, whistling and hollering. And then there came a spontaneous chant of "Jolson, Jolson, Jolson." Edna loved the excitement, the electricity of the crowd's enthusiasm. Some special magic had jumped off that screen and filled the whole theater. The movies would never again be the same.

When Edna and Jimmy walked out into the Houston sunshine, Edna felt transformed. "That was the best movie I've ever seen," she told Jimmy excitedly. "It was thrilling. I'd love to be able to entertain people the way Jolson did." *People respect Al Jolson. They love and admire him.*

Jimmy laughed, took her hand and put it through his arm. "Yes, he's a hot feet boy, and sure can warble."

Edna, caught up in the movie's afterglow, started singing, "Blue Skies, nothing but Blue Skies …" imitating Jolson's jazzy version, as she strutted a bit and did some Charleston and black bottom moves she had just watched. Jimmy joined in. The two of them continued their spirited singing and dancing all the way to Jimmy's car which was parked three blocks away. "Nothin' but blue skies from now on …"

CHAPTER FOUR

THE SODA SHOPPE

Edna stared out the window of The Soda Shoppe, watching the hot air wafting up from the sidewalk. She occasionally sipped on her chocolate soda. *Laurabeth should have been here by now. She's thirty minutes late. What is wrong with that girl?*

Jimmy had worked extra hours recently and it had been some time since the two of them had been on a real date. Edna understood that Jimmy's earnings were important for their future, but she missed him. He had promised that tonight would be a special evening for the two of them. *Maybe he'll ask me to marry him.*

Laurabeth had been Edna's girlfriend since they were eight years old, when the incipient fashion mavens enjoyed dressing up their paper dolls with home-made couture and comparing their outfits. Recently with Jimmy's long hours, Edna was spending more time going shopping or visitng with Laurabeth, but Edna was tired of her always being late.

Edna's home life had continued to be strained, but that served as an added incentive to save money for the future. Even if she and Jimmy did not marry soon, she now had almost enough to move out of her relatives' spare bedroom. *It's just a matter of time and planning.*

"Edna, looks like you could use another soda. How's about if I refill you? Still have some of your soda here in the mixer."

"Okay, Bobby. Thanks. That Laurabeth better get here soon or I'm taking off. She knows I have to meet Jimmy tonight. She's kept me waiting too long now."

Edna went over to the magazine rack and took a *Photoplay* back to her table. She thumbed through the magazine, studying with keen interest the outfits the movie stars were wearing. An extraordinary white crepe dress on Gloria Swanson caught her eye. It was "bead-embroidered" and had a trim of "gilt-edged mousseline de soie." Edna appreciated the detailed descriptions of the gowns that complemented the photos.

Bobby came over and filled Edna's glass with the leftover chocolate soda from the metal mixing canister. "Here you go."

"Thanks, Bobby." Bobby had been a year behind her in school and she could tell he had a small crush on her. She looked up from the magazine and gave him her kindest smile.

As she glanced out the window, an attractive low-waisted two-toned sleeveless dress caught Edna's eye. The outside of the pleats, which looked to be a brown jersey, swayed and contrasted with the lighter taupe inside as its owner briskly walked. On the head of the dress wearer was a glistening flapper-style, form-fitting hat. *Well, I'll be*, thought Edna. *That's Laurabeth. I love her new outfit.*

Laurabeth hurried into the shop, spotted Edna immediately, kissed her on the cheek and sat down facing her. "Honey, so sorry I'm late, but I had to get you a copy of this." She shoved a *Houston Times* paper in front of Edna.

"Laurabeth, your outfit's terrific. Aren't you the fashion plate."

"This hat was designed by Patrice, all hand sewn pheasant feathers. It is gorgeous; isn't it? It cost me a small fortune. But isn't it somethin'? Don't you think it's stunning with my copenhagen and tan dress. Nice, huh? I must maintain my appearance."

"You must maintain your vanity, you mean."

"Now, now, Edna. I'm worth it. Don't get catty with me. Plus, I'm still on the search for my Mr. Right. But there are more important things to think about. I have to tell you something you won't want to hear."

"Laurabeth, you're over a half hour late. I've had almost two chocolate sodas, and I'm trying to lose some weight for Jimmy. What in the heck could be so important to keep me waiting this long?"

"Honey, you know you're just like a sister to me. There's some gossip you need to hear."

Edna realized that scolding was not making any impression on Laurabeth, so she focused her attention on what Laurabeth was so darned worked up about.

"Honey, I'm so sorry to tell you this, but Jimmy was out on the town the past few weeks, on some of those nights he was supposed to be working late. A group went into Hotsie-Totsie's one of his work nights and he wasn't there. They said he was down in Galveston dancing. That was a night you told me you were staying at home because Jimmy was working late.

Another time he was seen at the movies with a blond. A little bird told me her name may be Myrna, but whatever her name is she apparently likes dancing because they were spotted down at the Galveston Pavilion again the other night. Maybe she's his long-lost Yankee cousin? I hope so. I had to make sure that this wasn't just rumor before I let you know.

Edna's spirit fell as if it were being drained from her body. She became numb. She looked up at Laurabeth with a dazed expression. Laurabeth, who had often seen Edna erupt with spirited well-deserved anger, was stunned at Edna's reaction.

"That son-of-a-gun has his nerve, doesn't he," Laurabeth offered, trying to get a feel for what Edna was thinking. "How dare he take someone else out dancing when you two dance so beautifully together. Do you know her? Is her name Myrna? Is she his cousin?"

Edna would not, could not speak. No words came. No feelings arose. She could hear her heart pounding in her head. But where were her tears? Where was her anger?

"Honey, Edna, you okay? You want a glass of water? How about a piece of chocolate? I'll buy you a piece of milk chocolate."

Edna stared outside the window at the people walking on the sidewalk. They seemed to be enjoying the sunshine, or their errands, or their day. They all seemed too pleasant, too happy. *How can those people walk so easily, so cheerfully along those sidewalks?*

Laurabeth got up from the table, and walked over to Bobby.

"Listen, Edna just got some bad news. How about bringing us a couple Coca-colas and two pieces of milk chocolate. Maybe that'll cheer her up."

Then she returned to the table. "Honey, I've never seen you like this. Are y'all okay?"

Edna suddenly hated Laurabeth for acting so normal, for being so overly cheerful when she had told her the news, for being so late while making certain to bring Edna the painful message.

Bobby brought the two Cokes and chocolate which he silently and respectfully set down on the table. Laurabeth grabbed her chocolate and put half the piece in her mouth in one large bite.

"Here, honey, this will perk up your spirits. Coca-Cola always makes you feel better. And, I know that this chocolate is your favorite."

Edna took a small sip of Coke, a small bite of chocolate, but, no, there was no way to handle this betrayal, this blow that hit her like a final blow.

The man she had entrusted with her heart and her future had played her for a fool, and in such an obvious way that everyone would soon know if they didn't already. Nothing could ever be the same. *How long have others known? I can't take this. I can't go on. I …*

Edna started to get up from her chair and could not move her legs. Her feet were numb.

"Edna, Edna, are you all right? What's the matter, honey? You look disturbed. Sip more Coke. Eat another bite of chocolate."

"I -- I can't walk."

"What do you mean, honey?"

"I can't move my legs, Laurabeth. They won't work."

"Ah, c'mon, honey. Sure you can. Remember when you were the fastest runner at school? And, you're one of the best dancers I know. Of course you can walk."

"No, my legs aren't moving. I can't make them work. I can't walk."

"Oh, my goodness, honey. What are we going to do?" Laurabeth began to panic. She had only wanted to spread a little news, had anticipated from Edna a fiery response, but not this. "What can we do? How can you get home? I'm so sorry, Edna. I guess I shouldn't have told you. I guess I --"

"Hush up, Laurabeth," Edna calmly said. "Go to Bobby and ask him if he'll take me home when he gets off. I can wait. I might be better later."

"Sure, honey. Sure. I'll ask Bobby. Does he have a car? I took the streetcar today or I'd take you."

"I think he borrowed his brother's car today. I saw it down the street. Ask him."

"Sure, honey. Sure." Laurabeth walked up to the counter where Bobby was waiting on a couple of youngsters. She pulled him aside.

"Bobby, Edna is having some trouble walking. She wonders if you could take her home after you get off work? Do you have a car?"

"Yes, I have my brother's car today. Of course I'll help her," Bobby agreed. "I can take her in about an hour. Anything for Edna."

"Great." Laurabeth returned to the table.

"Honey, Bobby's shift ends in an hour. He does have his brother's car today. He'll take you hone."

"Okay, Laurabeth. You go on now. I'll be fine," Edna said.

Laurabeth appeared all too happy to get out of there as soon as possible but said, "You sure I can't help you more, honey? You want me to stay?"

"No. Good-bye, Laurabeth."

Laurabeth left her Coca-cola but made certain to take the rest of her chocolate as she left The Soda Shoppe, calling out joyfully to Bobby, "Good-bye, Bobby. Thanks. See you soon."

And, as cheerfully to Edna, "Bye, honey. See you soon."

I never want to see Laurabeth again as long as I live, thought Edna. *That bridge is burned.* Edna turned and gave a half smile of thanks to Bobby, who broke out in a big grin at Edna's attention. Then Edna returned to staring out the window at those people whose world now felt separate from hers.

It was two weeks before Edna was able to even get out of bed on her own. Aunt Lillie and Uncle Justin were solicitous of her. They had watched Bobby carry her out of the car into the house and then into her room. "She can't walk," was Bobby's sole explanation.

Edna refused to tell her Aunt and Uncle what had happened, not really understanding it all herself. But she gave them some indication when she said, "If Jimmy Griffin comes by I refuse to see him."

Uncle Justin notified the slaughterhouse that she would be out of commission for some time. And, Aunt Lillie got Dr. Hodges to stop by the house to try and determine what was wrong.

Edna told Dr. Hodges something vague about, "I have no feeling in my legs. I can't move. I can't go on." And, Dr. Hodges did his tapping-the-kneecap test which revealed that Edna's leg reflexes were normal. After further tests and some questions which Edna answered truthfully, Dr. Hodges came to a conclusion which he shared with Aunt Lillie and Uncle Justin. "Her nerves are strained as a result of emotional trauma. She doesn't want to walk because her heart and spirit are broken. Don't give her any added grief, and try and be cheerful and upbeat. Make her eat even if she doesn't want to. She'll work it out but it will take some time."

And time it did take. Edna lay in bed for days, and thought and thought, which did little to lift her spirits. Many of her friends from her job and her schooldays stopped by to visit with her, but she would see few of them. When Laurabeth stopped by with a gift of movie magazines, Edna refused to speak with her.

Jimmy knocked on the front door many times but was told by Aunt Lillie repeatedly that Edna did not want to see him, that Edna never ever wanted to see him again. That did not seem to dissuade his presumptuous nature until the evening Uncle Justin answered the door and told Jimmy, "Boy, if you ever come around to this house again I'll take my shotgun to you. You've been told to stay away, now do it."

All the way from her bedroom, Edna could hear Uncle Justin yelling at Jimmy and she was surprised by her Uncle's uncommon protective vehemence. *Uncle Justin loves me*, Edna thought. And, *his sticking up for me proves it*.

After that evening, Edna's situation took a turn for the better. She began thinking more positively, and started getting out of bed more often. As her strength increased, Edna began to think about what she needed to do. *I must move forward. I must make my place in this world. It's time to get out on my own.*

One day after Aunt Lillie went to the grocery store, she brought in with Edna's supper a magazine called *The New Movie Magazine.* "Sugar, here's something for you. They say it's new. You know I don't approve of such things, but I know you like them. It might make you feel better."

"Thank you, Aunt Lillie." Edna was grateful for everything her aunt and uncle had done to help her through this rough period. They were good people at heart.

After Aunt Lillie left the room, Edna carefully examined the magazine cover. It was not as glossy as *Photoplay*'s cover but one front caption jumped out, "Hollywood seeks Young Starlets."

That's it. I've nothing left here in Houston. I'll go to Hollywood where I can start a new life. It's silly to think of becoming a starlet, but I can get a job, maybe in fashion. I can meet new people, leave my past behind. For the first time since Edna had learned about Jimmy two-timing her, she felt focused and exhilarated. This was the next step, her future. This was the path that resonated. *I must get well. I have to start planning my future. California, here I come.*

PART II

HOLLYWOOD, CALIFORNIA 1930

CHAPTER FIVE

HOLLYWOOD, CALIFORNIA 1930

I can't believe I'm here, Los Angeles, California. Hollywood! Edna's Southern Pacific Railroad car pulled slowly into the small Spanish-style train station. The Golden State Limited had taken three days from Houston. As her brochure had proclaimed, the train travelled the "comfortable low altitude way."

Edna had developed an appreciation for the enormity of her home-state as the train crossed the barren miles of prairie from Houston to El Paso. Striking white cumulous cloud configurations contrasted against the deep blue wide sky forming a captivating view from her window. Edna envisaged people, animals and angels in those clouds. In one peculiarly shaded puff she thought she saw Charlie Chaplin, complete with bowler hat and cane. And in a spectacularly luminous cloud she could see her mother watching over her, which she took as a sign, *Mama must approve of my move.*

When the flat, wide-open spaces of the Texas prairie switched to desert landscape, Edna was fascinated by the miles upon miles of sand dunes and cacti, with the occasional mountain range to break the horizon. The wide-open spaces of the country were daunting.

"Miss Edna," asked the porter, "are you ready to disembark for your new life in Hollywood?"

"Yes, Bill. I'm as ready as I'll ever be."

Edna had fastidiously reorganized her few possessions more than once during the three days. She wanted to start her new life in a proper manner, yet felt nervous about what the future held. Her re-inspection of the contents of her two suitcases just this morning gave her certainty that all was in order, and nothing was left behind. She had even rearranged her purse contents after the early breakfast. And a few minutes ago, the slant of her hat, as well as her lipstick application had passed a second mirror check.

"Well, all right then. Let's go," the porter said as he took in his large hands the two Woolworth's suitcases Aunt Lillie and Uncle Justin had given her for this move.

Edna stood up in her three-inch heels. She smoothed out the skirt of her blue cotton dress.

"Thanks for your help during the trip, Bill." Edna handed him a quarter. It was extravagant considering her resources, but he had been conscientious all along the train route, answering her questions in an intelligent and respectful manner.

As Edna climbed down the steps from the car into the California sunshine, she smelled a sweet, fresh fragrance.

"Bill, what's that wonderful scent?"

"Orange blossoms."

This air felt somehow newer, crisper, cleaner than the muggy Houston summer. *Southern California is like the brochures described.*

"Miss Edna, where do you want me to take these bags?"

"I'll need to catch a bus, Bill, so wherever the busses stop."

"To the front then."

As Edna followed the porter to the street in front of the Mission-Revival depot, some of the bustling crowd turned to look at her. A raw energy exuded from her excitement, giving her a commanding presence. *They must like my blue dress or my hat,* thought Edna, unaccustomed to such outright ogling.

A sudden jolt caused Edna to almost lose her balance and cry out "Hey." Bill turned around to look and saw a man holding a folded *Variety* catching her by the elbow.

"So sorry, Miss," the man said.

"You almost knocked me over."

"My sincere apologies. I didn't mean to bump you. Wasn't looking where I was going. Let me make it up to you. Where are you headed? Do you need a ride? Let me take you in my car."

Edna was tempted to accept the ride, but Bill had warned her that men in Los Angeles hung around the train and bus stations specifically waiting for vulnerable new girls in town.

"No, thank you. I don't need a ride."

"All right, tootsie. Sorry about bumping into you."

Tootsie? I'm no tootsie. Edna was indignant but kept it to herself as she watched the man continue walking to his right and then intentionally bump into a somewhat unkempt woman that Edna had seen on the train. *He can 'tootsie' her all he wants.*

Edna followed Bill to the bus stop where he set down her bags at the end of a line of people. "See you in the movies, Miss Edna." Bill smiled as he turned and left.

"Thanks, Bill." Edna looked around for a place to sit. The one bench was full. She could sit on her suitcases, or stand with the others. *I'm grateful*

I can even stand again. It had taken her weeks to regain her strength before embarking on this move.

Standing in the bus line hundreds of miles from home with all she owned in two suitcases on the sidewalk, Edna started to worry. *I have no place to stay. That brochure said you could find hotel rooms for one night or even a month at a time. What shall I do? Where can I spend the night?*

There were people waiting for the bus who also looked somewhat lost. *Maybe one of them can suggest a good place to start.* Edna decided to ask the young woman standing in front of her who was wearing a flapper hat. She looked about Edna's age.

"Hello. I like your hat." Edna knew a compliment was usually a sure opener.

"Well, thank you."

"Are you new in town also?"

"Well, I've been to Los Angeles before. I'm here to visit my older sister. She's lived here a few years. This is my second time out to see her."

"How nice. Since you've been here before maybe you might know of an inexpensive hotel?

"Oh, I'm sorry. I've never had to stay at a hotel." The woman paused. "I can tell you though that we went to a very friendly coffee shop called 'Johnny's' one time, and everyone in there seemed to be talking about places to stay and how to get along in this city. It was a real smart crowd, young and stylish. That might be a good place for you to start out, get some information."

"Sounds good. Is it near here?"

"The bus goes right by there. I'll point it out to you. I know it's on Wilshire, but I'm not sure of the cross street. Oh, here's the bus. If you sit with me I can show you where to get off."

"Thank you."

Edna took her suitcases in her two hands and started to follow the young woman up the narrow bus stairs. Edna's high heels made it impossible for her to get up on the first step carrying both suitcases. So she set her luggage down on the sidewalk, and lifted them one by one to the top of the entrance stairs. Then holding on to the side rail she climbed to the top.

"Five cents," the bus driver said curtly once she had made it to the top of the stairs. *These Californians aren't as polite as Southerners.*

Edna opened her purse and took out a nickel which she handed to the bus driver. Then she pushed one suitcase and pulled the other along the bus aisle until she reached the young woman's seat.

29

"Put your luggage up there," the young woman pointed to a rack above the seat.

Edna lifted her suitcases one at a time up into the rack, then sat down on the aisle seat, momentarily out of breath.

"I'll sure appreciate a cup of coffee once I get to this 'Johnny's' you mentioned."

"You're from the South, aren't you?"

"Houston, Texas. Some Southerners don't even consider that to be the real South. But yes. I know my drawl gives me away. I like to kid people sometimes and say I'm from Goose Creek, Texas."

"I'm from Iowa." Her tone implied she did not really want to talk anymore. Edna took the hint. "Oh."

As they rode in silence, Edna looked with interest at the buildings and storefronts. Los Angeles looked similar to Houston in the way that any large city resembles another, yet the buildings here were taller, more plentiful, and the architecture was striking. Many buildings conveyed a unique style with decorative flourishes. Fleur de Lis, lions, mermaids adorned the various buildings as if this city were a movie fantasyland. *Appropriate*, thought Edna.

They had ridden in silence for a while when the young woman pulled the stop request cord for Edna. "There it is, right there on the corner."

"Oh, thank you."

When the bus stopped, Edna pulled each of her suitcases down from the rack. She placed one in front of her in the aisle and this time held one under her right arm, with her purse hanging from her left forearm. She pushed the aisle suitcase forward with her right high heel until she reached the steps. A friendly-looking gentleman with a panama hat was waiting to enter. He saw Edna's struggle and climbed up the steps to help her out. He lifted both suitcases down the stairs for her and set them on the sidewalk.

"There you go, pretty lady."

"Why, thank you."

Some Californians are nice. She stood there catching her breath and waived good-bye to the young woman who had helped her. The girl managed a slight smile in reply. *Not the friendliest type but I'm grateful for the lead.*

Edna was in front of 'Johnny's Coffee Shop Restaurant.' It was around noon and when she entered, the place was bustling. The hostess greeted her and pointed out two seats at the counter. "Take either seat."

"May I leave my suitcases here?"

"Yes, we'll put them here behind the cash register. They'll be safe."

"Thank you."

She sat down at the closest open seat and removed the menu from the metal holder. "Coffee, 5 cents. Hamburger, 15 cents. Bacon, lettuce and tomato, 10 cents. Chili, 5 cents."

Edna needed to conserve money but decided she should eat some lunch to keep up her strength. *Who knows what the day will bring* and *those suitcases are heavy.*

"I'll have the chili with plenty of saltines, please, and coffee."

"Sure, sweetie."

Edna's coffee was set in front of her in less than a minute.

"Thank you."

"Sure."

Edna added the counter cream and sugar, and sipped the coffee, trying to focus her thoughts in the middle of this noisy lunchtime crowd. She needed to find someone who knew the area. *I need a place to stay for at least a few nights to get my bearings.* Edna took another couple sips of her coffee and began to feel her strength and resolve returning.

"Here you go, sweetie." The waitress set a large bowl of chili in front of her, and a basket full of cellophane-wrapped saltine crackers.

"Thanks."

"Sure." The waitress was off again working the long counter before Edna could even think to ask her a question.

Edna took five packages of crackers and slipped them into her purse. They might suffice for dinner later.

"I do that, too."

Edna looked to her right to see a neatly dressed young woman.

"Those crackers are a lifesaver in my apartment at night when I just have to have a snack."

"That's what I was figuring on. Hello. I'm Edna Mae."

"Oh, a Southerner. I'm Mattie. Given name is Martha, but everyone calls me Mattie."

"Nice to meet you, Mattie."

"Likewise."

"Say you might be able to help me out. I'm new in town."

"I thought you might be. I saw you carrying your suitcases."

"Yes. Just got in from Houston on the train. I need a place to stay short-term while I look for a job and an apartment. I'm on a budget, so it needs to be safe and clean but the bare minimum."

"I was in the same situation a few months ago when I first got here from Missouri. There's a hotel I stayed at that fits your description. Each floor has one bathroom with a tub. Management works out the bathtub schedule. There's also a downstairs lobby bathroom. Most of the patrons when I was there were either tourists or short-term tenants. And they were a friendly group."

"What's the name of the hotel?"

"Hotel Marquis. It's just a few blocks west on Wilshire, on this side of the street."

"If it's in this neighborhood it's probably beyond my pocketbook. Would you mind telling me what the rooms cost per night?"

"A few months ago my room cost $1.50 a night, or $9.00 for seven nights. I stayed there a couple weeks."

"Oh, good. I can afford that." Edna thought about the $300.00 she had in her purse, all conscientiously saved from her slaughterhouse wages.

"Good. There's a cheap restaurant next door to the hotel with pretty good food, and about a block away there's a small store that sells the necessities, you know, coffee, milk, cereal, canned soup. Real convenient. And, the trolley car goes right by. You can catch it out front."

"Wonderful. Mattie, you've helped me feel a whole lot better."

"Maybe it's that good coffee and chili."

The two of them laughed.

"Say, Mattie, would you watch my seat? I'm not through yet but I'll just go call Hotel Marquis and see if there's a room available."

"Sure."

Edna took her purse over to the pay phone she had spotted on the wall by the restroom hallway. She took out a nickel, put it into the telephone slot, and placed the call. After two rings, a female voice with a California accent answered, "Hotel Marquis."

"Hello. Would you have a room available for tonight, and probably for at least one week, maybe more?"

"Why, yes. We have two rooms left. One's $1.50 a night, and the other is $2.00 per night. If you stay a week or more, we'll give you a discount."

"Wonderful. My name's Edna Mae King. Could you save the $1.50 room for me? I'll be over in less than an hour."

"Yes, Miss King. If we don't hear from you in an hour, however, the room will once again be available first come, first serve."

"I understand. I'll see you within the hour."

I better finish that chili and coffee so I'll have the energy to carry those suitcases the few blocks to the hotel. Edna returned to her seat and told Mattie the good news.

"Thank you, Mattie. I very much appreciate your help."

"That's all right, Edna. People helped me out when I first came here. This is, for the most part, a friendly place. So many people are starting out new, from different cities and states all over the country, that everyone tends to help each other. I've had a grand time the past few months. You will, too. I'm certain of it."

Edna focused on quickly finishing her meal. Her first morning in Los Angeles had already given rise to a number of feelings, but certainty about her future was not one of them.

Just like in Houston, there are good and bad people everywhere. Who knows what will happen to me here? At least I'm relieved to find a place to stay. That's a good beginning.

CHAPTER SIX

THE SALESGIRL AND THE SUPERINTENDENT

Edna awoke this Saturday to a clear and sunny Los Angeles morning. Her one month of Southern California life had been productive. She applied for and got a job at B.H. Dyas Department Store as a cashier and salesgirl. Management also promised her occasional modeling jobs in their fashion shows. She felt lucky to even be working and earning a paycheck.

The streetcar line was two blocks away from the tiny, furnished utility apartment she had rented at the Marguerite Apartments. Her only additions to the unit's decor were her mama's ruby red creamer and a table made from her two suitcases.

A girl at work had told Edna about this Westlake area which was safe and well-kept. Edna loved the combination of Spanish revival and art deco mansions with beaux-art. Many newly-built apartment buildings held other newcomers to Los Angeles. A brief walk across Wilshire Boulevard, and a short streetcar ride took her close to Dyas Department Store at the southwest corner of Hollywood and Vine. The convenient commute was a carefully planned consideration on her part. And she was actually working in the center of Hollywood, a fashionable, stimulating environment.

Although Edna had been watching her money very carefully, her original stake had now dwindled to $225.00, but she had received her first paycheck and was planning to start saving some rainy day money again.

Some days she and other gals from work would go to the automat or cafeteria. They would take a glass of water, and a few packages of the free saltine crackers set out for the soup and chili patrons. They would then take the ketchup, mayonnaise, mustard and relish condiments that were set out for the hamburger and hot dog customers and lavishly spread their saltines. Ten crackers piled with condiments, along with a large glass of water could fill up a stomach.

Edna's usual Dyas shift was nine to five, which gave her plenty of time at night to listen to the radio that came with her apartment furnishings, and to relax and lay out her clothes for the next day. But this Saturday her shift was one p.m. to closing.

Edna had a natural eye for fashion, a style sense that served her well at her job. She conscientiously dressed as neatly and fashionably as her limited budget allowed. She would completely change an outfit by adding the right scarf or costume jewelry, or by mixing different skirts and tops. Her ingenuity helped her convert her few clothes and accessories into many different looks which earned her a reputation as a clothes horse whom other clerks would come to for advice. And, her good taste enabled her to aid the customers in choosing their best colors, form and fit.

One of the benefits of working in the Dyas Department Store was the employee layaway plan. Not only could employees get a discount of twenty percent applied to their employee purchases, but the layaway plan also encouraged them to buy clothing by paying a small amount out of each paycheck. Edna already put one sea foam green dress with an ecru bolero jacket on layaway, and a new pair of leather three-inch pumps.

Edna had been promised at her time of hire that when she modeled in a fashion show, she would be given one dress or another item of clothing she wore. She particularly looked forward to the haute couture modeling.

Mattie had called Edna at the Hotel Marquis, and after she had moved to the apartment building they stayed in touch. Edna found Mattie to be fun, so one night Edna agreed to double-date with her and two young fellows Mattie knew. The men splurged and took them to dinner at The Brown Derby, down the street from the Dyas building. The four of them had a fabulous dinner of Caesar salad, sirloin steak with baked potato, chocolate cake and milk. Edna ate every single bite, and was kidded by her date that it was great to see a woman enjoy her meal and not worry about her waistline. Edna did not let on that she had not eaten a complete meal in a couple of weeks. It was exciting to see the inside of the ritzy restaurant where movie stars ate. They didn't spot any movie stars but still had a pleasant time and a terrific dinner.

Many of the women at work had talked about what they called "dating for dinner." They encouraged Edna to do the same. Although there was a store policy against dating customers whom they met at the store, many girls would sneak their names and telephone numbers to interested men. Even when they were not attracted to the customer or when the customer was married, many of the sales clerks would still go out to dinner with them in order to get a free meal.

Edna understood the survival instinct and tried not to judge the other girls too harshly, however, she did not want to break store policy, could not bring herself to go out with any man she did not like, and particularly would not even think of dating a married man. Edna steered clear of friendships with any of the salesgirls who knowingly dated married men. In her mind, a woman who would do that did not truly respect herself or other women, and could probably not be a loyal friend.

This Saturday, Edna's streetcar ride to work was less crowded than her weekday commute. She boarded one of her favorite "Hollywood" cars, with the zebra-patterned mohair seats and was happy to find a left *Photoplay* magazine on her seat. The cover proclaimed, "Gossip Never Hurts." Edna was amused as she knew otherwise, however, but she admittedly enjoyed learning about the latest Hollywood liaisons and fashion faux pas as much as the next person. It was useful to follow what was going on in the movie world so she could dish knowledgeably with the other girls at work. Every scandalous detail occurring in the lives of moving picture idols was always a surefire topic of conversation.

Edna opened the *Photoplay* to page 36, and read about Mary Pickford and Douglas Fairbanks. *What a terrifically attractive couple.* Mary Pickford appeared to be as nice as she was talented and cute. Mary's husband, Douglas Fairbanks, combined dark good looks with a devil-may-care personality. The two were always in the social columns, mentioned out dancing at the Cocoanut Grove or some other nightclub. It was difficult to fathom how they kept up their work schedules with their busy social life. They were Hollywood royalty, the first two stars who placed their hands into Grauman's Chinese Theater's lobby cement.

Edna looked through the magazine at the various ads about the "Meeker Made" handbags, "No more shiny nose," and "How Famous Movie Stars Keep Their Hair so Attractive." There were so many different products advertised. Edna became so engrossed in the magazine she almost bypassed her stop but looked up just in time to pull the cord. She rolled the magazine and put it into her purse to share with the girls at work.

Edna quickly left the streetcar by the rear door. As she walked towards Dyas she heard a quickening step behind her. Then the footsteps moved right up alongside her. "Hello, miss. I couldn't help but notice your handbag is unlatched. Some unscrupulous type might reach in and take your billfold."

Edna turned to look up at the face of one of the most strikingly handsome men she had seen. His dark curly hair, chiseled features and a finely trimmed mustache gave him a movie star look. Edna's trained eye swiftly observed the gentleman's bespoke suit and gleaming leather shoes as he took off his hat with a slight head bow and continued, "My name is Ray."

Edna stopped and smiled, "I'm Edna. Thanks for noticing. That's so gracious of y'all to notice my open purse."

"Well, you all must be a damsel from the South. Or, are you a Hollywood starlet practicing for a role?"

Edna saw a good-natured humor in his eyes. "Your first hunch is right. Houston born and bred. I've been in Los Angeles for about a month."

"Well, we can't let a beautiful young woman such as yourself stay here without knowledge of all the wonderfully diverse places this area offers. How about I take you on a grand tour of the Los Angeles basin? I happen to be a truly experienced guide to the area, having been born and raised here."

The thought crossed her mind that he might be a debonair con man, but he had called her attention to the dangers of her open purse. Her instincts signaled he was sincere.

"A native of Los Angeles? Well, that'd be fun. Wednesday's my next day off from work."

"Well, although Wednesday's not my usual day off, for this occasion it will be. I'll pick you up Wednesday at 10:00 a.m. It isn't often I get the opportunity to share my hometown with a lovely newcomer such as yourself." Ray's dark eyes glimmered with amusement.

"I'm at the Marguerite Apartments in Westlake, near MacArthur Park and the Palace Hotel."

"That's a lovely area. Many new apartment buildings have been built there recently. And Miss Edna, for whom shall I call? What's your last name?"

"King. How about you, Ray? What's yours?"

"Gibson."

"Well, Mr. Ray Gibson, this is where I work. Thanks again for helping me safeguard my handbag. I'll see you Wednesday at ten a.m." Edna smiled at Ray with her most flirtatious smile, then turned and entered the employees' door of the Dyas Department Store.

Between Saturday and Tuesday night, Edna did her nails, conditioned her hair, and tried on a number of different outfits in an attempt to decide on the right look for Wednesday. Where would Ray take her and what would be appropriate for any place they went? Would he wear a suit like he wore when she met him? Or, would he dress more casually?

By Tuesday night she had decided upon a royal blue two-piece suit, with a white blouse. She could take off the jacket and bring along her white sweater for a more casual look. She had her costume pearls if the day turned into an evening dinner. She would wear heels, but take a pair of flats in her purse.

Edna heard a knock on the door. It was eight o'clock. She had been home from work a couple of hours.

"Who's there?"

"It's Russ Newman, your neighbor from down the hall, Apartment G. We haven't met yet, but I was on my way out and the lobby telephone rang. You have a call from a Ray Gibson. He's waiting on the line. I told him I would come upstairs and see if you were in."

Edna peeked out the door to find a balding gentleman in a grey double-breasted business suit holding a fedora in his hands. He had smiling eyes and a friendly, sincere-looking face.

"Thanks, Russ, I'll be right down."

"You're welcome. I'll let him know you're coming to the phone as I leave." Russ turned and left.

Edna switched from her slippers into a pair of flats, and hurried downstairs to answer the telephone. As she picked up the lobby phone receiver, she watched Russ exit the front door of the apartment building then put on his hat.

"Hello?" She answered in her warmest, most Southern tones.

"Well, there you are," Ray responded. "I'm calling to confirm our date tomorrow and to let you know where we'll be going so that you'll know what to wear."

"How thoughtful of you. I'll bet you've had women ask you about what to wear before," Edna teased.

"Well, I grew up with a mother who insisted on dressing in the appropriate clothing for every occasion. That puts the fear of God into a gentleman, and an awareness that women want to know where they're going so that they can dress appropriately."

Ray continued, "I'd thought we'd take a drive up to Mulholland, then down to Malibu for lunch. We'll head back to Griffith Park, see the stables, the observatory. Then, to dinner and dancing at the Cocoanut Grove."

"You've planned quite a day, Ray, and I'm looking forward to tomorrow. Thanks for calling and confirming."

"My pleasure. See you tomorrow at ten."

"Bye-bye. See you in the mornin'," Edna drew out the word mornin' then gently rehung the receiver. This man was charming. A take-charge type. Edna liked that. And he wanted to spend the whole day and evening with her. She smiled as she climbed the stairs.

Entering her apartment, Edna walked straight to the closet and pulled out her short green chiffon. She examined the front and back. *It doesn't need ironing, thank goodness, and not a tear or a stain on it.* Her one party dress from Texas would have to do for evening.

Edna's radio was now playing live music, direct from the Ambassador Hotel's Cocoanut Grove Orchestra. She carefully returned to her closet the dress she would wear dancing there tomorrow evening.

CHAPTER SEVEN

FIRST DATE: TOURING LOS ANGELES

Raymond Gibson's chauffeur, Thomas, pulled the limousine over at a captivating stretch of Mulholland Drive which overlooked the Los Angeles basin. Edna waited for Thomas to open the heavy door for her and help her out. Ray walked around the car, took her hand, and led her carefully along a worn path through the ground cover to a clearing about fifteen feet from the edge of the cliff.

Thomas soon followed carrying two portable folding chairs for them to sit on. He went to the car again, and returned with a picnic basket and a small folding table which was opened then set between the two of them. Out of the picnic basket, Thomas took a small, blue-checked tablecloth which he laid over the table. Edna did not show her surprise when Thomas next shook open with a flourish a blue cloth napkin which he placed over her lap. He then did the same for Ray.

Oh, that's what he's doing. I'm glad I didn't say anything.

He then pulled out two china cups and saucers which he positioned on the table.

"Coffee?" Thomas revealed a portable coffee pitcher he had kept properly balanced and concealed in the picnic basket.

"Sounds good," responded Edna, now truly amazed by this whole process. Thomas skillfully filled each of their cups.

"Did you care for sugar or cream?"

"No, thank-you," Edna said. She watched as Thomas poured cream into Ray's cup and stirred the contents with a silver demitasse spoon.

Thomas then returned to the car and left Ray and Edna alone. Curious as to how Thomas had fit so much into the picnic basket, Edna peaked into it and saw an array of pastries. "Oh, Ray, there are breakfast pastries."

"Help yourself. That's why they're here." He reached over, looked in, and took a glazed donut.

Edna chose a bear claw. *What? No plates?* She kept her thought to herself. *Such special treatment. I feel like a plutocrat.*

"Ray, Los Angeles is sure big. You can see for miles from here." Edna took a bite of bear claw, followed by a large sip of the strong coffee.

"Yes, Los Angeles basin is over 400 square miles. Today's exceptionally clear. Look out in the Pacific Ocean. You can see Catalina Island. That's 26 miles off the coast."

"That's the first time I've seen Catalina that vividly." Edna took another couple of sips of the strong coffee and continued talking.

"The area has such a wonderful streetcar system. It's even better than Houston's. My second weekend in town I took the anywhere-for-a-nickel Sunday special. The trolley cars were filled with families on their weekend outings. I saw farms with dairy cows and a few new suburbs springing up along the streetcar tracks." Edna realized she was babbling. *Must be the excitement and the strong coffee. Stop talking.*

"Yes. Los Angeles is undergoing a growth spurt. People are thronging here for its good weather and its tremendous opportunities. The streetcar system is the best system in the world. There are a 1000 miles of trolley lines, and 2700 scheduled trains daily, which take citizens to most points of interest. For people without cars, it makes it easy to get around. But Los Angeles is large and to see all the hidden gems, a person needs a car."

Edna was relieved that Ray had responded to her nervous talk with an intelligent reply. Now maybe she could relax somewhat. "How long has your family lived in the Los Angeles area?"

"Since the 1790's," Ray responded. "My great-great-grandfather got a land grant from Spain which gave the family thousands of acres of what was then desert-like wilderness. This area was a slow-starter compared to the East Coast, or the Northwest, or even your Texas.

In 1850, before California's statehood, the population of Los Angeles was only 1,610. We have some photos of the old family house and surrounding structures you'd find amusing. Los Angeles was like the Wild West, haciendas and ranch land. The 1876 transcontinental railroad completion spurred the area's growth, and by 1900 the area population was over 100,000."

I like the way he speaks, Edna thought. *He's full of information.* "Are all your days spent providing historic tours to new women in town, or do you have a place you usually have to go to during the week?"

Ray laughed at her direct playfulness. "Actually I am employed, yes. Since our family name held some weight, it helped me to become elected Superintendent of the Los Angeles City School District. The job keeps me pretty busy, often turning into twelve to sixteen hour days."

Edna was impressed at Ray's position. She had always respected education. "What sorts of things does a School Superintendent do that keeps you working that much?"

"Well, my responsibilities include choosing sites for new schools to service the growing population, budgeting, periodic city, county and school board meetings, and curriculum decisions, among other things. And then at night it's important to attend society functions to hob nob with the movers and shakers. There's a strong interaction between the Los Angeles area government and the monied interests who are instrumental in helping to further develop the area."

Edna watched Ray intently as he spoke enthusiastically about his work. The sunlight bounced off his dark hair and his eyes glistened. He obviously loved Los Angeles and his job. His enthusiasm was palpable. "How interesting," was all Edna could manage to respond.

"For example, you mentioned your streetcar ride. Those tracks were very carefully planned to correlate with where subdivisions would be built, along with placement of schools, public buildings, and various services for communities. A great deal of wheeling and dealing took place to obtain certain of those streetcar routes. Years ago, my father who owned land in many of the proposed development areas was involved in some of the planning, along with the railroad men. Every step forward in this region has been a confluence of many powerful forces behind the scenes vying to obtain the best for not only the area but their own pocketbooks and corporations. Nothing, nothing at all came easily."

Ray's voice became more forceful, faster and louder as he spoke about the streetcar growth. Edna had never thought in terms of streetcar routes being controversial. She'd never even thought about regional development. *I've always taken these types of things for granted.*

Ray started talking again. "The electric companies, to drum up more power usage, were also instrumental in the spread of the trolley system throughout the Los Angeles area.

This transportation system has served Los Angeles well for a number of years despite competing interests, consolidations and takeovers that at times stalled direct progress. But that happens in many industries. Look what happened with the hundreds of car companies. They've been whittled down to a handful over the years."

I could listen to him for hours. Try not to look too dreamy-eyed. Say something.

"Yes, I heard about the car companies," Edna shook herself out of her reverie. "My Daddy had a Ford and he was so proud of it, particularly when a lot of other auto makers went bankrupt. I learned to drive at fourteen out on the Houston country roads. But, we also took the streetcars around Houston a lot, even though we had a car. It was quick, easy and economical."

Ray looked at Edna, "Since fourteen, huh? Well, aren't you Southerners early bloomers. What else did you learn at fourteen?"

Edna ignored Ray's insinuation. "Well, Ray, honey, I hate to admit it but ..." She drew out her pauses as long as the slowest Texan she had ever heard. "I -- I -- I learned to, to ..." Edna slowly took a small bite of her bear claw, and then a slow sip of coffee while looking up at Ray who was totally focused, watching her very attentively, awaiting her next words.

"...smoke."

Ray burst out laughing. "I thought you were headed in another direction. Smoking, huh? Every woman on the silver screen has been smoking for years. Can't blame you for identifying with some of those glamour girls. You're every bit as gorgeous and a heck of a lot more spirited than some I've met. I'm not a smoker. I try to keep my temple clean. Clean body, keen judgment. But, hey, I don't judge others. Feel free when you want to indulge."

Edna briefly considered going to the car and getting her pocketbook which contained her cigarettes, but decided against it. She didn't want to change the tempo. Ray's company, the view, the coffee were stimulating enough.

But Ray had different plans. "How about us finishing up here and moving on down the road. We've got a full day ahead of us."

"Sure enough." Edna took her last bite of the bear claw, her last sip of coffee. Then with a toss of her hair she turned to look directly at Ray, smiling with her mouth and eyes. Ray reflexively smiled back and held her gaze for a few long seconds.

Edna felt a queasy feeling in her stomach. She recognized it to mean attraction or excitement. *Ray certainly knows how to make a woman feel she matters. He seems too good to be true.*

From Mulholland Drive, Ray told Thomas to drive west on Sunset Boulevard to the Pacific Ocean. Along the way they toured the growing University of California campus, and then stopped briefly at the Will Rogers Ranch where they watched some polo skirmishes.

When Sunset Boulevard ended at the ocean, Thomas turned right and travelled for a few miles north up the coast until Ray told him to stop at a Malibu restaurant for lunch. The tiny restaurant was built out on pillars into the ocean, with full length windows hanging directly over the Pacific.

The water setting reminded Edna a bit of Galveston, but the sea here was grayer, darker, and the crashing waves were much more powerful than the warm, clear Galveston Gulf water.

"Two crab salads and two ice teas," Ray ordered, then turned to Edna. "What's the matter? You have a sad look on your face. You like crab, don't you?"

"Oh, yes. And I love ice tea. Sorry. I was just imagining what it would feel like to be adrift alone out on that vast ocean, half-way to China."

"What a thought. Well, concentrate on this beautiful coastline. You can even see red tile roofs on the Palos Verdes Peninsula today."

"Yes. It's beautiful."

During lunch, Ray shared the recent history of Malibu. "The family who purchased the Malibu Colony portion of an old land grant slowed this area's expansion. Builders fought in court for years to merely construct roads here. The owners were against any development and wouldn't even allow railroad tracks. It wasn't until recently that heirs permitted sections of Malibu land to be leased for ten-year periods."

Edna was surprised. "You mean people who own these homes and businesses don't own their land?"

"Right. They're willing to pay the ongoing land leases in order to overlook the Pacific Ocean. To some people there's a status attached to paying to lease land."

"To lease the land your house sits on holds more status than actually owning the land?"

Ray ignored her question and continued, "In many instances there isn't even much ground that the houses were built upon. Pillars or pylon foundations are pounded into the beach, with supports built into the cliff sides somewhat in the manner of a hillside mountain cabin. Or, like this restaurant. The ocean waves crash right underneath this restaurant at high tide."

"Sounds shaky to me. I'll take solid ground any time."

As they were finishing their meal, a couple of gentlemen came up to their table and said hello to Ray. Ray introduced them to Edna. There was a brief exchange of small talk and mention of a meeting next Tuesday night. After the men left the restaurant, Ray explained to Edna, "Those are two executives from Standard Engines. They've been in town for a few weeks trying to put together some business deals for their company in the Midwest. I've seen them around town at various functions. Nice guys."

"Oh," was all Edna could muster.

Ray continued, "A national petroleum company and rubber company are also involved in the consortium. The companies are working together to benefit their mutual interests."

"How interesting," Edna appreciated that Ray was sharing his business with her but her nicely full stomach was the focus of her interest right now. *I've never had such a good crab salad,* Edna thought to herself. *This was a wonderful meal and setting.*

Out in the restaurant's parking lot, there was an above- ground saltwater pool which held four sea lions. Two of them were sunbathing on a large rock-type structure in the pool's center.

"How clever." Edna was delighted by the one of the large sea lions lunging for a tiny sardine in one bystander's hand.

Ray went and bought a bag for Edna to feed them and returned.

"I think I'll pass, Ray. Thanks, but I don't want to get that sardine smell on my hands."

Ray handed the bag to a young boy who was standing there. They watched the child toss the sardines to the animals. The largest sea lion swam right up to the side of the pool and barked for more. Edna found it thrilling to be in such close proximity to these powerful ocean creatures that were friendly to humans.

"Ray, I wonder if they could be trained like dogs, to do tricks," Edna asked.

"Well, yes, they can be. I've seen them perform in the circus. They're smart animals."

"Well, they sure are quick at figuring out who has the fish and where to go to get it."

"That's a good first step in any animal training, food bribery and reward. Carrots and sticks. What would you want to train them to do?"

"Clap their flippers on cue? Swim through a hoop? Bark? Their faces are so alive. They remind me of Freckles, the fox terrier my father had when I was a child. He would follow my dad everywhere."

Edna was suddenly saddened by thinking of her father.

"What's the matter?" Ray was sensitive to her mood change.

"Nothing, Ray." Edna snapped out of her momentary blues. *Thinking of the past doesn't help when there's nothing that can change it.* She turned and gave Ray a flirtatious eye-twinkling, head-tilted smile.

"Well, let's go back towards downtown and I'll show you what else the Los Angeles area has to offer."

Leaving Malibu, Ray had Thomas drive them past Marion Davies' house on the Santa Monica Beach. "She has over fifty rooms in her place," Ray told Edna. "I've been to some wonderful parties there. At one party, some exuberant souls wound up swimming in the ocean at night in their dress clothes. Quite a wild bunch, some of these Hollywood people."

"Did you join them in their swim?" Edna wondered.

"No. It didn't seem to me to be the most reasonable action, ruining their tuxedos and ball gowns for a few minutes of alcohol-fueled thrill. My nature's more practical."

Edna fell silent. She was thinking about how alcohol could make people do odd things. She thought about how her father drank day and night after her mother died. *Mama could have climbed down from their car just fine on her own, but daddy wanted to be chivalrous and lifted her in his arms. He dropped her and she hit the ground hard. He blamed himself for mama and baby brother's death. Daddy was never again a fun drinker. He became a sloppy drunk. He had trouble even continuing his iceman's route. Daddy loved mama so much. He had been so heartbroken, so very, very heartbroken.*

"Hey, beautiful, you're staring at the ocean. What's on that pretty mind of yours?"

"Nothing, Ray. Nothing."

"Well, if you've seen enough, let's head up to Griffith Park."

Edna looked at Ray and felt better. "Terrific. Yes, let's go."

Griffith Park was a wonder to Edna. "Houston has a lot of trees, but not a huge park like this."

"Few people realize that Griffith Park's 4,253 acres make it the largest city park in America." Ray sounded as proud as if he had built the park himself.

They were now passing through an area called "Fern Dell." Large tropical fern trees were artistically landscaped to form an exquisitely groomed tropical forest. Edna rolled down the limousine's window to get a better look.

"How beautiful. Exotic."

"This park has unique enclaves," Ray responded. "The fern garden is a wonderful place to stroll but we should probably save your feet for dancing tonight."

Edna laughed, appreciative of his concern. She rolled up the window as the limousine moved on.

Ray continued his audio tour, "Some of that Kennedy-Von Stroheim fiasco that Gloria Swanson starred in was filmed in this area we're driving by now. It was supposed to resemble the German countryside."

Edna's eyes lit up. "I read about that movie. *Queen Kelly.* It wasn't released. I'm not a Gloria Swanson fan. She seems pretentious to a southerner like me. But I sure wanted to see the movie to find out what all the fuss was about."

Ray continued his tour guide monologue. "A lot of the studios film in Griffith Park. In Los Angeles you never know when you'll see a production at work. Many of the Arabian desert scenes are filmed down in the sand dunes between Santa Monica and Manhattan Beach."

"I caught a movie being filmed on Hollywood Boulevard last week when I was on the streetcar. It was so exciting." Edna continued, "This park is so beautiful. Too bad there isn't a streetcar line up here. It's such a wonderful getaway and more people should have easy access."

"Well, developers can't build here since it's a city park, so there's not the incentive to advocate getting tracks up here. But, if you promise not to spread the word, I'll ease your concern about access."

"Mum's the word."

Those executives I introduced you to down in Malibu are trying to increase bus lines around the Los Angeles area, and plans are that new buses from their company will take people all throughout Griffith Park and to other area in the near future."

"Well, good," Edna said.

They'd now arrived at the impressive observatory dome, which sat on the south slope of Mount Hollywood, overlooking the vast city basin. The view from there was similar to what they had seen that morning up on Mulholland Drive. Thomas let Edna and Ray out of the car in front of the observatory. "I'll be back in one hour, sir," Thomas said to his boss.

Ray bought two tickets and they entered the Griffith Park observatory. Inside the door was a huge hanging pendulum structure. Ray led Edna over to it and they both looked down.

"This is a Foucault Pendulum. It demonstrates the earth's rotation by acting like a gyroscope, staying in a fixed direction while the earth rotates beneath it."

"Impressive."

"Yes, it is. It's 240 pounds, and swings 40 feet."

Ray led Edna to the planetarium next, where they sat down and awaited the show. After a brief time, the lights went out and Edna was thrilled to see the ceiling transform into a daytime sky like the beautiful blue Texan sky with its white cumulous clouds. Then the day changed to night and stars began to twinkle. Some of the stars turned brilliantly bright, but appeared to glow from within.

The planetarium narrator focused the audience on the big and little dipper, and other constellations. When the speaker mentioned the "lovers constellation," Ray reached over and gently took Edna's hand.

It fascinated Edna that many star configurations formed a familiar shape and had a name and meaning attached to them. She knew about the big and little dipper, and the north star, but some of the more esoteric structures were new to her.

When the show was over and the overhead lights went back on, it was at first difficult for her eyes to readjust to the full light.

Ray started talking in his tour guide mode once again. "Okay. You've seen some of the park. There's also a zoo, riding stables, a merry-go-round, and a children's train. Did you want to explore more? We could go ride the merry-go-round. Or, are you ready for dinner and dancing? The Ambassador Hotel's Cocoanut Grove has palm trees like you saw in the Fern Grove or like the Canary Palms in Echo Park. Plus, they have a terrific dance band booked there now."

"Ray, I'm having a wonderful time, but am getting just a little tired. It's been quite a day already. And, what about changing? Where could I freshen up?"

"The limo has lights, mirrors, and privacy curtains. Plus, Thomas has been instructed to have a pick-me-up waiting for us."

"You've thought of everything. If your planning and follow-through at work is as thorough as for this date, the Los Angeles School System must be in terrific condition."

"That's it, build me up. You know how to make a guy feel appreciated. Let's go show you off at the Grove."

Edna and Ray were met by Thomas at the side of the observatory. Thomas offered them a martini from a silver shaker. Despite prohibition, Edna had an occasional drink as did most people she knew. After the full day she felt a cocktail might hit the spot, and perhaps would replace some of her flagging energy. They both sat in the back of the limousine with the doors and windows open to the fresh air, and sipped their drinks.

When they were through with their conversation and cocktails, Thomas drew all the curtains in the passenger compartment, and Ray and Thomas left Edna to prepare for the dinner and dancing to come.

In ten minutes she was ready, and carefully climbed out of the back of the limousine.

"Don't you look beautiful," Ray complimented.

"Well, thank you."

Ray then took his turn to change into his evening attire. Thomas offered Edna one of the portable chairs they had sat in that morning up on Mulholland but she declined. She stood and watched the crimson sun float on the horizon for a few minutes, before it began to sink into the ocean.

Ray joined her as the western sky was changing to a vivid red. Edna felt literally an electric spark as his hand took hers. They stood silently together and watched the sky turn mauve, then pinkish, then begin to grey. Once the sunset colors had completely disappeared from the sky, Ray gave her a light kiss on her cheek and helped her back into the car.

"Thomas, on to the Ambassador."

"We have a dinner reservation for 6:30 p.m., an early seating. I realize it has been a long day and I won't keep you out too late. Dancing starts at 8:00. We'll have time for a leisurely meal, then can catch a couple of the band sets."

Edna felt the day had already been magical. She had met some nice people in Los Angeles in her short time here, but Ray was someone very special. *How could a day be more perfect? I could very quickly get used to this pampering.*

As the maitre d' led them into the large, open room of the Cocoanut Grove, Edna was awed by the sophisticated, tropical atmosphere, with groves of palm trees and faux monkeys that were posed in various positions on the palms. The whole setting was exotic. Ozzie Nelson and his orchestra were playing background music. They were the lead-in band for the main entertainment, The Cocoanut Grove Orchestra.

Heads turned to look at Edna and Ray. The Grove was a place where everyone wondered if the next couple entering might be the latest hot screen couple. The tropical decor that decorated the room was only outshone by the attractive patrons. Edna felt a palpable excitement in the air, as if all the luckiest souls in the world were together tonight in that one unique room.

The maitre d', who knew Ray, sat them at one of the best tables, near where the orchestra was playing. Easy access to the dance floor. Perfect location. Edna's chair was pulled out by the maitre d', then gently pushed in as she sat down.

Her linen napkin was taken from the dinner setting and laid carefully across her lap. *Twice in one day.* Los Angeles was full of surprises, both small and large.

"Ray, this place is the cat's meow," Edna gushed. "I love the palm trees and monkeys."

"Some of these palms were the originals from the set of Valentino's *The Sheik*," Ray explained.

"It's so exotic," Edna replied. "I'd love to have one of these palm trees in my apartment. They create such an ambience."

"Yes. This place is a lot of fun. At midnight, more monkeys drop from the ceiling."

They sat and talked awhile before ordering dinner. A few people stopped by the table to say hello to Ray, and he introduced Edna to all of them as "this little Southern gal has just arrived in town and I'm showing her what Los Angeles nightlife offers."

It was cute the first time, but a bit much by the third. Edna smiled at each new person, stayed quiet beyond a polite "hello," and played along with Ray's apparent need to be the big shot. His friends all seemed friendly enough and were certainly dressed exquisitely. Some of the women eyed Edna's blue Texas dress up and down with that critical look the haughtiest women have mastered. Edna knew her dress was inexpensive but, overall, it appeared that she passed inspection in Ray's friends' eyes.

Ray had caught some of the women's attempts at eye put-downs and after they left he leaned over and whispered to Edna, "Don't let those women get to you. They're just jealous. With your face and figure you'd look gorgeous in a gunny sack."

Edna burst out laughing, then Ray joined in. He was sensitive to her moods, and knew how to get to her.

Ray pointed out to Edna the son and daughter-in-law of Edward Harriman, who Ray explained had made a lot of money off of the streetcar route that was extended out to Santa Monica, Manhattan, Hermosa and Redondo Beaches. "See that dress she's wearing? It cost a fortune, but she doesn't hold a candle to you."

Edna took Ray's hand and squeezed it.

After a wonderful dinner of filet mignon with baked potato, the Cocoanut Grove Orchestra began to play its music. When they played "Dancing In the Dark," Ray asked her to dance. He led expertly, in perfect time with the tempo. They moved well together and as the dance numbers progressed, Ray seemed to invent some new dance moves which Edna seamlessly followed. It was as if they had known each other and danced together for years.

True to Ray's promise of an early work night, Edna was to the front steps of her apartment building by 11:00 p.m. After the long day, she was in bed within a half hour. As she was falling asleep she thought of the way Ray had kissed her lightly on the cheek at the door, and had said "I'll talk with you soon."

Edna's Los Angeles move had begun as a whirlwind of insecurity disguised by necessity and bold courage. But lying in bed tonight, thinking of her day with this appealing man who had shown her such a terrific time and treated her with such respect, she felt safe and secure. *My life is looking up. Thank you, God. I'm very grateful.*

CHAPTER EIGHT

PICKFAIR

Edna and Ray had now been dating for over six months. As she awoke this Sunday morning she looked over at the palm tree with attached faux monkey that decorated one corner of her apartment. Ray had sent her the gift after their fourth time dining and dancing at the Cocoanut Grove. The accompanying note read "May this be merely one of many future wish fulfillments. I appreciate the splendor of your company. Ray."

He was spoiling her at a dazzling rate while expanding her knowledge of the entire Los Angeles area. Ray took her up to Lake Arrowhead and Big Bear Lake one day, where they went ice-skating, made a snowman and threw snowballs at each other. Another day they walked across the oriental bridge, then saw *Blue Boy* and *Pinkie* at the Huntington Mansion in Pasadena. Bicycling on the Hermosa Beach Strand, and then going to the jazz club down there filled one wonderful, warm afternoon and evening.

Some days Edna struggled out of bed and through the work day. Ray's fast-paced lifestyle was demanding. With the depression, work was scarce. She knew it was critical to be reliable at her job no matter how late her nights were.

Since they spent so much time together, the relationship was more and more comfortable yet her heart still beat faster whenever she first spotted his handsome face.

There had been only one cautionary note in their relationship. One night Edna accompanied Ray to the Los Angeles City Council meeting where he made a presentation. He explained to the Council what the School District's anticipated expansion would entail over the next decade.

Edna saw there the two gentlemen she had met at the Malibu restaurant on their first date. The two men were members of a group that pulled Ray aside and started speaking to him in the hall down from the Council Chambers' door.

When Edna approached to talk to Ray, one man brusquely told her, "This is a private conversation."

Another man directed, "Why don't you walk down to the opposite end of the hall while we're talking."

Ray nodded when she looked to him for some support.

Seeing no alternative, she walked down the hall and stood there off to one side alone. She worked at appearing nonchalant by lighting a cigarette and standing next to one of the ashtrays. *After all this is probably about some business deal*, she rationalized Ray's behavior. But she was angered by the treatment.

Some of the men raised their voices at one point. When Edna looked she noticed they were talking directly to Ray, and the urgency in their voices sounded like they were criticizing him for something extremely serious. When they raised their volume, Edna heard something about "gasoline," "bus routes," "Cadillac." The disjointed concepts did not make sense to her. *Maybe they're discussing the budget needs for school busses but what's that have to do with a Cadillac?*

When the conversation abruptly ended, and everyone in that group dispersed, Ray took his time in slowly walking down to the end of the corridor to join her.

"What's wrong, Ray? What did those men want?"

He coldly and curtly cut her off, "Nothing. None of your business." Edna was hurt by his first sign of rudeness. But he was sensitive enough to notice the look on her face and quickly changed his mood. "Don't worry your pretty little head. It's just business. Better for you that you don't know about it. Business sometimes means business. I'll take care of it." Ray's confident assurances soothed her concerns for the moment, but Edna's intuition told her there was an underlying issue that should not be taken lightly.

Today, Ray was going to pick her up at noon and they were to attend a charity brunch at *Pickfair*. Edna was thrilled. It would be wonderful to see where Mary Pickford and Douglas Fairbanks lived. Photos of the house and grounds had been displayed in *Photoplay* and *Modern Screen* magazines, but to actually go there to visit was tremendously exciting.

She had discussed with many of her co-workers what she should wear for the Pickfair brunch today. The girls had suggested a new sleek, fitting, shorter-length dress would be suitable, preferably in a blue fabric to match her eyes.

Edna lacked funds for an expensive new outfit, and there was not enough time for layaway so a friend in the high-fashion department lent her a dress sample that had been taken off of a store mannequin. The blue rayon dress fit her beautifully, and the display's matching small hat with a navy blue veil also looked fabulous on her.

Edna preferred the veil to be worn up so that her forehead and eyes shown. She also wore her gold charm bracelet that Ray had begun building for her. The bracelet had two charms thus far, a heart with an arrow through it, and a tiny bicycle. The expensive dress gave her the confidence she needed for this social occasion with the hoi-polloi of Hollywood.

That afternoon, as Ray's limo drove through the gates of Pickfair, a thrilling surge filled her whole body and gave her goosebumps of excitement.

She had never been to a home of this magnitude. It was grand and gorgeous. The magnificent grounds contained the deepest green freshly-mowed grass, dotted by flowers, fountains, tennis courts, and an Olympic-sized swimming pool. This lifestyle was extraordinary.

The party was outside and the most attractive people were scattered about the vast area. Ray whispered in Edna's ear, "You're the prettiest woman here."

After the shrimp salad, melon balls and champagne she and Ray consumed from the buffet, Edna excused herself and escaped to the restroom for a few minutes to reapply her lipstick and use the facilities. While washing her hands in the black marble sink, she saw a gold ring sitting by the washbasin. When she picked up the ring she was surprised to see that one side was a watch face encircled by small diamonds. *A watch ring. How unique. I've never seen one. I wonder who left it here?*

She took the ring with her when she left the restroom. She had been keeping her distance from Mary Pickford all afternoon since Ray had first introduced them. Now Edna had a compelling reason to approach her again.

Miss Pickford was sitting with two other women in tall director's chairs out in the sun. The three women were chatting while observing the mingling crowd. Edna walked over to where the three sat. "Mary," she said. "I found this adorable ring in your black and pink guest restroom by the rear door. Do you know who it might belong to?"

"Why that's mine," one of the women spoke up. "How forgetful of me. My head would fall off if my neck didn't anchor it to my body." All four women laughed.

"Well, it's a terrific watch. What an unusual design," Edna said.

"Thank you," said the owner as she took the ring and placed it back on her finger.

"And thank you so much, darling, for taking care of my friend here," said Mary. "One of these other not-so-honest guests would have walked off with it. You're a doll. Why don't you --"

Just then Ray walked up and interrupted. "There you are. I thought someone might have kidnapped you for a moment. I'd like for you to meet someone. Excuse me, Mary, ladies. You don't mind if I steal her away, do you?"

"Ray, you know whatever you do is fine with me," Mary retorted. "You've got a gem of a gal there."

Ray led Edna away from the three women.

"Thanks again for finding my ring."

"You're welcome."

"What ring, Edna?" Ray asked as they walked down to a nearby brick pathway cutting through the grass.

"Oh, I found the cutest ring-watch in the guest restroom and took it over to Mary. It was lying next to the sink as if someone had taken it off to wash their hands and forgot about it. It happened to belong to one of the women who was sitting there with her."

"How thoughtful of you. Well, in the meantime I ran into a man I want you to meet. There he is. Now, turn on your brightest charm."

They walked up to a gentleman dressed in a hand-stitched navy blue suit, with a white, high-collared, bespoke shirt. His black leather shoes Edna recognized as being the most expensive men's shoes sold at Dyas Department Store, and they were exclusively custom fitted and ordered by the pair. Although the gentleman was not classically handsome, there was the aura of money and power about him. If clothes made the man, as so many magazines and books were preaching lately, this man was obviously playing at the top of his game. All his clothing was exquisitely tailored. But steely eyes gazed coldly at Edna as Ray introduced them.

"Mr. Blaine, this is Edna."

"Edna, this is Mr. Blaine. He noticed you earlier and wanted to meet you."

"Hello," Edna said, while smiling at Mr. Blaine, trying to charm as instructed. *I wonder if he'll warm up.*

"Hello," replied Mr. Blaine, his chilly demeanor not melting in the slightest.

"How are you enjoying the afternoon, Mr. Blaine?" Edna inquired, making an extra effort to be polite.

"Fine. Nice place. Good food. Need to get to the airport soon, though. Have to return to the Detroit snow."

"Oh, you're from back East," Edna responded warmly to the stilted voice.

"Well, technically the midwest, but, yes, east of here. I travel a lot," his monotone almost whined.

Ray interrupted. "Edna, Mr. Blaine is the President of Standard Engines. He's in Los Angeles on business. A number of us local community leaders had dinner with Mr. Blaine last night. He has some progressive ideas for our area. Mr. Blaine is a brilliant businessman."

"Why, Mr. Blaine. You must be famous. Standard Engines is one of the most prominent companies in America. Have you met President Hoover?"

Edna finally got a slight smile out of him, perhaps at her own naivete, but at least it was a smile.

"Yes, The President and I are good friends," replied Mr. Blaine.

"Is President Hoover going to get us out of this bad economy soon?" Edna asked.

"He's an engineer, an international businessman, has served on many Boards of Directors and was Secretary of Commerce. He knows business as well as anyone and certainly knows what's good for the economy," stated Mr. Blaine in his blunt, now clearly arrogant manner.

Rather abruptly, two men in poorly-cut suits and sloppily-worn hats walked up to the three of them, and without introducing themselves one whispered into Mr. Blaine's ear.

"I must be going, Ray. Edna, nice to meet you. Ray is a lucky man," said Mr. Blaine.

"It was a pleasure to meet you, Mr. Blaine," Edna responded with a smile.

Mr. Blaine and the two men left.

"He sure is a cold fish," Edna told Ray after Mr. Blaine was out of earshot. "And his two men look like thugs."

"He may be a cold fish, my dear, but he may be making me and some of my friends incredibly wealthy in the next few years. He has a grand plan to expand auto-related business in Los Angeles County, and those of us who are working with him on the ground floor will make a killing."

"Ray, it seems to me you have more than enough success and money already," Edna replied. "What is he planning to do that will make you wealthier?"

"Honey, business is a man's arena, and where big money is concerned, you either continue to grow your interests or by sheer inertia you start going backwards," Ray replied. "Don't worry your beautiful little head about the details."

"This is such a marvelous event, I don't want to worry about anything, much less the business plans of a man like Blaine," Edna agreed. She chose to ignore Ray's patronizing attitude.

"Good. Let's go get another champagne flute and take a walk down to the Koi pond," Ray suggested. "We can toss a coin and make a wish."

"Whatever you say. Lead the way." This was one of the better days of Edna's young life, and formulating her coin toss wish was as serious a pursuit as she wanted to think about at the moment.

CHAPTER NINE

EDNA, MARIE AND RUSS

This Tuesday's *Los Angeles Post* caught Edna's eye. The bold headlines stated *VANDALS HIT TRACKS*. She stopped in front of the newsstand near work and glanced through the article. Some of the streetcar tracks had been pulled up during the early morning hours after the trolleys stopped their runs. She was lucky it was not her route but knew some of the girls at work came from that direction. *Why would anyone do such a thing?*

Edna was assigned to work today in high-end women's sportswear. The department carried riding breeches, tennis dresses, bathing outfits, and even some of those risqué shorts. They also sold the long, wide slacks like Marlene Dietrich had been scandalously wearing around town. Very few women had the courage to try the shorts or the slacks.

Edna enjoyed the department because the ladies who shopped there were of the active, curious, thus fascinating variety. Most participated in the Southern California lifestyle and took full advantage of its beautiful outdoors. Like *Photoplay* had suggested, one sure way for single women to meet and mingle with men in the Los Angeles area was to watch or play sports. Last time she worked in this department, she met Babe Zakarias, the famous female Olympic gold medal winner, who bought several new outfits. Edna never knew who might be her next customer. That kept her job interesting daily no matter where she was working.

Today, however, was a switch-inventory day in the department, and that involved a lot of pure manual labor. After making three sales her first half hour, the customers briefly dwindled so she started removing a section of clothing from the front racks and taking it into the back room.

As she carried an armload of inventory from the back room out front she noticed three new customers browsing. The second salesperson in the department had not yet arrived and it was thirty minutes into the shift. Edna became concerned that this pace might continue without the necessary assistance for the customers.

In this economy there were the haves and the have-nots. So many people were without enough food to eat and yet inexplicably there were always women shopping. Since most people dressed up to go shopping downtown it was difficult to tell who had money and who didn't.

Edna hung up the new clothing then went over to the cash register area to quickly write a note expressing the need for additional help in the department. She loved the process of rolling the paper and carefully placing it into the pneumatic tube. She then popped the tube into the delivery system that immediately took her note downstairs into the administration office. She stood there awaiting a return message while observing the customers for signs of any obvious need.

The return swooshing sound of the tube came quickly and she took out and unrolled the message. "Velma was supposed to be with you today, Edna, but can't make it in until much later because of the track vandalism out where she lives. Try and hold down the fort and we'll see if we can locate extra help from some less busy department."

What could Edna do? Her parents had taught her that she must do the very best she could at anything she did. Doing the task well was in itself the reward. However, that philosophy became frustrating when she couldn't possibly handle all that needed to be done.

Edna shook her head in disgust, thinking again about the vandalism of the streetcar tracks. *How in the world could someone do such a thing? And to what purpose? Oh, well, get to work.*

She saw that the original three ladies still seemed satisfied as each was searching through the clothing racks, so decided to help a new customer who had just begun looking at the riding habit rack. "Hello there. May I help you?"

"Well, yes. I'm looking for some riding breeches, Edna."

"Marie. Hi. I hadn't recognized you from the back. That chignon is stunning. You somehow look different outside of our apartment building. Why aren't you at work today?"

"My job's located out on the broken trolley line. I can't get to work because of the torn-up tracks. Tomorrow I'll get up extra early and try to share one of the scarce cabs available. Can you imagine someone destroying the transportation line?"

"That's just what I was thinking. We count on those streetcars. It's shameful you can't get to your job because of some idiotic act of vandalism. What is wrong with some people?"

"Edna, I don't know. It makes no sense. I can't afford it but I'll have to use some of the small savings I've scrimped to build. Cabs are expensive." Marie was obviously upset and looked sadder than Edna had seen her. They had had cocktails together at the apartment building and knew that each had come from a difficult background. This was another blow that Marie didn't need.

"Well, honey. I don't mean to be rude, but how in the world can you afford these riding breeches?" Edna asked.

"I really can't, Edna. I'm just looking. Thought I'd try some on. I've always wanted to go horseback riding up in Griffith Park like the movie stars do, and see if maybe as a bonus I could find an interesting or interested man," Marie said. "It sure doesn't hurt to look and try on these fun clothes; does it?"

"Of course not, honey. Here, try these. These are top-of- the-line riding breeches. I've seen a photograph of Mary Pickford in this brand. You're a size eight; right? Let me open up a dressing room for you. Dream a little bit."

"Thanks, Edna. I appreciate it."

After Edna got Marie settled into the dressing room, she went over to help another woman who was looking at some of the new casual wide-legged slacks. "May I help you?"

"Just browsing," the woman replied.

Edna noticed a three-carat plus radiant diamond ring, with matching diamond wedding band on her ungloved hand. *Wealthy married woman,* Edna categorized. "Well, if you need any help, please don't hesitate to ask."

Other customers looked preoccupied so Edna returned to her stocking duties. As she went to get some of the new merchandise from the back, she thought about Marie. It could as easily have been Edna stuck without the trolley to get to work.

Marie had moved out here from the midwest and did not yet have a steady beau. More reserved than Edna, she didn't meet people as easily. Yet Marie had such a solid dignity and warmth that Edna admired. She was a terrific young woman with good values.

Marie was about Edna's size, yet resembled more a pretty librarian or schoolteacher. Her wavy brown hair and warm brown eyes would be a magnet for men if she would let herself open up more. She tended to be guarded and proper. Yet she was a woman that other women could trust. Edna loved meeting women like that. Although Edna was extremely loyal she did not always receive that same consideration in return. Some women found Edna's beauty combined with personality a target of envy. With Marie, Edna had found someone who, like herself, could be counted upon.

After hanging the new merchandize, and ringing up one statuesque lady's choice of ecru wide-legged slacks on the cash register, Edna returned to the dressing room area. Marie was still in her stall. Edna heard some sniffling.

"Marie. It's Edna."

Marie slowly opened the door and Edna could see that her eyes were red from crying. She still had the riding breeches on and they looked elegant.

"Marie, those fit you beautifully. You look fabulous in those. Are you all right, honey? I know you've been in here a while."

"Oh, Edna. Yes. I guess I'm just worn out. I got dizzy, almost fainted. I haven't eaten a full meal in days."

"Oh, honey. I didn't realize. Well, I can help you resolve that. Ray is gong to take me to dinner tonight. You must join us."

"Oh, no, Edna. I wouldn't want to intrude. I'll be all right."

"Marie, I won't take no for an answer. We're going to dinner at the Cocoanut Grove, and, who knows, you might meet some elegant bachelor there. Why don't you change, and go on back to the apartment building to rest and plan for tonight. Ray will pick us up around 7:30. I insist you come with us. You've been so kind to me at the apartment building these past few months."

"Well, I could use a night out. It would get my mind off myself. And, a good meal might work wonders to improve my spirits."

"Great. It's settled."

Edna went back to her purse which was hidden in a nook beneath the cash register, and removed about eight packages of crackers she had there for just such an emergency. When Marie came over to say good-bye, Edna said, "Here, this will tide you over," and handed her a tiny Dyas accessories bag.

Marie looked into the bag, saw the crackers and said, "Oh, Edna, thank you. I was planning to go by the cafeteria to get some on my way home. This will save me the trip. I'll go rest and get ready for tonight."

"And, Marie, if you want those riding breaches, I can put them on my layaway plan and you'll get my employee discount. You can pay me each month and I'll make the payments for you."

"Oh, Edna, that's so sweet of you."

"Well, think it over and let me know."

"I will. See you later."

"Okay. Eat, rest and get some strength back, honey."

An employee arrived in the department that day only to help Edna break for lunch. Because the other salesgirl could only stay fifteen minutes, Edna went to the break room downstairs and ate some saltines, accompanied by coffee with cream and sugar. At least the time went by quickly. She liked busy days that consumed her attention.

When Edna arrived home that evening, she was surprised to find a vase of tropical flowers, a box of See's candies, with a card sitting outside her apartment door. Ray was so full of surprises. Edna took the flowers, candy and card inside, placed the flowers on a side table, and sat down to open the card. What romantic notion did Ray write to warm her heart this time? The note stated:

"Edna, Am so sorry but an important business matter has arisen. Am unable to make this evening's engagement. Please forgive me for this late cancellation. I'll make it up to you as soon as possible.

Sleep well dear one,

Ray"

Edna was disappointed mainly because of Marie. She was tired from work and would have been just as happy to stay in and rest tonight, but Marie needed a good meal. Edna opened the See's candies and chose a milk-chocolate covered caramel. Perhaps the sugar would help her sort this out. She turned on her radio to her favorite music station. Her door wasn't yet closed since she walked in with her arms full, and she now heard a knock. She looked over to see Russ, the neighbor from Apartment G, standing in the hall.

"Hi, Edna. How're you doing tonight? I saw those lovely flowers you were sent earlier. An ardent admirer, huh?"

"Hi, Russ. Yes, so ardent he stood Marie and I up this evening. Come on in."

Russ entered. This was the first time he had actually been inside Edna's room and he looked around, taking note of what she had done in the small space. Cozy. Not too cluttered; not too stark.

"Nice apartment. Homey."

"Thanks."

"So Marie and you are free? So am I. How about letting me take you out for dinner tonight? I've been wanting to get to know both of you better. You seem to be two of the nicest women in the building. I'd be honored to escort you. What do you say?"

Edna could not believe how perfect the timing was for Russ's invitation. Russ had a fine reputation among the other apartment house tenants whenever his name came up in conversation.

"Russ, that would be wonderful. I've been wanting to get to know you better also. I'm sure it will be fine with Marie. Why not give me forty-five minutes. We'll be ready around 7:30. I know she was dressing for the Cocoanut Grove. Where did you want to go this evening?"

"That would be fine with me as long as we make it an early evening. Tomorrow's a busy work day," Russ offered.

"A man after my own heart. An early evening would be just great tonight."

"All right. Then I'll stop by at 7:30. See you later."

Edna smiled. "See you in a bit."

As he went out the door and closed it behind him, Edna realized she had not even had the good manners to offer Russ a piece of candy or a cocktail. *Oh, well. A tired working girl can't always be the perfect hostess. I'd better hurry and get ready.*

Russ pulled up to the Ambassador Hotel valet parking area and the valet helped the two women out of his Buick. Russ was dressed up in a dark suit with bow tie. Marie and Edna were in their short evening gowns, high heels and held clutch handbags. It was a handsome trio that walked into the Cocoanut Grove that evening.

The Maitre d' recognized Edna from prior visits with Ray and gave the three of them a lovely table. Russ quickly ordered Oysters Rockefeller as an hors d'oeuvre.

Edna found Russ to be personable and calmly confident. He entertained the ladies with talk of his work. "I'm West Coast Manager for a rubber company headquartered in New Jersey. Rubber sales are growing along with the auto business. As population growth and cars multiply, my responsibilities are increasing. And, there's talk of synthetic rubber on the horizon which can eventually replace much of the foreign rubber imports."

Russ said that " …the auto and oil companies have a vested interest in increasing sales, and that will also benefit the rubber companies. The more cars and busses on the road, the more rubber tires sold."

"Yes, I've heard that," Edna chimed in. "In fact I met Mr. Blaine, head of Standard Motors, at a party recently. He was apparently in town working on some development deal to increase automobile and bus sales in Los Angeles."

"Yes," Russ replied. "I heard one of his men at a recent chamber of commerce meeting discussing the anticipated increased auto-related sales."

For their main course, Russ ordered rare prime rib and baked potatoes all around. They enjoyed each others' company while eating a wonderful dinner that should keep hunger pains at bay for some time.

As they were finishing their meal, Russ asked Edna to dance with him to a fox trot, and she was delighted to do so. As they whirled around the dance floor, Edna saw a man standing by their table talking with Marie. He was dressed in a white tuxedo with black bow tie. They seemed to be having a pleasant conversation. By the time Russ and Edna returned to the table, the gentleman had left.

"Who was that man you were talking with, Marie?" Edna inquired.

"His name is Alfred -- Al for short. He asked for my telephone number. He said he'd like to take me to dinner sometime. Let's see if he calls. I certainly wouldn't turn him down." Marie said.

"Yes. Attractive man," Edna replied.

"Hey, now, ladies. I'm your date tonight, remember?" Russ gently kidded. "Marie, how about our dance now?"

"Sure, Russ. Be glad to." Marie stood up, and Russ escorted her to the dance floor.

Edna sat at the table watching Russ and Marie for a minute, and then looked around at the other tables for the first time this evening. She loved to see how the women dressed when they came here. There was quite the variety, from women in dressy suits to floor length gowns, but everyone dressed up or they would not even be permitted inside. Edna thought back to her first night here with Ray when she wore her Houston party dress. She had felt intimidated by the glamour. But time brings familiarity and tonight she was feeling quite at home. There were strict dress codes in the town's nicest venues. And, that made it a clotheshorse's paradise. Edna loved that the latest trends were on view tonight.

As Edna looked around the large room, she spotted the back of a familiar head a few tables away. *No, it couldn't be.* The Maitre d' didn't tell her Ray was here. She looked closer and realized that two of the men that had argued with Ray in the hall after the City Council meeting sat at that table facing her direction. The three men were huddled closely together, talking intensely. As the back of his head turned sideways with a chin movement down to emphasize a point to one of the men, Edna confirmed that the third man was indeed Ray.

Well, I'll be. However, he did say that he had a business matter. But here at the Cocoanut Grove? Well, I can't very well say much under the circumstances. Better play this down, pretend not to see him, and get out of here as soon as possible.

When Russ and Marie returned to the table, Edna explained that she was tired and asked if they would mind leaving. Russ and Marie were both willing to comply. The three of them would have that early evening after all.

I'm not going to interrupt Ray and let him know I'm here. "Business means business." At least he isn't with another woman, but what was so urgent to make him cancel our date this evening?

CHAPTER TEN

STUDIO PHOTOGRAPHER

Edna switched off her alarm, then turned her radio on low to help her wake up. Looking out the window, she saw the sun casting its early morning rays over the city. She could hear birds chirping outside. It would be a hot one today. She would wear her short sleeve blue jersey dress, and take that matching rayon bolero jacket for later if the wind brought cool air.

Edna had learned that in Los Angeles the wind could sometimes be very hot when it came off the eastern desert sands. The western wind from the ocean could be chilly. The Los Angeles winds were moody. *At least there are no tornadoes like in Texas*, she thought.

She started boiling her water for instant coffee on her hot plate, then opened her window to feel that fresh morning air while she dressed for work.

The radio broadcast abruptly changed her mood.

"And now we bring to you the morning news. An overnight explosion at an electric generating plant has caused the Red Car lines 71, 72, and 85 to be out of service in the Wilshire Boulevard and the Hollywood Boulevard area. Authorities are not certain as to how many hours or days it will take for the trolleys in that section of the city to be up and running again …"

Edna began to panic. That was her route to and from work. What would she do? What if it was days or weeks before the streetcars were running again? It was at least five miles each direction.

Quick enough her common sense kicked back in. She would take care of today and think about the future later. It never helped to get ahead of oneself, particularly in the worry department. She would hurry to get dressed and go downstairs to use the phone.

When Edna finally made it to the phone there were three other girls -- one of them Marie -- in front of her also trying to arrange transportation in lieu of the Red Car trolley line. A new tenant was on the phone with a girlfriend and he did not want to let others use the phone before he got a date confirmed for that evening. Edna talked to the other three women about sharing a cab and they all agreed. They were all headed west, some closer; some further, but it would work out just fine.

Although none of them could afford the extra funds even to share a cab, the monetary consequences of missing work or being late could be much worse.

After all the morning turmoil, Edna arrived at work early and had time to sit in the back room and have a cup of coffee before starting her shift. No one was there, so she had time to think. She thought about Marie who would be the last one in the cab, but would be dropped off at a streetcar transfer line that would get her to work, so that would save her some money.

Marie said she wanted to get together with me to discuss something serious. What could it possibly be? She looked distressed. Well, we were all stressed but were trying to make the best of it. But Marie had looked particularly worried and somehow sad. It isn't her usual nature to be so glum when everyone else was trying to deal in a positive manner with the trolley car problem. Marie's such a wonderful person, always thinking of how she can help others. What could be bothering her? Oh, well, I'll find out soon enough.

Ray surprised Edna after her lunch break that afternoon. His handsome grin disarmed her as if it was the first time she had seen him. "Hello beautiful. I was in the neighborhood on business and thought I'd personally stop by to deliver a message," Ray started, in his always confident manner.

"Ray, you know I can't talk with you at work for long," Edna said, "but it's terrific to see you."

"Well, help me look at dresses. You would look beautiful in a new evening gown when I take you out dancing," Ray offered.

"That's not my department today. Oh, well, everyone already knows who you are by now anyway, but make it quick. I don't want to get in trouble for flirting with my boyfriend. What's up?"

"Well, I ran into Mary Pickford last week. She asked about you. She thought it was so honest of you to return that watch ring that you found when we were out at Pickfair. But, more than that she mentioned you to a studio photographer who now wants to do a photo layout of you. Mary thought you were very attractive and the studio wants to see how you photograph. What do you think of that?"

"Gee, honey, this is really a surprise. I'm not sure what I think. I sure liked Mary. She seemed to be a real down-home gal like some of the girls I knew in Texas. No false airs. Direct, with a fun-loving spirit."

"Yes, she's terrific. Well, look, just wanted to deliver the news. I'll give the photographer your apartment house phone number if it's all right with you?"

"I guess so. And, Ray, did you hear that my trolley car line is out of commission for a few days because of some explosion?"

"Ah, yes, I had heard. So sorry. It will sure put a dent in your work commute." Ray was teasing her.

"Do you think you could help me out a few days this week? It's a little too far to walk in my high heels."

"Why not buy some flats?"

Now he had gone too far.

"Forget I asked." Edna's commute worries caused her to miss his playfulness. Her ire was raised.

Ray started to laugh. Her spirited nature was exciting. "Calm down. I was just toying with you. Of course I'll help. Thomas can pick you up and take you to work after he drops me off in the mornings. I'll have him pick you up after work also. Let him or me know if your hours change."

"Would it be all right if some of my girlfriends who work near here also share the ride?"

"Sure, just as long as Thomas is available afterwards in case I need the car for business."

"I wish I could kiss you. That is a load off of my mind. I was worried about the commute. Thanks so much."

"I must take care of my future movie star, eh?"

Edna focused her blue eyes directly and intently into Ray's brown eyes and delivered her best, most loving smile.

"Oh, and Edna, there's a beautiful green formal gown on a mannikin in the front window. I already bought it for you to wear dancing next Saturday. Go try it on at your convenience to make sure it fits." Ray winked, smiled and headed out of the department. Before he walked too far, he turned and reiterated, "I mean it. I want to see you in that Saturday at eight."

Edna shook her head. This man filled her heart and head. She had been in dangerous territory from the moment they met, but now she was becoming deeply involved.

Thursday night around seven p.m. while Edna was listening to the radio and laying out her clothes for work Friday, there was a knock on her apartment door.

"Edna, it's Russ from down the hall. You have a phone call."

Edna was still dressed from work. She opened the door to Russ.

"Thanks, Russ. You going out on a date in that good-looking suit?"

"Business dinner," he replied. "Come on. I'll walk down with you. There's some fellow on the phone who says he's a photographer. Works at a studio taking pictures of the starlets. Now that's a job I'd love to have."

"I bet you would."

Edna joined Russ and they walked together down the hall towards the phone. "Russ, I rarely see you home anymore. You're a busy man these days."

"There are some very large sales contracts being negotiated in the rubber and tire business recently. Most of the business is done over entertainment," Russ gave a wink.

"Men sure have it made in this world," Edna said.

"I think it's the exact opposite. Women can wrap men around their little fingers whenever they try."

They both laughed. "Thanks for coming to get me, Russ. Good luck with business tonight. Monkey business."

"You're welcome. It's less luck I need than my superlative business sense. See you soon." Russ left Edna at the lobby wall phone and walked toward the building's front door.

"Hello," Edna answered the phone. "This is Edna King."

"Edna, hi. This is George Harlan, a photographer friend of Mary Pickford's. Mary said that you are attractive and might be very photogenic. I'd be interested in taking some photographs of you to see if the camera lens finds you as appealing as Mary and her friends did. How about it?"

"Well, George, my boyfriend, Ray, thinks it would be a good idea so I guess I'm in. Next Wednesday is my next day off."

"Great. We'll make a day of it. Let's plan to get together next Wednesday around 7:00 a.m. so I can get some of the outdoor early morning light. I'll pick you up at your place. What dress size are you?"

"A 6 or 8," Edna replied.

"Oh my, you're quite a woman. Mary is a size 1."

"Yes, she's tiny, petite. I'm 5'5 inches, 115 pounds."

"Well, fine. I'll have some clothes for you to change into. You bring a few outfits that you own and love. We'll make a day of it, beach, park, indoor studio lights. Okay?"

"Sure, George." *It would be wonderful to have some professional photos of myself to trade with girlfriends and send back to Texas. It's quite the rage to have a studio style shot, movie star pose made these days if one can afford it. Ray might like an attractive studio photograph of me.*

"Where shall I pick you up?" George asked.

"At the Marguerite Apartments near Westlake. I'll meet you out front. See you next Wednesday at 7:00 a.m."

"All right. Looking forward to it. See you then."

Edna hung up the phone and was a bit stunned. *I need to get some outfits together. Who knows what will come of this.*

She started walking back to her apartment. As she walked past Marie's place, she was suddenly saddened. Marie had told her the other night that she was pregnant. Al, the man Marie had met that night Russ and they went to the Cocoanut Grove had been dating Marie. The guy had pressured Marie. One thing had led to another.

The "father" did not want to get married or have a child so he gave Marie half of the money to get a Mexican abortion. Marie was despondent and afraid. Edna had suggested that Marie seriously think about having the child and putting it up for adoption. But Marie had no money to survive unless she could work, and she had little family she could count on. None lived around Los Angeles.

Edna had told Marie that she would help her in any way she could and might be making her first trip to Mexico soon as support for Marie. This was such a difficult situation. Edna could relate to Marie's feeling lost and alone. She felt empathy for Marie, and resolved anew to never allow herself to get into that situation.

Wednesday morning at 7:00 a.m., Edna stood by the curbside with her riding breeches and jacket, her new green evening gown she had worn when Ray took her to Earl Carroll's, and her beige trench/raincoat that she could wear over all outfits. She was dressed in her blue jersey short dress she often wore to work, with her Lane Bryant blue hat. Besides the outfits on hangars, she carried a large hatbox containing a pair of shoes and a pair of boots to complement her other outfits.

In her large purse, she had packed herself a peanut butter sandwich, and some saltines in case this photo outing did not include a good meal. *I need some strength to smile, pose and model.* Edna had seen models pass out on the Dyas Department store runway when they had starved themselves to be thinner for a fashion show. Edna had clearly learned since the time that she had dropped twenty pounds after Jimmy betrayed her, that one had to have food to live, to have strength and energy to move forward. She had not wanted to even live back then. But now she had a lot to look forward to.

A man in a black Ford pulled up to the curb, parked and got out. He walked up to her.

"You must be Edna. Hi, I'm George Harlan. Mary was right. You're a striking woman. This day looks promising."

He took the clothes and hatbox from Edna and placed them in the back seat of his car. Then he opened the front passenger seat door for her. "Hop in. Let's get started."

Edna climbed into the Ford and, with a bit of nervousness, tried to settle in. *What will this day bring? After all, George does work for a studio and knows Mary Pickford. He's a professional photographer. Relax. Enjoy yourself.*

They began with a photo shoot at the beach in Malibu, at the base of Castle Rock. George told her he had taken a number of prior photographs in that area. He liked that spot because there were boulders right at the water which added a dramatic flair to the photos. "Charlie Chaplin made his 1927 movie, *The Adventurer* right here in the same place," George told her.

"Put on that trench coat over your dress, and climb up on those rocks."

"I'm a bit shaky about these high heels on the boulders," she told him.

But George took her arm, and helped her steady herself climbing up there. He encouraged her and told her that "these types of gymnastics are often required if you want to be an actress or even a photographer's model."

Edna's practical nature and wish to be a good sport compelled her to follow his directions.

George was quickly pleased by the photos at the beach, so they soon left there and headed up to Griffith Park. Along the way George stopped and took a few photos of Edna poised at the side of the highway with cliffs in the background.

At Griffith Park, they headed to the stables where George told Edna to "Use the ladies room to change into your riding breaches, boots, blouse and jacket."

While she was complying, George arranged with the stable head to borrow a horse for the shots, promising to send a copy or two of some photos in exchange for using the horse. He also arranged to borrow a dressage riding hat to complete Edna's look.

When Edna emerged from her change, George handed her the hat and asked her to put it on.

"No, I'm not going to ruin my hair with that helmet. I worked very hard on my hair this morning, and the ocean air already ruined some of my efforts. If you want to make a full day of this, the hat stays off." Edna was adamant.

"All right, Miss Kind. You win this round. But, hold the hat in one hand, and hold the horse's reins with the other."

Edna's was a more strong-willed personality than a lot of models George had photographed. Most were so thrilled by the prospect of having their photos taken by a studio photograper that they complied completely with every request. Edna was of a different mold, with her strong southern will that bordered on stubbornness. In the movie business, it could mean trouble, or it could spell star. Time would tell.

The Griffith Park stable pictures were completed without too much difficulty. The horse was one of the tamer versions usually rented out by the hour to beginning riders. Edna initially balked at getting up on the animal for some shots, but gave in after some persuasion and a boost up. They again had some terrific pictures, according to George.

This woman was extremely photogenic and didn't seem to take a bad photo. Development of the photos would be the proof, however. Sometimes shots looked terrific as one was taking them, but later the lighting or background distraction, or model movement would disqualify them. Much could be fixed by burning in or dodging during the development process, however, if the model just didn't come through the camera, or if the chin, nose and cheek bone angles were not good on film, the photos would fail. A photographer could not definitively tell by feel or process whether a photo in the final analysis would work, but his years of experience were telling George that this woman's photos were probably going to turn out fabulously. She emanated a magnetism, that "it" factor that was so often revered in the movie magazines, and it appeared to jump through the camera lens.

Edna stayed in her riding breeches as they drove to George's commercial studio, which was on Gower Street in Hollywood. The rear portion was where he lived.

Once they arrived, Edna was told to change into her evening gown behind a curtained dressing area. George set up the lights for the more formal movie star style photos, both full-length and head shots.

Edna was hungry and ate half of her sandwich while she was changing into her beautiful new evening gown. It was now after 2:30 and though the day was passing quickly, she was surprised at how much energy had been expended in modeling so far. Photographic modeling, posing, changing outfits was more difficult work than the end result indicated. Edna took some extra time to refresh her make-up and check her teeth, then brush her hair.

"Come on, Edna," George said, "time's a wasting." Edna finished her primping then walked into the lighted studio area. After a few full-length poses in the gown, George told Edna to relax for a minute. He went back into a storage area of the studio and returned with a large furrier's box. He laid the box on a table, removed a beautiful white fur jacket, which he handed to Edna. "Here, put this on and let's get some glamour close-ups."

"How beautiful," Edna admired the jacket. She took it and threw it over her shoulders then walked back to look at its placement in the full-length mirror. She examined herself closely. Edna admitted silently to herself, she had never looked more glamorous. This jacket was exquisite. Its light fur accentuated her facial features. Her blue eyes seemed to emit sparks. She felt fabulous.

"Turn your right shoulder this way. No, no, a little more to the left. Now, your head like this," George physically moved her head to the exact angle and chin tilt he was looking for, then walked back to the larger format camera he was now using.

"Great. That's it. Now shine. Show that Southern spirit, that spark. Good. Now, turn your head to the right more. Good."

Edna was a natural and was now truly enjoying the process. They took a number of poses with and without the fur. George appeared pleased by what he captured. He told Edna he was confident they had some decent shots. He would share a portfolio of today's best photos with the studio.

"They might have a new star. The raw material is certainly there. You are photogenic. Now you can change back into your dress and I'll take you home."

Before Edna left the dressing area, she carefully examined the fur jacket. *All the wealthy, smartly dressed women of the day are wearing fur. They are treated with respect. Maybe some day I'll have one.*

Fur was the status symbol for women. Fur recently eclipsed even jewelry. In this depression, only the wealthiest men could spend their money on a fur for their wives or girlfriends.

George took Edna home and stopped right in front of the apartment building. He helped her to carry all the clothes items she had brought into the downstairs lobby. Edna asked him if he wanted to come up for a cocktail or coffee.

"No, thanks. I'll call you when the film is developed and you can pick out the photos you want. The studio will contact you after seeing them if they're interested."

"Thanks, George." Edna was impressed at how focused and professional he had been all day.

A whole new world was opening up to her. She had never considered herself to be an actress, yet she did love the movies like everyone else. *As a child in Houston, I remember singing and dancing on the street corners whenever I'd hear music playing. I'd draw a crowd. I guess I did love the attention, the limelight. My parents were sure amused, and the people who gathered around to watch me seemed like they were enjoying my antics. One thing I know for sure, people in the movies are treated with respect.*

CHAPTER ELEVEN

TIAJUANA

The drive to Tiajuana took a lot longer than Edna anticipated. San Diego was only about 125 miles from Los Angeles, but the coast route this sunny day was filled with bumper to bumper vehicles. Marie and she had started driving at 9:00 in the morning and it was now noon. They were supposed to be at the doctor's office by 12:30 and were only now leaving San Diego proper. Edna hated to be late, but there was not much that she could now do. She had not slept much last night worrying about today, which made her more nervous than usual.

At Edna's urging, Russ had been nice enough to loan them his Buick convertible for the drive. He was out of town on business for a week and was traveling this time by train. Both Edna and Marie agreed that he was a great guy. Russ had been to Mexico a number of times and told Edna and Marie that if they decided to spend the night, one of the best hotels to stay at in Tiajuana was Caesar's, where the Caesar salad had been invented.

Edna and Marie had both arranged in advance to take a vacation day off from their jobs to be able to drive down today. It would be ideal if they could return to the apartment building tonight. Both hoped that the procedure would go well and there would be no problems. They had heard horror stories about what could happen and both were apprehensive, but Marie was steadfast in her resolve that if she was to continue to survive and be able to work, this was the only solution. A single girl without money or family had few options, particularly in this depressed economy. Single girls were lucky if they were now even able to find a job, and though the pay was quite low, less than that for any man, by scrimping, they were able to survive. But hundreds of people would jump at the opportunity to replace Marie or any other woman who was not able to continue working.

Marie and Edna had both searched for a local doctor to perform the operation. They had both confided in girls at work who had recommended certain doctors they had heard about in the Hollywood and Los Angeles area. But when contacted, those doctors seemed to cater only to the rich. A couple of thousand dollars was out of the question for Marie. Al, the so-called father, had recommended to Marie this doctor in Tiajuana that he knew about. "A friend of a friend had gone there." The cost was three hundred dollars and Al had given Marie half.

Three hundred dollars was an enormous amount of money to Marie, but she would have no job and no money at all if she did not get the procedure done. Marie had arranged to borrow her half from a number of different sources including a small loan from her employer. Marie had told her employer and others that she needed the loan because someone in her family was in trouble and Marie needed to help them out. Marie hated to tell even a white lie, but survival made people have to do things they would never otherwise do. Marie would be paying off the $150.00 for a long time. It would be a nagging, weighty reminder of what she had done.

Edna had not told Ray about the procedure. She had told him that Marie and she wanted to have some girlfriend time and thought it would be a lark to drive down to Tiajuana for a day. Ray was his usual accepting self and thought it was great that she and Marie could get away. "A different environment clears the head," Ray told her. He did not ask about transportation and lodging, and Edna did not offer any details.

Edna had trouble understanding Marie's sweet nature regarding this whole matter. The whole situation made Edna angry at Al. He had dated Marie for a few weeks, had pressured her to have relations with him, then did not want anything more to do with Marie. Yes, he had given Marie half the money for the abortion, but Edna thought him to be an awful cad and wanted to tell him a thing or two to his face.

But Marie had not a drop of vengeance in her. She was as nice as they came, and seemed all too willing to claim her part of the responsibility for what had happened, and to do what needed to be done to move forward with her life. Marie would not let Edna talk to or even meet with Al.

Edna hated to see Marie be taken advantage of and believed that at the very least Marie's "gentleman" friend should pay for the whole operation. Marie was the one who had to take off from work and have the dangerous procedure done. Edna had heard of women who had died from the operation and was frightened for and protective of Marie. Women were too often the scapegoats of men's egos.

Edna had seen a few cads in her life and knew how women could too often be treated as bothersome, useless possessions by some arrogant, self-centered males. Thank God Ray was confident without needing to display his power by denigrating women. And Russ, also, was respectful of women. Those were two men who must have had wonderful mothers who taught them that women deserved their respect and kindness.

Too many men because they were taller and stronger thought that that confirmed women were inferior to them. How silly some men were in their perspectives, and sometimes downright cruel because of their ignorance. Women were just as clever as men, and their intuitive nature was sometimes capable of bringing about superior outcomes and solutions. Height, brawn and bulk did not truth make. And a woman's nature complemented that of a good man. Edna had heard men talk over the years about how the tallest man in a group usually got more respect just for his height. Women were not nearly as silly as to divvy out respect based on how tall someone was. Although, perhaps women were just as silly to give so much weight to how well someone was groomed and dressed.

Edna had been lost in her thoughts for a few minutes. "Marie, here we are at the border. It's going to be another half hour to an hour before we find this place. What street did you say it was on again?"

"Avenido de los Constitution. Number 557." Marie had been holding the address in her hand for a few miles now. She was prepared for this question. "Edna, don't worry. We'll find it."

"What time is it now?" Edna inquired as she inched the car forward towards the California-Mexico border.

"12:15," Marie answered. "We're doing fine, honey. Calm down. We'll be there soon."

As they pulled up to the border, the Mexican border guard leaned and looked into the car at Marie, then asked Edna in a no-foolishness voice, "Where are you ladies headed?"

"To Tiajuana for the day, sir," Edna responded and smiled at the serious guard. "Would you happen to know where we can find Avenido de los Constitution?"

"Yes, senorita. Drive about 4 miles straight ahead on this road and you will see that street intersecting this street. There will be a street sign with the street name at that corner, and a divorce attorney's building with a big sign in English. The sign says 'Cheap American Divorces. 24 hours a day.' You can't miss it."

"Thank you, sir," Edna responded.

"You two ladies have a nice day. Be careful. There are many hombres who will be interested in you. Stay safe."

"Thank you, sir." Both Edna and Marie smiled and said good-bye to the border guard, moving forward into Mexico.

"We might make it on time yet," Edna said as she drove the car along the Tiajuana street. Now that they were in Mexico itself there were a lot fewer cars to slow down the traffic. People were walking, and there were carts with burros, but few cars were in front of them to slow them down.

They soon came to a corner where a large building had painted on its side "Cheap and Easy American Divorces. 24-hours."

"That must be the lawyer's building the border guard mentioned. There is the street sign, Avenido de los Constitution. Edna, please turn right here."

Edna followed Marie's instructions and they drove along slowly looking at the storefronts.

"There it is," Marie said. "557."

Edna pulled the car over in front of an adobe building with a red-tiled roof. There was nothing inviting about the building nor the neighborhood, and the two women each felt some apprehension.

"See, Edna. We made it. 12:30 on the dot," said Marie, trying to add a positive note to the circumstances.

"Yes. Let's go." Edna responded, urging them both on.

Edna and Marie got out of the car and walked into a tiny, dimly-lit, dingy front room. One tired-looking Mexican woman who appeared to be around 50 years old sat in a chair at a wooden table. Four straight-backed chairs lined the walls which had no pictures. There were no tables, magazines, plants. Merely the bare room.

"Bueno," said the Mexican woman with long gray hair. Looking from one woman to the next, she asked "Marie?"

"Yes, I'm Marie," Marie clarified.

"Three hundred American dollars," the woman said as she held out her hand in Marie's direction.

Marie removed the bills from an envelope in her purse and handed the money to the woman who took it and began to slowly yet silently count each bill.

After she was apparently satisfied, she got up from the table, opened a door at the rear of the room, entered and closed the door behind her. Edna and Marie stood in the room quietly waiting. After about one minute, Edna broke the silence, "I hope she didn't run off with your money. Let's go see."

Before Marie could respond, the woman opened the door again and spoke, "Doctor ready."

"Okay," said Marie with some hesitation.

"Are you going to be all right, honey?" Edna asked. "Do you want me to go in there with you?"

"No, Edna. I'll be fine."

"Are you sure you want to go ahead with this?" Edna had to ask.

"Yes, Edna. You know I have to. Please. I'll be fine." Marie tried to reassure her.

"Well, I'll be right out here waiting for you."

"All right. Thank you." Marie followed the woman through the door and left Edna in the small front room. Edna sat down in one of the small wooden chairs by one wall. As her eyes adjusted further to the dim light she noticed the room's walls had cracks in them. The room did not look to have ever been painted. The flooring was some crude type of cement with cracks. This room did not feel or look particularly clean, except for the simplicity provided by the lack of clutter or décor. Edna hoped the back room was more antiseptic, more sterile, like the hospital she had seen when her mom died.

Edna thought back about how she had sat in that hospital in Houston after her mama had fallen and hurt herself. Aunt Lilly and Uncle Justin had come and gotten Edna after school and had taken her straight to the hospital to see her mother. Edna had walked into the room and her mama was in a coma. There was no response when Edna had told her mother, "I love you, mama. I love you."

Edna had then been relegated to the chair in the hall while the grown-ups, her dad, Aunt Lillie and Uncle Justin stayed in the room with her mother. After a couple of hours of waiting, Aunt Lillie had come out of the room and hugged Edna and told her "Honey, your mom has passed. She's in heaven now. You're going to come and stay with us tonight. Your daddy needs to get things arranged for her funeral."

Edna started crying. She could not believe that her mama was gone. How could she have left her? And how could Aunt Lillie be so calm about this great loss. This was not right.

"I want to see her. I want to say good-bye," Edna said between sobs.

"No, honey. Not now. Your daddy's in there with her, grieving with Uncle Justin. You'll be able to see her when she's laid out in all her glory."

Edna's heart and stomach felt as if she had been kicked and beaten. "What about my baby brother?" Edna asked. "Mama said I'd have a baby brother or sister."

"Honey, the baby boy's gone to heaven with your mama. I'm so sorry, sugar, but the baby's gone, too."

The Mexican lady had returned to the front room and broke Edna's reminiscing. *Thank God.* Edna had been picturing again her baby brother and her mother together in the coffin in the living room.

"How is Marie?" asked Edna.

"She okay. She okay. She get sedative," said the woman.

"How long will this take?" asked Edna.

"She will need rest for a while after operation," the woman answered. It might be one hour, two depending on how she do. Doctor want tamale. I go get. You want?"

Food was not on her mind, but Edna figured she needed to keep her strength up. One never knew what might happen. "Yes," said Edna. "Thank you." *How could the doctor eat a tamale while he was doing the procedure? Hadn't he eaten before?*

With that, the woman got up from her chair and exited the front door.

Edna was left alone in the dingy front room, lost in her own thoughts. She would not cry. The past was past. Plus, the present worry was enough. *How well would the doctor perform his task if he hadn't eaten?* Edna had heard that the actual procedure was fairly short, but the recovery time was longer. Maybe the doctor hadn't done the procedure yet. Perhaps he needed to eat before he began.

Edna got up and stepped out the front door into the sunlight. *I better make sure Russ's car is all right. Oh, oh …*

A young boy about twelve was leaning against the car. "This your car, lady?" the young boy asked.

"Yes," Edna responded, somewhat surprised to hear such good English from this young Mexican boy.

"I watch for you. I take care. One cent?"

Edna smiled at the youngster and his enterprising ways. She was relieved he meant the car no harm. "Okay," she said and took an American penny out of her handbag and handed it to him. It would make her feel better to have him watching Russ's car.

"What's your name?"

"Jose," he answered.

"Well, I'm Edna. Thank you, Jose. It might be a couple of hours, though."

"That's okay, lady. I watch good for you. You very pretty senorita."

"Well, you're quite the flirt, Jose."

Jose looked at her with puzzled eyes.

"Flirt means--" Edna struggled with how to explain the word appropriately to this youngster-- "warm-blooded, loving guy. A young man who likes the senoritas."

"Ah, *si*, I like the senoritas," Jose responded with a warm smile, his eyes lighting up.

Edna laughed out loud, tickled by his worldly attitude at such a young age. "Do you have a girlfriend?"

"Yes, senorita, Jose have many girlfriends, but my heart still has room for you."

Edna laughed out loud again. This young Romeo had quite the personality. "Well, I feel lucky to have a charming young man such as yourself watching the car. Now, don't run off with any girlfriend before I return."

"No, beautiful lady. You are my only one now."

Edna laughed again, and turned to reenter the building. If Marie needed her she wanted to be close-by. "I'll be in there, Jose. Come and get me if there is any problem," Edna offered.

"Yes, lady. Jose take care. Jose good watcher." The boy grinned at Edna and Edna returned the smile. This young man was gong to be a heartbreaker one of these days.

She went back inside the building and returned to sit in a chair by the wall facing the door in the empty, dark abortionist's front room. Russ's car was safe, and in watchful hands. She just wished she felt as secure about the situation with Marie.

In about fifteen minutes, the woman came back with the tamales. She handed one of the wrapped tamales to Edna and said, "five cents." Edna looked into her handbag, took a nickel from her coin purse and placed it into the woman's extended open palm. Then the woman left and went into the back room. In a couple of minutes she returned with her tamale, and sat down at the wooden table to eat her lunch. Edna and she ate their respective tamales in silence. After Edna finished eating hers, she leaned her head back against the unfinished wall surface, shut her eyes and tried to take a nap.

Edna must have dozed off because she was startled out of her rest by the sound of a scream. At first she thought she was dreaming, but then she remembered where she was and she recognized Marie's voice now half-moaning, half-yelling, "No, that hurts. Don't. No more. It hurts. Please. No. No more."

Edna immediately stood up and walked toward the door to the back room but was met by the woman blocking the door. Edna literally pushed her aside and entered the back room. She could not believe what she saw. Blood was all over the sheet-covered wooden table that Marie was lying on.

The abortionist was leaning over Marie's face and saying to her, "Silence. You okay. It's over now. Quiet."

"What is this? What has he done?"

Edna was horrified by the sight of a bloody knife lying over on a wooden counter.

"Honey. Marie. Are you all right?"

"Yes, I think so." Marie's voice was weak and slow. She seemed in shock.

The abortionist turned to Edna. "Go. She rest. We clean up."

"I will not. I will stay until I know Marie is out of danger."

"Go. We clean. Then you can come back in." The abortionist was insistent. He was a strong, rotund man who gave Edna the impression he was used to always forcing his own will.

"Marie, I'll be back as soon as they clean up. You rest. I'm right outside this door."

As Edna turned to go, she saw in a very large dirty glass jar on the counter what appeared to be a large pinkish tadpole-like creature floating in a clear substance. She quickly exited the room to sit once again in the front.

Edna knew that Marie had struggled for weeks about deciding to have an abortion. Edna knew that Marie wanted to get married and have children and that the decision to end this child's life was the most difficult decision Marie had ever made. Yet, as Marie had said, she had no close family she could return home to, had no money so could not take off from work, would not be able to eat or have a roof over her head if she continued with the pregnancy to full term.

There was no place Marie knew to go. And, even if she had had the money to live on for a few months to have the baby, she would not have had a job to return to in this job market. Her employer would fill her position while she was gone. Too many men and women were out of work and waiting in line. How would she have raised a baby without a job?

Edna knew Marie's religious background gave her the strong belief that if there was a soul yet in the growing baby, that the soul would return to God and be just fine. It would be Marie who would bear the guilt and sorrow for the rest of her life of the decision she knew she had to make for her own survival.

Edna thought about all that Marie had told her, but now worried that perhaps after all of this, Marie might not make it. This place was not safe. That room was not sanitary. Edna was frightened by what she had seen of Marie's blood loss on the sheet, and Marie's obviously weakened state. This procedure was much more dangerous than either of them had imagined.

About ten minutes later, after the blood had apparently been cleaned up, Edna was permitted back in. Marie was sleeping on the wooden operating table, without a sheet underneath. A Mexican blanket was laying over her.

"Will she be all right?" Edna asked the abortionist.

"She okay. She sleep for one hour. Then you two go." Edna noticed that the abortionist wore jeans, cowboy boots, a big metal-buckled belt and cowboy shirt under his now-removed bloody medical garment.

"What about the blood she lost?"

"That okay. That normal," The abortionist replied. "Go. Sit. She be fine."

Edna was not sure that Marie was fine or would be fine, but was at a loss as to what to do. She returned to the waiting room once more.

Very upset by the circumstances, and tired of the dingy room, Edna decided to again go out front and check on the car.

Little Jose was sitting on the ground, leaning against the Buick. He jumped to his feet when he saw Edna.

"Pretty lady. I watch car good."

"Jose, are you around this building a lot?" Edna asked him.

"Many days, senorita. That's my uncle in there." Jose offered.

"Oh, he is." Edna couldn't help but ask, "Has anyone ever died in there?"

"Oh, yes, senorita. Many times. I help my uncle get the *policia* when it happen." Jose said this cheerfully, as if he were helping Edna by sharing the information.

"Jose, what if someone bleeds too much, what does your uncle do?"

"He can do nothing, senorita. He feels badly sometime but nothing he can do."

"What about a hospital. Is there a hospital around here? In the city?"

"Not good, senorita. Best across border. San Diego."

"Do you know the address, how to get there?" Edna asked.

"Across border, downtown San Diego. Tall building. Hospital sign. Easy to see."

Edna began to worry about how much a blood transfusion or other treatment might cost at the hospital. She fell silent.

"Pretty lady. Don't worry. Many people gets scared. Lots and lots of blood always. No problem. After they sleep, those who don't die, they okay most time."

Jose again thought he was being helpful. Edna was feeling a sinking, sickly feeling in her stomach. But, she must stay strong for Marie.

"Pretty lady? You okay?" Jose seemed truly concerned.

"Yes, Jose. I'm fine," she said convincingly, as she decided to not let her feelings get the best of her. Worst things had happened in the past. *I can handle whatever needs to be done.*

"Jose, thanks for watching the car. Thank you for the information."

"Claro. I be here 'til you go."

"Yes, Jose. See you later." Edna turned, lifted her chin and pulled back her shoulders. She again resolved to handle this situation well no matter what happened as she re-entered the dark front room to await Marie's awakening.

About forty-five minutes later, the waiting room woman who had been sitting at the table staring into space, stood up and went into the back room. She was gone for about ten minutes. When she came out again she looked at Edna directly and said: "She go now. You go now."

Edna stood up, and walked into the back room. The abortionist had apparently left through the back door at some point. Marie was sitting up on the table, her clothes having been helped on by the assistant. Marie seemed dazed and half-asleep.

"You ready to go, Marie?" Edna asked.

"Yes, Edna. Let's go."

"Okay. Now take it easy." She helped Marie slowly climb down from the wooden table. With the woman on the other side, they held Marie steady as they walked very slowly out to the car. As the woman helped Marie to stay standing up, by helping her to lean against the Buick, Edna got the keys out of her purse and handed them to Jose.

"Open the door for us, please."

Jose quickly opened the door. "You want me to drive, pretty lady?"

"No, Jose. Thank you." Edna couldn't help but smile.

Edna pulled forward the passenger side front seat and helped Marie get settled into the back seat where she could lie down and sleep on the way back to Los Angeles. No way now that they were going to stay in Tiajuana for the night. Marie needed to be near an American hospital in case she started bleeding again, or some other serious complication occurred.

Edna asked the woman, "What if she bleeds again in the car?"

"Get towel. Use for blood," the woman answered.

"Jose, thank you for all your help."

"Yes, pretty lady. You good person."

"You, too, Jose."

"Jose, do you know where we could get a towel in case we need it later?'

"My uncle have in back room. Only five cents for you, pretty lady. I go get." Jose ran into the abortion clinic and very quickly returned with an apparently clean towel which he handed to Edna." Edna handed Jose the dime she had taken out of her purse and then gave him a hug.

Jose at first said "No, no. No want extra money." But she insisted and he relented.

Edna got into the driver's seat of the Buick. As they drove off she waved good-bye to Jose. The young boy waived back, smiled and then winked at her. Despite Edna's serious concern about Marie, she burst out laughing at Jose's wink. *He's the one bright spot in this whole situation.* As Edna drove through the streets of Tiajuana in the stark, hot afternoon sunlight she could hear Marie quietly snoring. Marie was already asleep in the back seat.

Edna checked on Marie every twenty minutes or so on the drive back. Marie slept the entire way. Two times, Edna pulled over to the side of the road to feel Marie's pulse and to be certain there was no blood on her skirt. Marie continued sleeping hard.

When they arrived home it was dark. Edna was lucky enough to find a parking place close to the front of the apartment building. She went inside and saw a uniformed deliveryman in the lobby. She asked him if he could help her with Marie. He was a large man and was able to pick Marie up from the back seat, and carry her all the way up the stairs to Edna's apartment. Edna hurriedly unlocked her own door and pulled back the covers on her bed so Marie could be laid down.

"Thank you so much," Edna responded. "You're so strong."

The man beamed at her remarks, said "You're welcome," and left.

Edna removed Marie's outer clothing and stockings, leaving her slip on. *So far, no more bleeding, thank goodness.* She covered Marie up with the sheet and blanket, then hung up Marie's clothes. She then removed the top spread from the bed and laid it down on the floor.

It had been a long day. Edna undressed and put on her nightgown. She set the alarm for work the next morning. Although Edna hadn't eaten since the tamale, Marie hadn't eaten since yesterday. If she woke up in the middle of the night, Edna had a can of soup she could fix for Marie on the hot plate, some canned milk, and, of course, the usual soda crackers from the cafeteria. Edna also had a bottle of whiskey Ray had given her to serve when friends stopped by. She poured herself a small shot from the bottle and drank it right down in one gulp. Edna lay down on half of the bedspread on the floor, turned on her side and pulled the other half over her. She felt like she could sleep for days.

"Edna, Edna, honey." Marie was shaking Edna lightly. "Time to get up. The alarm went off a few minutes ago. I turned it off to let you sleep a little longer."

Edna turned around and looked at Marie. "Thank God you're all right."

"Well, I must have slept 16 hours. I'm not strong, but I'll be fine. I just went downstairs and called in sick for today. I need another day's rest before I can face that crowd at work. I took the stairs very, very slowly."

"Sure, honey. Let me fix you some tomato soup with soda crackers." Edna got up from her makeshift floor bed.

"Edna, no, honey. I think I'll get over to my apartment now and let you get ready for work. I've got some soup and cereal there. Thanks ever so much for all you've done. I can never thank you enough. You're a true friend." Marie gave Edna a hug.

"If you need anything today, call me at work. I know they don't like that but in case of emergency I don't care. You lost a lot of blood and need to regain your strength, but if you start bleeding again, call me."

"Edna, it's great to have someone that I can count on. Now, go on, get ready for work."

"Okay, Marie. I'll check in on you after work tonight," Edna gently closed the door, then began to get ready for work.

CHAPTER TWELVE

THE MOVIE STUDIO AND TENNIS

Edna was excited. Ray had lent her Thomas and the limousine to drive her to the studio this afternoon. They would later meet for dinner.

Although Ray had pointed out the Nation Studio before when they had driven past its gates, Edna had not been inside any movie studio lot. The gates were quite impressive, and driving by the guard booth this Wednesday afternoon, Edna felt like a swell. *This is a moment to remember, my first time inside a movie studio.*

Edna was to meet with a studio vice-president at 3:30 p.m. in the executive offices. The photographer's photos had gone over well with the studio heads and they wanted to meet Edna. She was photogenic, certainly, but did she have the "it" factor in person? And, could she act?

George had let Edna pick out a few of the photo shots they had taken and she had sent an eight by ten of her fur glamour pose back to Uncle Justin and Aunt Lillie in Houston. Edna wanted her Uncle and Aunt to know that she was doing well, or certainly appeared to be doing so in the photo. Edna knew that despite Aunt Lillie's religious protestations about movies, make-up and worldly goods, her aunt would show everyone the photo and spread the word about how well Edna was doing in Hollywood.

Edna felt good today. She had seen Marie early this morning, and Marie was back to her old self after only a couple of weeks of eating well and resting more than usual. What a nightmare that whole incident had been. It made Edna feel better that Marie was recovering quickly.

Today Edna was dressed in a knee length, form-fitting satin dress. Blue again to complement her eyes. Her auburn hair was pulled back in a chignon and her heels were high enough to show off what Edna considered to be one of her best features, her shapely legs. Even Edna had to admit she looked fabulous. She had a small stylish hat that was tilted, set on only a portion of the top of her head, so as to reveal her shiny hair, and leave her face fully uncovered. Edna was clearly wearing this outfit, it was not wearing her.

Thomas pulled up into a parking area in front of the executive offices, stopped the limo, and came around to open her door. "It's right in there, Miss King."

"Thank you, Thomas."

Taking Thomas's hand, she gracefully emerged from the limo and walked into the building. A receptionist directed her to Mr. O'Malley's office, and told her he was awaiting her arrival.

Edna knocked on his door, and entered upon hearing "Come in." She was surprised at what she saw. The office was four times the size of her efficiency apartment, and was furnished in what she recognized to be expensive art deco furniture in a light blond wood. A large hand-carved, black-lacquered Chinese bar added a sophisticated flair along the left side of the office. The length of the wall behind the bar was mirrored. The room resembled the decor of high-end modern New York apartments Edna had admired in some recent films.

"Well, hello there." Mr. O'Malley rose from behind his large desk and walked around in front to shake Edna's gloved hand. "Aren't you a pretty one. Have a seat right here."

Mr. O'Malley helped her into one of the two Arabian Nights' motif silk upholstered chairs in front of the desk, and then returned behind the desk to sit in his large, white leather desk chair.

Edna crossed her legs and smiled at him.

He returned the smile with a large grin, his eyes slowly taking in every inch of her.

"Now, my dear -- 'Edna', is it?"

"Yes."

"Have you done any acting before?"

"No, sir, unless you count the song and dance performances I used to give for neighbors and on Houston street corners as a child."

Mr. O'Malley laughed loudly. "Well, you have the performer's instinct it sounds like."

"Yes, sir."

"Please, stop with all the 'sir'. My name is Joe."

"Okay, Joe." Edna flashed her best smile and looked him straight in the eyes.

"Now, Mary Pickford recommended you, and it seems she was quite right. You are a stunning woman. Modeling in front of a still camera, however, is different from the acting required in front of a movie camera."

"I understand," Edna agreed with a smile.

"I'm the gatekeeper to decide if you are what we need right now. If we proceed, it will be necessary for you to take a screen test. That test will be shown to other executives, and then, in consultation with Mr. Hannity, the studio head, a final decision will be made."

Edna listened carefully, intentionally giving Joe O'Malley her rapt attention.

"First, if you are going to be an actress, your name is not right. Edna Purviance was famous in all those Chaplin films, and we already have an Edna here under contract at Nation Studio, so we would need to give you a new moniker if we place you under contract. Think about what new glamorous name you might like. We can have the publicity office come up with a few suggestions that might suit you. That will be dealt with after the screen test results."

"Fine. I've never really liked my name anyway. My mother named me after an opera singer from her era. I've never felt like an Edna."

Joe O'Malley started talking faster. "Would you like a cocktail? I'm going to have one."

"No, thank you."

O'Malley went to the bar, opened a side panel and took out a glass. He then opened the top of the bar and took out a bottle of Haig Scotch, which he poured into the glass. "Are you sure you won't join me?" he asked.

"No, thank you," Edna declined politely. Best to keep her head about her. *This is strictly business, possibly my future.*

"Okay, well, cheers." Joe raised his glass up towards her, drained the glass of its contents and immediately poured another shot. He took the cocktail glass and sat back down behind the desk.

"Now, I don't see a wedding or engagement ring. That means you're still single?"

"Yes."

O'Malley's eyes lit up. "Terrific."

"I am now dating Ray Gibson, Superintendent of the Los Angeles School District."

"Oh, yes. I know Ray through some studio business dealings. He's a great guy. His family owned a lot of Los Angeles land at one time."

"We've been seeing each other since shortly after I arrived in Los Angeles. It was through him that I met Mary Pickford."

"Yes, Ray knows most of the movers and shakers in this town. He's very politically astute and is quite adept at getting things accomplished."

O'Malley had now downed his second glass and was up at the bar for a third refill. Edna was becoming uneasy.

"Ray is helping the studio with its investments in the automotive expansion area. We keep our hand in a number of other investments besides just movie making. We work to make a profit in whatever arena is promising."

Joe now sat in the matching chair next to Edna. He placed his hand on her lower thigh.

"When you're in pictures, you need to spread yourself around," Joe offered.

"What actually do you mean by that, Mr. O'Malley?" Edna spoke cooly as she removed his lingering hand from her thigh.

"You need for your public to believe you're available. As a young woman, the possibility of your availability to the public adds to your popularity and potential star power. An engagement or marriage would cut that short. The public fantasizes that they could possibly wind up in a relationship with their favorites." As he said this, Joe again placed his hand solidly on Edna's thigh.

Edna stood up carefully. "Mr. O'Malley, when and where shall I go for a screen test?"

"Well, I haven't made my decision yet. We haven't finished our discussion. Sit back down here and tell me about your upbringing in Houston. We'll need to create a biography of you if you are hired by the studio. The insistent tone of his voice meant business. Edna reluctantly sat back down in the chair.

"My mother and father were down to earth. They loved each other tremendously and loved and cared for me the best they could. My dad was an iceman in Houston. He was born in New York City, but moved to Texas as a young boy with his family. My mother's family lived in Texas for about a hundred and fifty years before my dad's family arrived.

My parents, who have both passed on, instilled in me that education and common-sense were both very important. They gave me moral guidance in a warm, fun-loving home. I loved them both very much."

"Well, sounds like you're from good people. Now, let's see how we would push you. You do have the all-American girl look, yet it is a cut above the normal girl next door. You're not quite the sophisticate yet, and certainly not with that honey-toned Texas accent. We'd have to give you diction lessons to get rid of the Southern drawl. You could fit into the ingénue category to begin with, with a path toward leading lady if things work out." Joe looked at Edna as if he were searching out her reaction to his statement.

Edna did not like the way his words slowed down when he said " …if things work out." He was implying something more than work and she was certain it was not her imagination.

Joe once again placed his hand on Edna's thigh and smiled at her. Edna again stood up, this time more agitated than the last. "I don't think this will work out, Mr. O'Malley. I am not for sale. I am not a girl who will trade favors. I work for a living." Edna was surprised at the forcefulness of her own voice.

"Well, you can't blame a guy for trying. Calm down. Don't get so upset. However, you've shown me your animalistic spirit. That could be terrific if it comes across on screen. Remember that feeling. If it translates well on film, you'll be a star."

Edna was startled by his response. She started walking towards the door.

"Don't go. We're just beginning," Joe said.

Edna had the distinct impression he was toying with her, playing with her like she had seen garden spiders do, when they circled the bugs caught in their webs.

"I really must leave now, Mr. O'Malley. A car is waiting for me. Please phone me to let me know if and when you wish me to take a screen test. In the meantime, I will think of new names that might have more marquee appeal. Thank you for your time. It was a pleasure to meet you." Edna smiled, turned, opened his office door and left.

She could not get out of there fast enough. Although she felt thrilled at the thought of being in the movies, if it was going to mean selling her soul, she wanted no part of it. *I need some time to clear my head, to calm down.*

She heard Joe through the open door shout after her, "Hey, come back. We weren't finished."

I'm finished, Edna thought to herself. *I might be completely finished. We'll see.*

She was happy to see Thomas, and to climb into the safe, secure environment of the back of the limo. Edna was now doubting whether her nature would permit her to participate in this fast Hollywood lifestyle. It certainly wouldn't if she was to be consistently considered the main course.

Thomas dropped Edna off at her apartment to change before meeting Ray later. Waiting for Edna upstairs in front of her apartment door was a vase filled with two dozen red roses. Edna took the vase inside, set it on top of her small side table, and read the card:

"Hello, Beautiful. Looking
forward to tonight. Wear
something casual. I might
teach you some tennis. Ray."

Edna was surprised. Tennis? At night? Ray had previously indicated dinner at Cafe Trocadero, and dancing to Phil Ohman's band. Oh, well. Ray could be spontaneous at times. He might be taking her to some friends' house, or a country club. What should she wear now?

He said "casual." Her new wide-legged slacks would work. She also had some white rubber-soled deck shoes that wouldn't harm a tennis court surface.

Forty-five minutes later, Thomas came to the door to pick her up. Edna was dressed, refreshed, and ready. Ray was waiting in the back of the limousine and when he saw her he expressed surprise. He had never seen her in her wide slacks before, and she looked as gorgeous as ever. "You can certainly wear clothes," he said. "How's my starlet?"

"Starlet? No, not so fast." Edna leaned over and gave him a kiss on the cheek. "That studio guy, Joe O'Malley, wanted me for an afternoon snack and I was not about to play that game."

"Sweetheart, you can't blame a guy for trying. Any red-blooded American male who saw you would love the opportunity, and those studio guys have twice the opportunity, and three times the aggressive confidence of the average guy."

"Well, I was at full alert to fend him off without causing injury." Edna brushed it off lightly, even though she had been more offended and shaken than she let on to Ray. Sometimes her Southern girl upbringing helped her; sometimes it hurt her. In the South girls learned early how to do plenty of flirting, but expected no serious consequences. Women and men both engaged in that playful pastime. But in Hollywood, it seemed there were males who wanted much more than flirting.

Ray took out of the limo ice bucket a bottle of imported champagne which he gracefully opened, and poured each of them a glass. "To tennis," he said, clinking Edna's glass with his.

They each took a sip. "You know, Ray, I've never played tennis in my life. I'm afraid I won't be much of a challenge for you."

"Don't worry. It'll be fun to help you learn the game. We may not be playing a match right off, but we can hit balls back and forth. It's a fun sport and I've always needed a good doubles partner."

Edna smiled at Ray, and took another sip of champagne. He was about the nicest man she had ever known outside of her daddy. *This man always knows the right thing to say to make me feel good. How can I be so lucky?*

After they had been talking for a few minutes, the car drove up in front of a large Spanish-style house in an upscale area of Los Angeles. Edna had not seen this well-manicured area before. All the houses were grand, not quite Pickfair-scale mansions but much larger than the normal homes one found in most Los Angeles neighborhoods. Ray climbed out, came around to her side and helped her out of the car. Thomas brought two tennis rackets and a bucket of tennis balls around and followed the two of them. Ray led the way by the side of the house, through an unlocked closed-in fence gate, to reveal a tennis court in a portion of the backyard of the house.

"Whose house is this?" Edna was curious.

"Just someone who's letting us use the court," Ray replied.

There were tall lights on the sides of the court, which Ray turned on to reveal a large, well-surfaced and perfectly clean tennis area, with a new-looking net. It was quite an extravagance to have lights on a tennis court when many households in the country could not even afford electric lighting in their homes.

Ray patiently taught Edna how to hold the racket, how to hit balls over the net, and within the half hour, she was rallying, albeit slowly, with Ray.

"I knew you'd learn quickly," Ray complimented his pupil.

"Well, I have a terrific teacher, but, honey, I'm getting tired. This has been quite an emotional day for me."

"Well, that's enough for your first time," Ray said. He went around the net, took the tennis racket from Edna's right hand, and laid it down carefully on the court. Come with me, I've got something to show you." Ray took her hand and gently led her out of the tennis court, towards the back door of the house.

"Oh, Ray, I'm not in the mood to meet anyone," Edna said.

"Just come with me," Ray urged. When they reached the back door, Ray turned the unlocked doorknob and walked right into the kitchen without knocking. He pulled Edna behind him. Thomas was standing by the sink in the kitchen, washing his hands. Edna could smell hamburgers and French fries.

Ray led her through the kitchen, through what was an empty dining room, to a cavernous living room with fireplace. Edna looked up to see a series of high dark beams appearing to hold the ceiling up. A white blanket with red, marine blue, and yellow highlights was lying on the shiny wooden floor about five feet in front of the fireplace. An ice bucket with some cold bottled beer was sitting next to the blanket. The fire in the fireplace was lighting the room.

"What's all this?" Edna asked, surprised to see that no one apparently lived in this large house.

"I thought we'd have a picnic," Ray responded. "Hamburgers, French fries, chili and cold beer. How does that sound?"

"I'm famished. That sounds perfect."

Thomas brought in a plate for each of them. He then opened cold beers which he poured into tall glasses for each of them. "I'll be out clearing the tennis court, sir."

"Fine, Thomas."

Ray and Edna devoured their food as they talked and looked at the fire. This was about the most fun Edna could remember on a date with Ray. She liked the dancing and dinners out, but Edna was more truly in her heart a homebody, who loved quiet evenings without the social expectations of the nightclubs and the sophisticated crowd. The best times she had had as a child were the evenings around the dinner table with her family, as well as those Sunday suppers where relatives and people from the neighborhood would drop by to visit and perhaps join in the meal.

"Edna, what are you thinking about?" Ray broke a comfortable, shared silence.

"Oh, my family. The years as a child when we would have family meals. It was so comfortable and secure. Life was safe and nothing felt like it could ever go wrong."

"Sounds very warm and loving," Ray offered.

"It was. Life was good. Life is good. This has been a wonderful evening. I feel safe and secure with you."

"Well, let me try and make it better." Ray took out of his pocket a glistening ring which looked to be a two-karat diamond. He gently took Edna's left hand and started to place it on her ring finger. "Will you marry me?"

"Oh, Ray. What a surprise. How beautiful." Edna let Ray slide the ring all the way onto her finger. It fit perfectly. She admired the diamond, then put her arms around his neck and hugged him. "Of course I will. I can't believe this is happening."

"There's more," Ray offered. "I bought this house for us to live in. What do you think?"

"Oh, Ray. It's beautiful. I adore it. This is all too much. But it's wonderful."

"Okay, future Mrs. Gibson. Let me give you a complete tour of your new home." Ray stood up and lent his hand to Edna, to help pull her up from the blanket. She took his hand, stood up, then again hugged him. They kissed gently and lovingly.

Edna felt like the star in one of those fabulous silver screen love stories she had seen over the years. *Only this is real. This is happening to me.*

What a day this has been. Ray certainly knows how to treat a woman. Romance and respect. If my friends and relatives back in Texas could see me now.

CHAPTER THIRTEEN

SAM'S CHILI AND THE SMOKE SHOP

The trolley cars on Edna's route had been fully functional for some time now. This Monday morning Edna and Marie agreed that they would meet near the department Store for an early dinner after work.

"Marie, I'll see you tonight at Sam's Chili. Have a great day." Edna waved good-bye.

It was a beautiful, clear, crisp Los Angeles morning, the kind that everyone associates with California. It was going to be one of those perfect weather days, not too hot, but bright, warm, visually stunning. Edna turned around and looked to the northeast. She loved the sight of snow capping the San Bernardino Mountains. Los Angeles was paradise on days like this.

When Edna punched in at the time clock this morning, there was a note behind her time card. Early as usual, she went into the break room, sat down and opened the note. It was from her recent regular department supervisor stating: "Edna, today the fur department needs you to work with them to model furs for their fashion show. When you are through there, please continue working with them for the remainder of your shift. Then, we get you back tomorrow. Thanks."

She preferred to know in advance about schedule changes but understood that work flexibility was necessary. And she was just in the mood for something different today. This would be fun. Some one must be sick. Usually the women who had been modeling the longest were chosen for the fur shows. The fur modeling was easiest since it did not necessitate the complete wardrobe changes of the regular modeling jobs. Thank goodness she had spent some extra time on her outfit, hair and nails yesterday evening, in preparation for the week ahead.

Edna went up the escalator to the fur department, looking forward to getting to know more about the different furs, and eager to try on the different colors, styles, and brands.

Edna felt sorry for the animals whose fur had been taken to make coats and stoles, but having worked in that meatpacking factory back in Texas, she realized it was a part of the circle of life. *God made the animals beautiful, yet he also made them a food source for mankind.* Animal fur had provided warmth since mankind's beginning, and today it not only provided warmth in cool climates, but had become a status symbol for the modern woman.

The day passed more quickly than usual. Edna modeled ten different coats and stoles in the show. She then worked sales in the department. By her shift's end, she had learned a great deal about the different styles and types of fur. Mink and ermine seemed to be the preferred choice of those well-dressed women with money. One woman even bought a dark brown mink bow-tie collar that could be attached to a simple blouse or dress by snaps.

Edna liked for herself, even more than the white jacket she had been photographed in, an auburn mink stole that complemented her skin color and hair. The price was prohibitive, but she told the department manager that that was her favorite. The manager agreed that Edna looked best in that particular stole, whereas some of the other gals really looked better in the long black mink coats. One black full-length mink coat was striking on a platinum blonde. As in many areas of life, one style did not suit everyone.

After work, Edna walked the few doors down Hollywood Boulevard to Sam's Chili. Marie was late. She had told Edna she was supposed to get off early because of some errand Marie's boss had to run, and she would be waiting for Edna at Sam's when Edna got off from work. Edna sat at the counter delaying the order of her chili as long as possible. She sipped on her water and took another couple of packages of saltines from the basket on the counter. Besides dinners out with Ray, and the occasional leftovers, saltine crackers were still a mainstay of her diet on her working girl's salary. *Until Ray and I are married, I'll depend on myself.*

She had already put five packages into her pocketbook, which was saving the adjacent counter seat. The trick was to make certain to be as casual and quick as possible when taking and hiding extra crackers. Edna was opening her second cracker package to eat, and was pouring some ketchup on the crackers, when Marie finally arrived. Edna removed her purse, placed it on the floor in front of her feet, so Marie could take the seat.

"Edna, so sorry I'm late. The trolley from work to my transfer trolley was delayed. Apparently a number of trolleys were removed from their routes for routine maintenance. That left quite a shortage."

"Good to see you, honey. Gosh, you'd think the trolley company wouldn't do that during commute hours. I wonder who planned that?"

"It is unusual. They usually do maintenance on weekends and off hours from what a fellow passenger was telling me. He thinks that some of the managers are getting payoffs to slow things up. He saw a neighbor of his who is one of the system schedulers driving a brand new high-end convertible. He said the guy didn't make enough money to buy it."

"Oh, honey. No one would intentionally make the trolley system less efficient. That wouldn't be good for Los Angeles or its workers."

"Well, I'm just repeating what the passenger said. There was a lot of grumbling about the late trolley cars. I hate to think anyone would take a bribe or make life more difficult for everyone. And, you're right. What would be the purpose?"

"None that I can see." Edna's rumbling stomach compelled her to interrupt Marie and turn to Sam who was standing in front of them to take their order.

"Sam, we'll have our usual. Two chili bowls with lots of cheese and onions. And, two ice waters."

"Okay, Edna," Sam responded. He was a frenetic bundle of energy, moving as quickly as possible between all the customers at the very long counter, always upbeat, never pushy though he sold more chili if the turnover was quicker.

"Marie, what else did that passenger say? Why would he suspect a bribe? The neighbor's father could have passed on and left him some money. There could be any number of ways a person could get a new car. Although I know a high-end convertible is awfully expensive for the usual wage-earner, even a streetcar scheduling manager."

"Honestly Edna, all I know is what the passenger said, but he seemed to know what he was talking about. He said he saw a bunch of men over at this neighbor's house recently who looked like thugs. He said a couple of days after that his neighbor who works at the downtown station came home with that new fancy convertible. He suspects something's up."

"I don't know, Marie. Why would anyone do that? It just doesn't make sense."

"Oh, Edna. A lot of things in this world don't make sense. Life isn't fair. It's not always orderly. You're looking at it through your personal perspective. You want the best for everyone and expect the best from yourself. But there are a lot of people who really don't care about anyone but themselves and their own selfish interests."

Sam set the brimming bowls of chili, cheese and onions down on the counter in front of them.

"Thanks, Sam," both women responded in unison.

95

"My pleasure, ladies."

"Marie, I guess I've been lucky enough to have been around people who have wanted to do what's right, except for maybe my ex-boyfriend Jimmy who only wanted to feel good himself and didn't care how he hurt others in pursuing that."

"Edna, you're lucky to not have seen some of the rot beneath the surface. There are many, many ruthless people in this world who would sell their mothers if they thought they could get a step up. And in this depression basic survival can cause people to do things they otherwise might not do."

"I guess so. Boy, this chili is sure good."

"Hot, but tasty. Edna, I knew a guy back home who sold his widowed mother's car without her knowing it, so he could get money to move to New York City."

"Oh, Marie. Really?"

"Yes. I grew up with him. He was bright, enterprising, but somewhere along the line he took a wrong, selfish turn."

"Well, the streetcars, although late, are still running, and my chili is good, so I'm satisfied with the world."

"Yeah, and you're engaged to a fabulous guy, and moving towards married life. You're going to include me in your fancy dinner parties once you're married, aren't you?"

"You'll be first on the list. And, we'll get Ray to invite all of his single bachelor friends to be your dinner partner. I bet you'll be married within a year."

"Honey, you're terrific. You're truly the best friend I've got in Los Angeles."

"Marie, I think you realize by now that when I make a true friend, I'm as loyal as a St. Bernard."

"Lucky for me. Pass me the crackers, would you, friend? I need some extras for my room."

Edna took a couple more packages of crackers and slid them into her purse on the floor, while moving the basket over in front of Marie.

As Edna looked around she saw Sam looking at her. She had a moment's apprehension, but then Sam smiled and winked at her. He understood a working girl's situation, and particularly liked these two.

"Say, when we get done, let's stop by The Smoke Shop. I want to look at the lighters. That may be what I get Ray for a wedding gift. He smokes cigars sometimes, and he lights my cigarettes for me. I want to see how much I'll have

96

to save up. I'd like to buy him maybe a sterling silver or gold-plated lighter, and have it engraved with meaningful words."

"Sure, Edna. I'm game. Never know who a single girl might meet in a smoke shop."

"Yes, but don't forget to conceal that onion breath. Sam piled those onions on tonight."

"I'll get close enough to smile but not too close to offend anyone with my breath."

"Great."

"I'll be finished in two minutes."

"Let's get the check and get out of here." Edna signaled Sam for the check.

As they walked out of Sam's Chili, they saw a Red Car pass by with passengers packed like a sardine can. The trolley passed the stop without even slowing down.

"Oh, my, Edna, look at that streetcar. I hope they all aren't like that."

"Well, let's go into The Smoke Shop and we'll see later."

"Sure."

There were two male clerks and about six male clients in the Smoke Shop. As Edna and Marie entered the store, a few heads turned and sized them up. One of the customers whistled. Another said, "Oh, boy, gentlemen, we've hit a bonanza tonight."

"Calm down, boys," Edna retorted. "I'm here to look for a present for my fiancé."

"Aw, the lucky stiff," said one of the customers.

"But Marie here may be willing to speak with you. She's a lady, so treat her right." Edna felt protective of her friend.

Two of the customers gathered around Marie and started talking with her while Edna waited at the counter for a clerk to help her with the lighters in the glass case. She spotted a beautiful gold lighter that looked like it would suit Ray. When the clerk came over to her, she asked him to see it.

"Well, you certainly have exquisite taste. This is our top-of-the-line model, the best we carry. It is covered in 14-karat gold plating. It has a lifetime guarantee for its function as well as for the gold surface. You couldn't have chosen a better model."

Edna took the lighter out of the box and turned it over in her hands. It felt solid, substantial. It was a little large and heavy for her hand, but it would be terrific for Ray.

"Do you do engraving?" she asked.

"We can send it out for you. It will be back in a week."

"Well, there's no rush. This will need to be a layaway, anyway."

"Oh, sorry, miss. We don't take layaways."

"You don't?"

"No. Sorry, miss."

"You can call me Edna."

"Sorry, Edna. But we have had this lighter for six months. Most of our customers want a less expensive model, or they go to a high-end jewelry store for a solid gold model."

"Do you think you might be able to save this one for me for a while? How much is it anyway?"

"This model is $25.00. Like I say, it has a lifetime guarantee and is top of our line."

"My, that's a month's rent. Well, he's worth it. Do you think you could put it aside for me?" Edna shined her best smile and looked into his eyes.

He melted. "If it were up to me, Edna, you know I would, but the owner won't allow it. How about if I call you and let you know if there's another customer interested in it? I'll tell them we cannot sell it to them until I check with you first? As I said, we've had it for six months. Start saving up. What's your phone number?"

Something in his grin made Edna believe that he wanted her phone number for more than that one reason.

"No. I appreciate that, but if you weren't here one day, someone else might sell it. I'll just have to take my chances and hope that it's here when I have the cash for it."

"Okay. If that's what you want. Sorry I couldn't help you."

Edna went over to Marie and saw that she was still flirting with the two gentlemen. Edna didn't want to pull her away since it had been a while since Marie had been interested in any man. The trauma of that abortion in Mexico had emotionally scarred her. Although she never talked about it, Edna had seen a change in Marie's demeanor with the men she met. It was hard for her to trust again after being abandoned in a tough situation by a man she had trusted.

Edna looked out the front window and saw another packed streetcar go by. What was going on? It was now 7:30 and the streetcars with the after work crowd usually had some room. She was curious. She went back to the clerk at the counter.

"Say, I notice the streetcars are still full and passing by this stop. Do you know what's going on?"

"Well, Edna, a customer about a half hour ago told me that a number of streetcars on a few lines had been taken off today before rush hour allegedly to perform maintenance. He was angry as hell -- excuse me -- heck. He was ranting about the Los Angeles Area Railway management being a darn bunch of fools. Passengers weren't notified in advance that it was going to happen.

I can't vouch for what he said, but I can tell you that a few Railway executives and financiers come in here for their cigars and they are as cagey a group of men as they come. Tough negotiators, ruthless businessmen types. They try to get their cigars wholesale. Not fools in the slightest. Something's going on is my suspicion."

"What do you mean?"

"Well, I've heard rumors from a number of different customers that the auto companies, along with the bus companies, rubber, oil and gasoline companies, want to increase their business in the Los Angeles area. Those special interests would be happy as can be if the streetcars were gone because people in Los Angeles would then either have to buy cars or take their busses to get around this big city."

"No. You're kidding. The street car system here is terrific. It's efficient and inexpensive. The routes are so well-placed."

"I know. Best system in the world. I take a trolley to work myself and I work odd hours. It's quick and convenient. But in the past two weeks they've even taken some of the late evening cars on my transfer line off the route completely. I guess they don't think normal working people stay out late. Only the limousine and cab crowd."

"That isn't good for businesses that are open late either."

"I know. And people from the theaters around here who get out of a movie late and need to transfer to get home sometimes find no trolley cars running. It's just been in the past few months or so where there's been an obvious change. It seems deliberate to me."

"I'd heard that more bus routes were planned, but I wasn't aware there was a scheme to get rid of streetcars. It's hard to believe. If they wanted to try to make more money they could increase their fares. People would be willing to pay more."

"I know. I agree. But I guess bigger fish with their own selfish motives are pursuing their own agenda. They don't care who gets hurt by their own personal pursuit of profits."

"You mean you truly believe those automobile related companies are somehow manipulating this streetcar situation?"

"From what I've heard and seen, yes."

"That seems far-fetched."

"You are an innocent."

"Well, who was it who told you the rumor about the companies? What was the source?" Edna was as skeptical of his information as she had been of Marie's gossip.

"A number of customers, like I said. There was, in particular, a well-known man of prominence in Los Angeles who comes in here a lot. He has been a customer for years. I'd rather not give his name."

"Oh, who am I going to tell? I'm on your side."

"Well, the conversation came up when he gave me a tip about buying some automobile company stock but of course I didn't have any extra cash to do anything about it."

"What company?"

"Standard Motors."

"Oh. Well, what else did he say?"

"He told me with a great deal of assurance that Standard Motors and other related automotive companies were going to make Los Angeles their next priority. That more and more people would be driving cars on the streets of Los Angeles, so I'd better buy some stock so that I could afford to get my own automobile in a while, because I'd need it."

"You'd 'need it'? Did he really say that?"

"Yes. Because all the streetcar lines are systemically going to become in 'disrepair'."

"He actually used that word 'disrepair'?"

"Yes. At the time I didn't take it seriously because I thought the Los Angeles railway companies would not let that occur. It seems now that railway management might be in cahoots with those large auto-related companies."

"Oh, my gosh. This is unbelievable. How can people be so ruthless? So greedy?"

"I don't know. They certainly aren't like my friends and family. I sure didn't grow up that way."

"You're a nice guy. What's your name?"

"John."

"Well, John, I appreciate your telling me about this rumor, but it's sure frightening to me. I can tell that you believe it, but I hope you're not right.

I hope the other people and the man who told you that were wrong. If what they said is true, there are some evil people with evil plots in this world. But I appreciate your sharing with me what you know about the streetcars. I'd better grab Marie and see if we can catch the next Red Car before the Pantages Theater crowd empties out of the movie."

"Sure. If you can't catch one, come back in and use our telephone. And, hope to see you soon about the lighter."

"Thanks, John." Edna went over to Marie and took her arm.

"Honey, we should get going before the movie crowd gets out."

"Okay, Edna." Marie turned and smiled at the prematurely grey gentleman next to her. "Bye for now, Eric. It was a pleasure to talk with you."

"It was a pleasure to meet you, Marie. I will be calling you soon. I look forward to our next meeting."

Edna and Marie went out the front door of The Smoke Shop onto the warm Hollywood Boulevard. The clear and fragrant air tonight meant more people were out walking, soaking in the fresh air and enjoying the bustling atmosphere.

"Marie, let's go wait right at the edge of the streetcar stop. A few full trolleys have passed by without stopping. We both need to get home. I want the streetcar conductor to see us standing there looking at him."

"Well, sure, Edna. He might stop for you."

The two gals walked in front of slowing automobiles to the streetcar stop near the center of the street. It was so crowded that there was barely enough room for them. But Edna moved through to the streetcar side of the four-thick group. She was determined to get home. She pulled Marie by her hand behind her.

In three minutes, a streetcar came by and stopped with its front door right in front of Edna. The driver smiled at Edna and said "Hello there."

Edna smiled back, got on board, placed her token in the box, waited for Marie to do the same, then walked all they way to the back where one man stood up and permitted the two of them to squeeze into the wide seat across the very rear of the streetcar.

"Well, honey, I'm glad this car is not completely full. At least all those people on the curb can get on. I felt badly about moving closer to the street.

Some of those people are like sheep. They might not have gotten a full car to stop. I was determined."

"Edna, you are a force of nature. I was embarrassed by what you did but I have to admit that the driver did stop right in front of you."

"We didn't cut to the front of the line. We just stood on the outside where the conductor could see us. There's no harm in that. There was no real line formed."

"Well, you do seem to know how to get things done. I admire your gutsy nature. Sure wish I had a little more of that."

"You're doing alright. Look at that nice gentleman you met tonight."

"I know. He's refined. Intelligent. I hope he calls."

"He will. He looks like the sincere type."

"I hope so."

Edna and Marie fell into silence on the way home. While Marie was thinking about the man she had just met, Edna was worrying about the streetcar situation and how it might effect working people in Los Angeles if there were no longer the frequent and reliable streetcar lines.

CHAPTER FOURTEEN

THE SCREEN TEST

Nation Studio's ornate black and gold gate looked intimidating this Wednesday morning. A studio car had picked Edna up at 6:30. Today was her screen test.

Apparently studio executives had not written her off when she refused to cooperate with O'Malley's advances. The studio was still interested in seeing if her "it" factor on the screen was as compelling as it was in still photos and in person.

As the large black car glided past the guard's station, Edna looked around for some of her favorite stars. Perhaps she might catch a glimpse of one of them this morning: Bette Davis, Joan Crawford, Clark Gable -- particularly Clark Gable. Edna adored him as did most women who had seen his films. He projected a virility and a can-do attitude on screen that also converted men into fans.

Edna wondered if Clark Gable exuded as much magnetism in person as he did on the screen. Some stars, she had discovered, were much shorter or smaller framed than they looked up on that huge movie screen, and many lacked any star presence at all when spotted in person.

She knew that Nation Studio did not own her favorite stars' contracts, however, reading *Photoplay* magazine for years had taught her that stars were often loaned to other studios for special projects in order to fulfill contractual or studio obligations. "Traded like horse flesh" was a phrase she recalled. However, she was disappointed this early morning because the studio streets were quiet and empty.

The instructions were that Edna was to appear at Soundstage 13, without any make-up on, at 7:15. The image consultant artist would decide the best image for her screen test. Once the right look was discerned, make-up would be applied, and hairstyle done in accordance with studio trends and style suitability.

She hadn't fully complied with the no make-up instruction since she often ran into other tenants in her apartment lobby. A light powder, some mascara, and lipstick made her feel presentable, more confident and comfortable.

Her sleep had come slowly last night as she anticipated today's events. *How exciting to see the inner workings of a soundstage where the movie magic is created. And to be part of it, at least for one day.*

"Here we are, Miss King," the chauffeur pulled to a stop in front of the door to a large hangar-like building. Edna was anxious to open her own car door and get started, but she forced herself to wait for the driver to walk back to open the door for her.

"Miss King, you enter right through there," the driver indicated. "I'll be here to take you home when you're done."

Edna steeled herself against any nervousness, raised her head high, and walked swiftly over to the indicated door. She tried the knob and it felt as if it were locked or closed too tightly. She knocked on the door and within thirty seconds a kind-looking man, slender, blond-haired, with twinkling intelligent eyes opened the door. "Miss King, I presume?"

"Yes," Edna answered and smiled her best, eye-engaging smile.

"Come on in. Please. I'm ready for you. My name is Maximilian."

"Pleasure to meet you, Maximilian," Edna responded as she walked through the door into her first movie soundstage.

The place was overwhelming in its size, filled with lights, cameras, various backdrops of cities, country roads, desert and mountain scenes. *An ocean liner could fit in here.*

"We've got about forty-five minutes to get you ready for your shoot before the director and the rest of his crew arrives so bear with me. It will be a bit frenzied. The make-up area is back here."

Edna followed Maximilian who was walking as fast as was humanly possible. Her heels slowed her down some, but her strong legs enabled her to almost keep up with him.

The lights were bright in a small room to the left of a set. Edna entered the area to find herself surrounded with mirrors on both sides of an elongated room. Light bulbs were lit around all the mirrors, with beauty shop-style chairs lined up in front. Glamour shots of movie stars hung in the space between the top of the mirrors and the false ceiling of the room. *So this is where the glamour begins.*

"Please sit here, Miss King," Maximilian said as he stood behind one of the middle chairs, waiting for her to catch up.

After she climbed up into the high chair, she kicked off her heels to the floor below her. Maximilian, with the flare of a bullfighter swinging off his cape for the ring's audience, covered her front in a pink rustling fabric. He quickly tied it in the back. Then before she could even settle in, he began pulling her hair back, studying her in the mirror.

"Is your hair dyed auburn?" he asked as he moved his fingers through her shoulder length, wavy hair.

"No. It's natural. And, also, naturally wavy."

"Let's take that powder, mascara and lipstick off." He handed Edna a few soft tissues and a pink jar of face cream. Edna complied with his request and removed her make-up.

"Freckles, huh?" Maximilian inquired pointedly.

"Yes. I keep them covered up for the most part. The sun brings them out more. Goes with the hair, I suppose." Edna spoke lightheartedly. She was at home in her body, freckles and all.

"Well, we can take care of those," he replied in a tone that indicated freckles were a liability.

Maximilian continued to examine her face and hair in the mirror. He looked closely at the position of freckles, he ran his finger down the bridge of her nose, he carefully looked at the spacing of her eyes and even took a small ruler to measure their distance. The curve of her eyebrows and the outer shape of Edna's ears were traced by his finger. She was totally compliant until he asked her to open her mouth so he could examine her teeth and gums.

"What? Am I a horse?" Edna balked at the request.

"We need to know if any dental work might need to be done in the future." Maximilian's attitude was purely clinical and professional.

I guess that makes sense. Edna opened her mouth wide.

After studying the inside of her mouth, he next examined the shape of her lips. Then he again started to play around with her hair, moving each side separately in various directions. He put her hair all up on top, then pulled it tightly from the rear into a chignon look. Edna was getting somewhat bored and restless.

"Can I call you 'Max'?" She tried to break his focused silence.

"Fine," Maximilian answered. "Many do."

"I thought there might be a hairdresser, too," she said, tired of the overly serious silence.

"I am the one who is the architect of your total look which will be my supreme vision of your most appealing image for the screen and the public. Many can do hair, but few can create the total image, the overall style that most suits a person's personality and features. I do the make-up, hair, and image consulting."

"How would you know my personality?" Edna was getting tired of the pretense. "We've barely spoken. You've merely been examining me like a bug under a microscope."

"Your personality radiated to me when we first met through your voice, your smile, your eyes. You're friendly, open; not the shy, reserved, elegant type, although your features are elegantly refined. You have more the down-home, woman-of-the-people feel. You kicked off your high heels immediately, indicating you are natural and not full of pretense nor do you have an overly self-conscious sense of propriety. You feel at home wherever you are and people can take you or leave you as far as you're concerned because you're comfortable being yourself."

"My God, Max. You've missed your calling. You should be a psychiatrist like that Freud guy. That's amazing how you pegged me. You're brilliant."

"Just an observer of people and beauty," Max replied. "It is a gift, but also a necessity in my line of work. But, thank you for your kind remarks.

Now let's begin your transformation. It won't take much for you, because of your natural beauty. A good foundation to cover those freckles, and the right shades and shapes for your eyes and lips will be enough. Your hair's good. I'll just wet it, then trim a bit to reshape it so it will frame your face beautifully. There are no features we need to hide or even disguise other than the freckles. This will be an easy one to do."

With the analysis concluded, Edna felt Maximilian become more relaxed and open. They began to talk more, and hit it off. They both had an irreverent sense of humor, once Max let down his formal reserve.

It did not take long for Max to turn Edna into a striking knockout. Her lively blue eyes stood out dramatically after his eye makeup application. Her lips were red and luscious after the moisturizing lip treatments and the lipstick brush shaped the popular lip outline. Her hair was tamed yet wavy enough to look neat and modern, hanging just above her shoulders, framing her face in the latest style of the year for the silver screen.

"You've worked your magic, Max," Edna complimented him as she surveyed her finished self in the lighted studio mirror. "Even I must admit I am one good-looking dame with your beauty secrets applied. Now all I need is a decent screen name."

"Let's see," Max offered. "How would 'Freckles' look up on that marquee?"

"Sounds like a dog," Edna countered.

"What about 'Red'"? Max teased.

"My hair isn't that red. It's more auburn," Edna responded with playful indignity. Besides there's already a Mr. Skelton on the radio that uses that name."

"Yes, there is. Just testing your entertainment education. What about 'Rusty'"?

"Well, that's a fun name, but I don't know how right it is for a movie career. Might limit me to westerns, B westerns at that. Might as well call me 'Dusty.'

"Or 'Dixie,' with that southern twang of yours. The studio will have you taking voice lessons at first light."

"No Southern name, Max. I may be a Texan, but I'm trying to leave the South behind and cultivate a more broadened California gal image."

"Okay, Missy King. More creative word types than I might need to work on your new marquee name. The studio might get the writers and P.R. guys involved. You're not an easy young woman to label. I see in you a mixture of spice, dice, and a warm, glowing heart, mixed in with old-fashioned values. I don't know what name can ever fully capture you. But, the studio will find one that will sell, that will pigeon-hole you into the type of woman they want to market you as, so be prepared. It's all about the publicity that they want the public to believe, and rarely about who you really are. Image is everything; reality not important in this business."

"Thanks, Max. I'll remember that."

It was 8:00 a.m. on the dot, and they both heard a loud knock.

"There is Herr Director," Max told her. "I thought he would have his key. I'll go let him in. Just one word of caution: don't laugh at him out loud, but do pretend to respect him no matter how outlandish his request. He takes his work extremely seriously, so go along and things will go well."

"Thanks for all the advice, Max. Your voice of experience is a great help."

Max went to greet the director and spoke with him as they walked from the front door to the make-up room. Edna could hear Max saying that Edna's movie makeover hadn't taken much and that she was a natural beauty of the Marlene Dietrich/Norma Shearer/Myrna Loy type, but with less sophistication than Dietrich, charm more Southern than Norma Shearer, and better legs than Myrna Loy.

As Max and the director entered the makeup room, Edna's eyes took in the director before he was introduced. The whip in his hands, his riding breeches, and his tall black riding boots indicated the director might be a horse aficionado.

"Mr. von Stronholm, this is Miss Edna King."

"Edna, Mr. Werner von Stronholm."

"It's a pleasure to make your acquaintance, Mr. von Stronholm," Edna said in her most inviting voice, accompanied by a special direct eye glance and smile. "You must love horses?"

"Horses?"

"Yes. The boots, the riding pants, the whip," Edna said playfully.

"This, Miss King, is my directorial outfit. One must maintain a uniform consistency, a discipline in dress and action in order that the creative product can be consciously formed, fanned and expanded in a determined, orderly fashion to reach its peak potential."

"I don't have a bit of any idea what you just said, honey, but I sure think your outfit is cute." Edna could barely restrain herself from breaking up with laughter at his heightened sense of the dramatic, so she countered it with some Southern drama of her own. She found the director's pretense hilarious. She did not dare look over at Max for fear she would burst out laughing. Thankfully, Max interrupted in an appropriate, respectful tone.

"Mr. von Stronholm, we've started Edna out with the general appeal look. I hope that will suffice for now."

"Yes, Max. Thank you. I plan to start the screen test with some off camera/on camera dialogue between Miss King and myself, then move into a scene reading with another actor. Could you have her change her dress into a long, frilly ball gown. There is a rack over there for the occasion."

Von Stronholm looked slowly at Edna from head to toe. Then he took her arm and silently turned her around full circle.

"Are you a size 8"? von Stronholm inquired of Edna.

"Yes, sir, 6, 8 or 10, depending upon the design."

"Good. Most of those outfits will fit. Max, choose one for her that suits her coloring and works well for the camera, and we'll begin as soon as she's dressed. I'll be over on the set preparing. Oh, and have her put on some shoes."

As von Stronholm exited the make-up room, his right hand whipped the floor with the black whip, making a loud cracking noise. Waiting a few seconds until he was completely gone, Max and Edna looked at each other and burst out laughing.

"You warned me, Max, but I wouldn't have believed it until I saw him with my own eyes."

"I know, I know. Unbelievable. He is recently on contract here and I don't think he will be around for long. The guy has a number of loose screws. He never or rarely cracks a smile. But, just don't let him know your true perceptions of him and you'll do fine. Follow his direction even if you find it ridiculous. He insists upon everything being done his way."

"I'll do my best, but this is going to be difficult. I'm not so great at hiding my true feelings. I'm much better at revealing what I feel."

"I've learned that about you. And, that will do well for you over time in the acting business once you team up with the right director, however, today, for now, just follow the nutcase's direction and you'll be fine. If you want to be an actress, well, this is your opportunity to start acting."

"Okay, Max, if you say so. Say, how about this blue taffeta?"

"Yes. That's exactly what I was going to choose for you. Put that on and let's see."

Edna went behind the screen at the far end of the room to change. When she emerged from behind the screen with the long blue taffeta dress on, Max whistled.

"You are stunning, Miss Southern Belle. Now go show them that wildfire you carry within you."

"I'll do my best, Max." Edna went to where she had sat in the make-up chair, bent down and picked up her high heels. She climbed back up into the chair for a moment to more easily put them on.

"They don't match the dress, Max," she complained as she stood up.

"Let's see. No, but that will be alright. The bottom of the dress just covers the shoes without dragging. The shoes won't be seen," Max offered. "And, on black and white film, this shoe color, if glimpsed, will harmonize."

Edna went over to look at the dress length with the heels in the full-length mirror. The shoes did not show much. Only a slight toe. In the mirror. A glamorous, sophisticated woman was looking back at her. Yes, a beautiful southern belle but, moreover, a radiant movie queen.

Other crew had arrived and had quickly readied their own areas of expertise. *This movie business is clearly a well-run machine*, Edna observed. Director von Stronholm told "Miss King" to sit in a tall chair in the middle of a now brightly lit stage area with a plain blue backdrop. Edna found the chair very uncomfortable, and it was awkward to cross one's legs at the ankle with her legs dangling above the floor.

"Are my shoes showing, because I certainly wouldn't want that. They don't match this beautiful gown."

"We are only photographing you now from the waist area up. Your shoes will not show." Von Stronholm dismissed her concern.

Edna watched the bustling motion around her. One man was moving a large, heavy metal object above where she was sitting.

"What is that?" she inquired politely.

The sound grip informed her it was the microphone and asked her to recite the alphabet for him while the sound was adjusted.

Edna complied in her own unique way. "A is for always, B for button, C is for cute, D for darlin', E for energy, F for feet with shoes that match the dress, G is for good, H for happy, I for Irene, J for jealous, K for kin, L for love—"

"Alright, Miss King. You can stop. The sound's fine."

Edna could barely make out movement behind the lights, apparently adjusting the lighting that had been turned on and was now being directed upon her. Edna was sparkling with excitement. She enjoyed this attention, all these people around, a group effort, working together for a screen test, *and of me*. The outgoing part of her nature was revving up in the spotlight.

"Take 1, Scene 1, Edna King screen test." The words were spoken and a man clapped together some board thing in front of the camera.

"Quiet on the set. Action," Director von Stronholm ordered through a large megaphone. Then he began a dialogue with Edna.

"Where are you from originally, Miss King"?

"Well, I tell everyone I'm from Goose Creek, Texas, for fun but I'm actually from Houston, Texas, born and bred."

"And when did you come to California"?

"I took the train to Los Angeles over a year ago. My life has certainly changed as a result of the decision to move out here."

"How has your life changed"?

"Well, I've met so many wonderful people who have so much going on in their lives. I've worked in a terrific department store where the fashions are fabulous and I've learned to model in the fashion shows. Dancing in the Hollywood nightclubs to the big bands has been a regular ritual. It's glamorous and exciting here."

"Do you like to dance"?

"I love to dance." Edna's eyes shot fire and her face was radiant when she spoke about dancing.

"Do you like to sing"?

"I love to sing, but my voice I've been told is not very good for singing."

"Sing us a few notes anyway, so we can estimate your talent in that direction."

"Oh, my. Well, I guess -- I did play the banjo and some piano when I was younger, and would sing a few songs along with my strumming or piano playing. How about --" Edna launched into:

"I wish I was in the land of cotton,

old times there are not forgotten,

look away, look away, look away,

Dixieland—"

Von Stronholm abruptly stopped her. "You're right. You are not a singer. Now turn your head to the far left for us so that we can see your right side more. Good. Now face the front again and lift your chin. Now look up at the ceiling. Hold that. Good. Now move your head to the far right. Let us see your left profile. Fine.

Now, look straight ahead far behind me. The lights I know are blinding. But imagine now that there is a sword fight going on right in front of you. Two men are fighting over you. One of the men you love with all your heart and you are afraid he might be killed."

Edna complied with all of von Stronholm's directions. At odd times the director would stand up and crack his whip against the floor to somehow accent his statements. Each time he did that, Edna wanted to laugh but held back, which only added to the sparkle in her eyes.

She was a natural. She reacted appropriately and quickly to whatever she was asked to do or imagine. Plus, the camera loved her. It magnified her natural beauty. She had what the studios looked for. Edna had the "it" factor. The whole crew could not take their eyes off her, and they laughed spontaneously at some of her fun-loving replies. Edna got such a kick out of the crew's laughing at her that she started laughing at herself at times, and the rigid structure of von Stronholm's direction dissolved, making him angry. But all in all, the screen test was going exceptionally well.

Next a young studio actor was asked to stand next to Edna and read from a shared script. The director insisted they both read the lines exactly as written.

But, Edna soon became bored with the recitation, and when the young man, devoid of feeling, read the line, "Would you care to dance?" in his monotone voice, she answered demurely "yes," as the script stated, but then quickly climbed down from the stool, and launched into a solo tap dance without music which segued into the Charleston. The crew could not contain their laughter and von Stronholm again became quite angry.

"Miss King. Stop. Stop it. Stop dancing now I say."

Egged on by the crew's enjoyment of her performance, Edna kept on dancing and smiling playfully until von Stronholm finally took his whip and snapped it a number of times loudly on the floor. She looked directly at him in surprise then stated as loudly but sweetly as she could, "Oh, honey, I'm not any circus animal. You don't have to use that silly old thing to get my attention."

The crew, startled not only by the ferocity of the whip snaps but by her daring to talk to von Stronholm that way, began to snicker again. This woman was a kick. And, fearless. She did not kowtow to anyone, not even this well-known director dictator. Such a spirited nature definitely was a portend of stardom.

The screen test was finally completed. Edna had made an impact. Now it was up to the studio heads to view the completed test and see if they were as pleased as were Edna and the crew. Von Stronholm gave no indication as to whether he was pleased or not. Edna would not find out about her film future until the film was developed, the Nation Studio head and others screened it, and a decision was made. No matter what the eventual outcome, it would be fun to tell Ray what had happened; and Marie and the girls at work would surely enjoy the story.

No matter what happened as a result of the test, this had been another memorable day in Los Angeles for Edna Mae King.

CHAPTER FIFTEEN

S.S. REX

Edna and Ray were on a motor launch with about ten others, headed toward the *S.S. REX*. The gambling ship was anchored three point one miles offshore from Santa Monica, and the ride out there tonight was bouncy and cold.

"Ray, I wouldn't have worn this evening gown if you had told me what we were going to do tonight. I usually love your surprises, but I'm overdressed for this adventure. Thank goodness my hair's in a chignon or it would turn to frizz in this foggy air."

"Edna, wait until you're on the vessel. There's a dance floor with a live orchestra, and a grand casino. I don't think you'll be overdressed on the dance floor."

"Well, I've heard it's fabulous. But, I wish I had known ahead of time. It's cold out here."

"Come on. Sit closer and I'll keep you warm. Don't be afraid. Please try and enjoy yourself. There are some business associates I need to meet. You can have some fun playing the slot machines while I talk with them." Ray took his jacket off and placed it over Edna's shoulders, then put his arm around her and pulled her closer.

"Thanks. That's a little better. Well, you owe me a few dances later, after my legs stop shaking."

"Of course. The night's young. The *REX* is open 24 hours. We'll fit it all in. Neither one of us has to be at work tomorrow."

"Oh, look, Ray. The moon's light is following us on the ocean. Doesn't it look like you could just reach up and touch it?" Edna raised her arm and used her hand to cover the moon.

"Yes. It's bright tonight. The moonlight shining on you shows you off beautifully."

Edna smiled at Ray and shivered from the cold. She realized he was trying to make her feel better and accepted his flattery without comment.

Ray continued to lay it on. "If I could, I'd buy the moon for you."

Edna couldn't let that blarney go by. "That's just silly. Why would anyone want to own the moon? The moon belongs to everyone."

"We're almost there." Ray changed the subject.

As the launch pulled up to the *S.S. REX*, Edna noticed the outside decks were empty except for three men standing outside at the upper deck rail. One of the men shouted down in a gruff low voice. "Ray, hey. There you are. It's about time."

Edna focused on the three men. They were standing below a deck light. They looked to be burly, longshoreman types, not Ray's usual society milieu. These men looked tough. The most noticeable of the three was short, stocky, dressed in baggy work pants, wearing what looked like a seaman's pea jacket. A lit cigarette dangled from his mouth. *What type of business does Ray have with these three?*

Ray helped Edna stand up, then steadied her by holding her elbow. The launch was bobbing two to three feet up and down on the ocean current. When it was her time in line to move from the launch to the *S.S. REX's* small floating dock, Edna made the mistake of looking down and saw that at least two feet of dark ocean water separated the moving launch from the *S.S. REX's* dock. It was frightening. Men did not realize how difficult it was to negotiate in high heels under the easiest of conditions, much less a boat bobbing on the Pacific Ocean's currents.

"Ray, please, take my hand."

"I'll do better than that." Ray picked her up in his arms and carried her across the gap between the two boats. When they arrived within the Rex, on flat surface, he set her down.

"Thank you, honey." Edna was truly grateful.

"Certainly. I'll take you over to the slot machines where you can sit down, then I'll meet up with the guys."

"Fine," Edna agreed, as she took a few steps forward on her wobbly legs and high heels. She focused on steadying herself on the Rex's deck which was also moving in concert with the ocean swells, although in a slower pattern than the launch.

"Ray, you can take your jacket back now."

Ray removed his coat from Edna's shoulders and put it on again. He and Edna walked to the ship's casino where Ray showed her the slot machine area. Almost all of the 300 shiny machines were being played. They finally located one that was open.

"Edna, here you are. Sit down here and relax a moment. I'll be right back."

Edna stared at the machine not quite certain of what she should be doing with it. It had a handle to pull, and a slot for coins. *I'll wait for Ray.* It was just good to be able to sit down and gather her composure.

Edna looked around. The place was absolutely packed. A quarter for the boat ride out gave people a lot of opportunity to have some fun. And there was the possibility of winning some money gambling.

She had never seen any place quite like this. There were a variety of slot machines, poker tables, blackjack tables and other gaming areas. They had walked by a large formal dining and dancing area, and there were a few more casual eating spots. The dance floor looked about the size of the Avalon ballroom on Catalina Island, but it was laid out differently, long instead of circular. Such an air of excitement permeated the atmosphere. Edna could hear the orchestra music playing in the background.

Even observing the assortment of people and the clothing they wore was stimulating on the *REX*. All levels of society mixed it up and there was a buoyant air of congeniality, of everyone being equals in humanity, that palpable feeling of shared community that comes when a group of congenial people are having fun together.

Edna had never seen so many gamblers. There were mostly women sitting at the rows of slot machines, which made her feel comfortable. And when Ray returned and handed her a coke, she quickly took a large sip to try and calm her jumpy nerves. She tasted a bit of whiskey spiking. She looked at Ray with surprise.

"I thought you might need a calming influence," Ray responded.

"You should have told me, but in this case I'll let it go."

He then explained to her how the slot machine worked, and handed her a bucket full of 100 silver dollars.

"Ray, no. I can't gamble with this much money. This is months of rent money. It's too extravagant."

"Well, sweetheart, get used to living larger. You'll soon be Mrs. Ray Gibson, and you need to become accustomed to what money can add to your life. But, if you want to start by playing with a smaller amount, call the change gal and get change. Actually, there's a dime machine right over there that just opened up, so if you want to move there and get some change, fine. Do what makes you feel comfortable. But that money is yours to play with, win or lose. Don't worry about it. Pretend like it's play money. I'll come back and find you as soon as I'm through."

"All right."

Ray headed off to his meeting, and Edna moved over to the dime machine. She started talking with the woman next to her. "Are you winning?"

"Winning and losing." The woman was intently focused.

Edna could not in good conscience play the dollar machine. There were too many people without money nowadays. And she was still earning each dollar she needed for her own support. When she was able to get the attention of the change person she traded twenty-five silver dollars for twenty-five dollars worth of dimes. That was as extravagant as she could comfortably be while still enjoying what she was doing. She finally settled in and began to play the dime machine with great enthusiasm.

It really is a lot of fun. When you put a dime into the open slot and pulled the handle towards you, red cherries, oranges and yellow lemons slid for a few seconds and then came to a stop. Depending upon how many of the same symbols were lined up on the middle line, you could win differing amounts. But the best way to win was to line up three gold *S.S. REX* emblems in a row. There were only three of those symbols, and aligning those paid the jackpot, which emptied out the entire machine.

As she played, Edna won a little here and a little there, but then lost until she was down to her last two dollars of the twenty-five. She was discouraged and decided she'd quit and sit and wait for Ray once the dimes were gone. She inserted another coin in the slot, pulled the handle forward, and watched as three *S.S. REX* symbols vertically moved flirtatiously with each other, then in unison abruptly stopped on the center line. Dimes started pouring out of the machine into the tray, and overflowing onto the carpet beneath her feet. "I won. I won." Bystanders stopped, and a small crowd gathered, curious to see what she had won.

The change lady came over and gave her two extra empty buckets for her winnings.

"How terrific."

"Wonderful."

"Good for you."

A woman showed Edna how to cup her hand to catch the coins as they flowed from the machine, and then she could transfer them more easily into the containers. Some people helped her pick up dimes from the floor, and a couple of scallywags took off with their findings. *That's okay. They obviously need them more than I do.* There had been many times Edna could have used an extra dime or two.

After the machine stopped its payout and the crowd began to disburse, Edna called the change girl over again. The woman had a machine which counted the dimes, and even with the dollar or so of missing dimes that bystanders had kept, Edna still had about $125.00 in dimes. Yes, she had put in almost $25.00 to win but that was still doubling of the hundred dollars Ray had given her for gambling. *That's a cushion for rent, and I can go back to the Smoke Shop and buy that lighter for Ray.* Thrilled by winning, Edna was feeling so good, she gave the change girl three silver dollars for her help.

"Buy yourself something wonderful," Edna suggested.

"Oh, thank you." The change girl appeared both surprised and grateful for the large amount.

"You're welcome. Thanks for your help." Edna decided to stop playing and sit and finish her whiskey coke while she waited for Ray's return.

Ray's business meeting was concluding.

"Okay, guys. It's a go. Afterwards, you'll get the completion payment. We'll be in touch. We've got to keep progressing to achieve our ends. Thanks for your help."

"Sure, Ray. Sure." The burly guy spoke.

"Now that we've got this settled, it's time to take my lady dancing."

"Hey, thanks, Ray. See ya."

Ray walked off without answering and went back to find Edna at her slot machine. Her eyes were sparkling with happiness and excitement.

"Ray, honey, look. She pointed at her buckets filled with coins. I won the dime jackpot. We're so lucky."

"Well, honey, you're the lucky one. It's all your money. I gave that money to you to gamble, and you deserve to win. You're a winner in my book already."

"Oh, Ray. What's with all this flattery tonight?"

Edna inserted a dime in the slot. "Here, you pull the handle."

Ray complied and pulled the handle. No win.

"Try again."

Ray tried five more times. No win.

"Well, Miss Edna, how about you and I cashing in your winnings and heading for some dinner and dancing?"

"Wonderful. Is your business all taken care of?"

"Yes."

"Good. I'm hungry."

Ray helped Edna up, took her buckets of coins, and they walked over to a cashier's window to exchange the coins for bills. The cashier handed Edna her winnings in bills.

"I had so much fun playing. You take it." She offered Ray at first. "At least take your hundred dollar stake back."

"It's all yours."

When he insisted she opened her purse and with great care neatly placed the bills inside. "Well, thank you." Then they headed to the large restaurant area for a hearty dinner of salad, porterhouse steak, and baked potatoes.

After their leisurely dinner, they danced to the REX orchestra which played a mix of lively and romantic songs. Edna enjoyed dancing with Ray to two of her favorites from the Hit Parade, "Cheek to Cheek," and "I'm in the Mood for Love." She was really a sentimental sap sometimes but why not? Those who said sentimentality was for fools did not know how to love.

"Life feels too good to be true," Edna smiled up at Ray's handsome face.

"Life is truly good," Ray echoed.

It was 4:00 a.m. when Thomas stopped the limousine in front of Edna's apartment building. The chauffeur opened her car door, and Ray came around and escorted her up to the front door. After making certain she could enter safely with the apartment front door key, he gently kissed her and said, "Get some sleep. I'll call you next week."

"Thanks for a wonderful evening," Edna whispered softly as she entered the apartment building.

CHAPTER SIXTEEN

MARIE AND KATHERINE KING

Edna slept deeply, dreaming of whirring slot machines and bobbing on the ocean like a fishing cork, until she was awakened by a knocking. She groggily emerged from her slumber, slowly climbed out of bed and put on her robe. "Who is it?" she asked.

"Marie."

Edna opened the door immediately. "Hi, honey," she said as she yawned and stretched. "What are you doing up so early on a Sunday?"

"Edna, it's noon. You must have had some night last night."

"I did." Edna's spirits immediately rose remembering last night, and her thoughts began to shake her out of her sleepy state.

"The night was wonderful. Ray took me to the gambling ship out in Santa Monica Bay. The transport launch wasn't much fun, but once you get out on the S.S. REX, it's grand. There's dancing, dining, slot machines, all types of gambling. Hoi-polloi and riff-raff mingle, and everyone's having fun together. I won four months rent on a dime slot machine. Didn't make it to bed until after 4:00 this morning."

"Edna, that sounds terrific. Wow, with that financial cushion, you're sure set until the wedding. How wonderful. You were lucky, but you aren't going to become a gambler now, are you?"

Edna laughed. "Of course not. It was just entertaining. And, dancing out there was wonderful exercise, great for the legs. The *S.S. REX* Orchestra played tunes from one of our favorite radio shows, 'Your Hit Parade.' It was one great song after another. And you should have seen the lively people on the dance floor. It's not like the usual sedate crowd we see at the fancy clubs around town. That gambling ship group really cuts a rug. There were couples dancing that new swing-style. It's fabulous to watch. I don't know that I'd like being thrown over someone's back, though."

"It sounds like quite an evening."

"How about some tea or Sanka?" Edna asked as she went over to her hot plate with yesterday's pot of water still sitting on it, and plugged it in.

"I've already had my tea, sweetie. Just returned from the service at Angelus Temple with Aimee Semple McPherson. Her One God philosophy was sure rousing that crowd today."

"Okay. Well, let me wake up. Sit down. I want to hear what's new with you."

"Well, I went out Friday night with the man I met in the Smoke Shop. Remember the distinguished gentleman, tall, slender, with the prematurely silver hair?"

"Oh, yes," Edna answered, not really sure she recalled at this moment.

"He took me to a wonderful dinner and show at Earl Carroll's. We had a lovely time together. I really like him."

"Oh, honey. That's great. But don't jump in 100 per cent this time. Take it slowly. Men like to be the pursuer."

"Edna, I learned my lesson. I can have a good time without falling in love. But he is really a nice man. Well-mannered. He brought me a corsage, pulled my chair out at dinner, stood up and gave me a tip for the gal when I went to go to the powder room. He was truly concerned about what I wanted for dinner. He actually listened to me telling him abut the small town I grew up in, and he seemed to enjoy what I had to say. He's from a small midwest town, also, but has been in Los Angeles for ten years."

"Marie, he sounds like a find, but take it one moment at a time."

"Edna, I told you, I've learned my lesson. I can enjoy myself without giving away my heart. Though I must admit that this man is definitely the type of man I would love to spend my life with."

"Marie, you're getting ahead of yourself."

"Edna, today Aimee McPherson's sermon topic was, 'love your neighbor as yourself.' I feel I can be loving and nice in all situations, even with a new beau."

"That's all well and good, let God's spirit inspire you, but human nature, our emotions can overtake the best of intentions unless you keep your head. Humans were given a brain to use as well as a heart. We're not built to just follow our heart and feelings. We're supposed to use our reason and common sense, too."

"When did you become so philosophical and religious?"

"Oh, it might not show now but as a young girl my parents had me baptized in the river, fully clothed. My head and I were fully dunked backwards into that cold water. I came up sputtering and coughing, thinking I was going to drown. I think the baptism took anyway. Those Southern Baptists take baptisms seriously and like to perform them authentically, literally in a river like St. John the Baptist used to do."

Both of them started laughing.

Edna poured some hot water into her cup of Sanka and stirred the cup.

"My family had me in church every Sunday growing up, but their church and my parents also knew how to have fun. After my parents died, Aunt Lillie and Uncle Justin's church didn't permit music, or dancing, or magazines, or make-up. It seemed silly in my mind for a church to teach people to be so removed from the current of life. I realized then that good sense was also a part of God's gift to humanity and that those who didn't use their own brains to think, as God created them to do, but who just blindly followed what they were told, were not utilizing their full self, their full potential that God intended for them in life."

"Edna, you're quite the philosopher. This is a side of you I didn't know about."

"Marie, my life has been wonderful, yet at times incredibly sad, and truly bad. I've learned life lessons from everything I've experienced."

"Yet you always seem to see the good in everyone and everything. Your spirit's usually up."

"Well, Marie, what's the alternative? There was that terrible time I was caught up in self-pity. I've told you what I went through when my parents died, and with Jimmy. I've hit rock bottom enough to realize that it's our own choice to get up and start moving forward again. No one is going to do it for us."

"You're right. I guess we each choose how we deal with what life brings. Talking with you today is as good as Aimee McPherson's sermon."

"Marie, life's hard knocks are one of the best teachers or preachers a person can have."

"Well, how about us getting a bite to eat together tonight? We could go to Clifton's Cafeteria, get a good meal, and visit their little chapel tower."

"Marie, today's my day of rest. I want to just fool around, get ready for work tomorrow and make sure everything is in order for the week ahead. Plus, I'd really like to listen to 'The Jack Benny Program,' on the radio this evening. How about if we meet after work tomorrow at Sam's Chili again? My treat. Then we can go over to The Smoke Shop and I can buy that gold lighter for Ray with my slot machine money. I hope it's still there."

"Okay. Sounds like fun. Then I'll get going, and I'll see you tomorrow night after work. I'm off at five o'clock tomorrow so expect me around 5:30."

"Great. Say, before you leave, how about helping me think of a marquee name in case my movie career ever gets off the ground?"

"Well --" Edna saw Marie look at the red glass creamer that Edna had brought from Houston-- "why not use your mother's name? 'Katherine King.'

That sounds like it could be an actress's name. I've always admired that creamer, you know."

"Katherine King?" Edna thought it over, and looked at the creamer her mother had always kept on top of her high bedroom dresser. "I like it. Yes. That might work. Thanks for the suggestion."

"My pleasure. Okay, Miss Katherine King. I think I'll head to Clifton's for an early Sunday supper. See you tomorrow."

After Marie left, Edna turned on her radio and listened to big band music as she looked through her clothes to make certain all her buttons were sewn on and nothing needed ironing. She checked her stockings to see if there were any holes that needed mending. She hand washed some clothing and hung it up to dry on a hanger she put on a nail in the window frame above her wall heater.

Then she went about deciding what she would wear for work tomorrow. *It's nice to be peaceful and to just relax.* Edna knew her nature. As much fun as she could have going out on the town, she also loved these quiet moments. She thought about the house she and Ray would soon live in, and rearranged some furniture in her mind's eye. And, she pondered more thoroughly the pros and cons of using her mother's name, "Katherine King."

Edna's Monday was busy at work and the hours passed quickly. She was hungry tonight. The counter at Sam's was full when she arrived, so she stood and waited for two seats to open up. Sam would let few people save a seat. Edna and Marie were two that were allowed that exception. They had grown to be friends in Sam's eyes and as favorite regulars were given special treatment. He recently started adding extra cheese and onions to their chili, plus making sure their cracker baskets were always full.

"Edna, here's two," Sam called to her attention. She sat down and Sam handed her a glass of water. Edna set her purse down on Marie's seat to keep a man waiting for a seat from taking it. "May I sit here?" he asked.

"I'm sorry, but this seat is saved," Edna replied.

"I thought you can't save seats here, lady," he persisted.

"Leave her alone, buddy. Go wait for the next seat that opens up," Sam helped Edna out.

"Sure, sure, Sam." The man backed off and went back to waiting by the front door. Sam had spoken.

Sam kept constantly busy, but as he walked back and forth serving customers, he would come by and hold a conversation with Edna.

"Edna, say, did you hear about the trolley cars?" Sam offered.

"Now what happened?"

"A generating station blew up. It knocked out transportation in one third of the Los Angeles area. So many streetcars are down that people are walking in large groups to try and get home. I can't believe you didn't hear about it."

"Oh, my gosh, Sam. That's terrible."

"I know. It will certainly curtail business and work activity."

"Here we go again."

"I know. I sure hope they can get the line up and running soon."

"Sam, I bet Marie is effected. Might as well serve me my chili bowl now."

"Sure. It might be a long time, if she even makes it here. I bet the pay phones have long lines, too. It's going to be a late and long night."

"A late and long week it sounds like."

"Yes. Why don't you let someone have that seat now?" Sam suggested. Edna took her purse off the seat so someone else could eat.

Edna ate as slowly as she could, but after a half hour, she felt certain the streetcar situation was causing Marie's absence.

"Sam, Marie probably will go straight home when she finds transportation. But would you tell her if she makes it in tonight that I'm headed to The Smoke Shop, then home?"

"Sure thing, Edna. See you soon."

"Thanks, Sam."

Edna walked over to The Smoke Shop, which was crowded tonight. John recognized her immediately.

"Still have your gold lighter waiting for you. No one has taken it yet."

"Great. I can buy it tonight, compliments of *S.S. REX* and its slot machines. Can you have it engraved for me?"

"Sure. What would you like it to say?"

"'Forever and a Day'."

"Nice. He's a lucky guy."

"Well, the feeling's mutual. How long do you think that will take?"

"It will be ready in a week, although with this transportation fiasco, better make it a week and a half."

"Isn't it awful, a generating station blowing up?"

"A guy in here earlier said that it was done on purpose."

"On purpose? Why in the world?"

"Remember what I was telling you last time you were in here? The streetcars were having problems that night, too."

"Yes."

"This guy who was in earlier today works for the electric company. He said what I told you before, that certain oil, rubber and auto companies are dead set on getting their products on the streets quickly to rapidly expand their markets and profits. As long as the trolley car system is so efficient and inexpensive people naturally won't want to spend a lot of their money to buy a car. If the transportation system is unreliable, then people will need to buy cars to get to work."

"Oh, John. You told me that, but I hate to believe it."

"Honey, you may be beautiful, but you need to take your blinders off. Big business is like war. Some corporations and businessmen will do whatever it takes to make more money. And, I heard that a couple of guys died in this explosion."

"If what you say is true, that's murder. Can't someone stop these greedy manipulators?"

"Who has the power?"

"Well, the city or county government?"

"Some of them have gotten cars and other incentives to go along with the plan. These executives are smart. They maneuver to get all the people that can be bought on board one way or another in order to accomplish what they want to do."

"How corrupt. How selfish and greedy."

"I know."

"Well, I'd better try and catch one of these full streetcars or get a cab. If my girlfriend Marie comes in looking for me, please tell her that I've gone home."

"Will do. The engraving will be ready in about a week and a half. Keep smiling and the streetcar will stop for your pretty face no matter how full the cars might be."

Edna laughed. "You're a charmer, aren't you?"

"I'm trying."

"Okay. Well, thanks, and see you soon."

Edna walked out the door and saw thirty people lined up to take the streetcar. And her streetcar line wasn't even one of those directly effected. She walked over and joined at the end of a long line that had spontaneously formed

Oh, well. I'll wait tonight. I can't believe that people can be so self-centered. Profits over people, greed over what's good for all. How can they live with themselves?

I need to talk with Ray about this. He's a businessman. He can explain this. Ray often says "business first," or "business means business," but he has ethics. He's not greedy. Being a school superintendent, he's the type of businessman people respect. He's responsibly successful. I'm a lucky woman.

CHAPTER SEVENTEEN

THE STUDIO HEAD

Edna was livid. "What is it with these studio executives? Who does he think he is?"

Marie and she were sitting in Edna's room on a Wednesday night. Marie had gotten home late again because of the trolley car problems, but she found a note from Edna on her door. "Come on over no matter what time you get home."

"He was certainly out of line, and taking a lot for granted," Marie was empathetic.

Edna was telling Marie about that afternoon at Nation Studio when Edna had met with the studio head, Mr. Hannity.

"The arrogance of that man. I can't believe that someone thinks they're so important that they can do whatever they want to do and say whatever they want to say without regard for anyone's feelings."

Marie's sweet nature urged her to attempt to calm Edna down. "I know, Edna. A lot of men don't seem to pay any attention to the golden rule. It's more like 'I rule.'"

"So true. I just don't know about my own behavior. I was so angry, I stormed out of there yelling something like "You treat me with respect or I'm not interested." I acted horribly, but it was so degrading. I was out to the car before I realized I'd left my purse in his office. Then I had to go back in to get it. So I went to the secretary's station and asked her to please get it for me. When she did, I overheard Hannity laughing with someone as if nothing had happened. I'm so angry. He treated me like I was worthless."

Marie tried to calm Edna's anger by reciting a concept she had heard recently at a theosophy lecture, "Well, I suppose we have to give others permission to make us feel small."

"Oh, Marie. You try and be in the midst of something like that and keep calm, cool and collected. Maybe you could. I guess I shouldn't have taken it so personally, but I couldn't let him think he could take advantage of me. My upbringing, and certainly Aunt Lillie's influence, have taught me differently. There was no way I was going to compromise my values for a job, even if the job is to be a starlet. No one is going to use or abuse me. And

I won't compromise my integrity even if it is to get a higher-paying, more glamorous job."

Edna was having trouble calming down.

"Edna, tell me again, as slowly as you can, what happened this afternoon. You went over it quickly and I'm just trying to figure out how the situation changed so rapidly. It seemed that everything was going well at the beginning of your meeting." Marie hoped that listening again in an understanding manner might help to quell Edna's anger.

"I sat down in Mr. Hannity's palatial office. It was even larger and more exquisitely decorated than Mr. O'Malley's office. Hannity's décor was powerfully elegant. He sat behind a large white and gold desk in a huge desk chair that was light buff leather. In front of the desk were two large, cushy, white armchairs, with a small gold-accented empire style table between them. Boldly framed movie posters covered the walls."

Marie chimed in, "It does sound like a beautiful office."

Edna had calmed somewhat while describing the furnishings.

"Marie, the first impression was one of opulence, done with great taste and refined style. Quite elegant in a semi-showy way. Plus, it showcased his power, making him look extremely important. I guess it fits his overblown ego. That man …"

Marie could hear Edna's anger rising again so intercepted the return of high emotion. "How about some tea? Do you have some here? I can go to my room and get some if you don't."

"Oh, honey, no. That's okay. Maybe I'll have a small bourbon. That will calm the nerves. Would you like one?"

"Not tonight, Edna. Thanks anyway. I had a short cocktail with dinner near work before I shared a taxi home."

Edna went to the small cupboard where she kept the bottle of bourbon. She took it out, along with a glass, and poured herself a small shot.

"Edna, what happened after you sat down in the white armchair?"

Edna went back to her bed and sat down, turned towards Marie who was sitting in a chair. Edna took one sip of her drink, set it down on the bedside table coaster, and continued.

"Mr. Hannity told me he had seen the screen test and loved the way my image jumped off the screen. He said he had not in quite a while seen such fire in a woman's eyes on screen, nor had he seen a screen test that conveyed such personality, plus the photogenic "it" factor at the same time. He said, 'you're going to be our new star, Edna. You have it in you to be one of the best. The camera loves you, and you jump out at an audience. That's magic.'"

"Oh, Edna, that's wonderful. You hadn't told me about that." Marie was happy for Edna.

"I thanked him for what he said."

"'I tell it like it is, and there's no use thanking me for what is, and for telling you what I see.'"

Edna was calming down somewhat as she conveyed in more detail what had happened.

"He said there were a number of things that the studio would need me to do. One was to change my name. I told him about 'Katherine King' and he seemed to like it. Second, I would need to take elocution lessons to completely lose my southern accent. Also, I was to take dancing, singing, and drama lessons."

Marie noticed that there was an ashtray full of half-smoked cigarette butts on the table next to her. That was so unlike Edna. She smoked occasionally, but had obviously been sitting there in her room thinking and stewing about what had happened before Marie got home.

"And, I was to go for a wardrobe fitting next week. They could start me out as an extra so I'd gain some experience. He mentioned a western that was starting in a couple of weeks."

Marie offered, "That was a lot to take in all at once, but it must have been exciting."

"Oh, yes. Up to that point, I was willing to do whatever was necessary. I intuitively know I can handle it. I didn't have any qualms whatsoever and was rather excited at the thought of this new career. Ray and I have spoken about the prospect, and he was supportive of my becoming an actress if that is what I want to do."

Edna finished her drink which did seem to be calming her down somewhat.

"Then what happened?"

"At some point, Mr. Hannity asked me to come over to where he was seated at his desk. He said I should take a look at the contract that he wanted me to sign. I stood up, and walked behind his desk and saw a contract in front of him. As soon as I got near him, he pulled me onto his lap, and put his big arms and hands around the front of my body to hold me there. Then he started trying to put the make on me.

His movements -- I could not believe what he was doing. I tried to pry away his arms but he was terribly strong. I had trouble getting away so I stomped on the front part of his shoe with my high heel which forced him to loosen his grip, and finally I got away from him. He was terribly forceful and aggressive. I might have even flirted with him a little, played along just a bit, if he had not been so brutish and coercive. I was shocked and angry."

"Oh, honey. What a surprise."

"Yes. That's when I quickly went towards the door and made that comment about disrespect, or something like, 'Mr. Hannity, if this is what it takes to get into motion pictures, I don't want any part of it,' or words to that effect. I really can't remember what I said. I was so upset I couldn't think straight.

How dare he do that to me? What arrogance. What a lack of respect for me. Who did he think he was? I guess his power has gone to his head. I am who I am and if they don't like it, too bad."

"He certainly was trying to take advantage of you, Edna. I'm so sorry that happened to you."

"Yes, I know. But who is going to believe me against the powerful studio head. I'd be made to look like a foolish country bumpkin if I tried to complain.

As I walked out the door I added something like, 'you can forget about me, Mr. Hannity. I'm not that kind of girl.'"

"He shouted back something about my being 'naive,' but I really wasn't paying attention at that point.

I slammed the door in a dramatic exit, and left. It wasn't until I got out to the car that I realized I'd left my purse."

Edna lit up another cigarette as she continued her rant.

"Some men think just because they're bigger and stronger they can take advantage. They think since they're more powerful, they can abuse you. Do they really have such little respect for their mothers and sisters and wives? I just don't get it, that attitude of supreme arrogance, with total disregard for the feelings of another human being."

"How I know," Marie commiserated. "It's as if some men's hearts, souls and consciences fly out the window when they want something. I don't understand it either."

"Well, your new boyfriend has been good to you though, hasn't he?" Edna was calming down some and was able to change the subject. She remembered what a difficult time emotionally Marie had gone through with the abortion.

"Well, yes. So far, so good. He's been quite the gentleman."

"Good, Marie. You deserve the best." Edna took a long drag from her cigarette.

"And so do you, Edna. That Ray's quite a catch. Are you going to tell him about this? Didn't you say he knows Hannity?"

"I don't know yet, Marie. Yes, he knows him from business and social functions. That makes it even worse in my mind. I've been completely honest with Ray so far. I told him about O'Malley, and he brushed it aside, seemed to think it was okay. That didn't feel as much a violation as this situation with Hannity did. I need to think it over.

I don't know how Ray would react to the details of what happened with Hannity. We'll see. I hate to keep anything from him, though."

"Thank goodness you're calming down some now. I'm so sorry that happened to you today, but your marriage is in a month. You probably need to start focusing on that now."

"I know, Marie. And I appreciate the help you have given me in planning the wedding so far. You're going to be a wonderful maid of honor."

"The honor is all mine," Marie responded, happy that Edna was getting back to her old self. Marie marveled at Edna's resilience.

The two women talked for a while longer, and then Marie left. Edna laid out her clothes for work tomorrow, took off her makeup, and set her alarm for 6 a.m. She crawled into bed and was sound asleep within ten minutes. It had been an emotionally taxing day, but she had learned after recovering from her leg paralysis in Houston that the next moment can bring a new beginning, and "I can start anew whenever I choose to do so." A new day could bring a new perspective. There was a lot to look forward to.

Friday night, Ray picked up Edna after work. "Well, gorgeous, that dress is a knockout," Ray commented as Thomas helped her into the limo's backseat. "You look every inch the movie star."

Edna smiled, kissed Ray on the cheek, and had no quick retort for a change.

"How's my girl doing?" Ray pressed.

"Fine, Ray. Everything's fine."

"Well, how did the meeting with Hannity go? You said you would tell me about it when I saw you."

"How about feeding a girl, first? It's been a long day. You wouldn't believe what it took to get the department head to let me borrow this gown for this evening. I promised to come in early tomorrow and single-handedly rearrange every rack in the department according to gown color and length. We can't make this a late evening."

"Why don't you just quit that job? You're going to be Mrs. Ray Gibson in less than a month. You don't need to be a working girl any more. Plus, you're about to be a movie star, aren't you?"

"Ray, first, during dinner I'll tell you about the Nation Studio situation. Secondly, until we are officially pronounced 'man and wife,' this little old Texan refuses to take anything for granted. You can tell me to quit my job after that. I've already scheduled my week's vacation for our honeymoon period."

"Well, Miss Independent. I like that in my woman. Okay. Whatever you say."

"Ray, there aren't any streetcars running in this area. The tracks are empty."

"Yes. Streetcars just aren't reliable."

"Well, thanks for having Thomas take me to and from work this week. I don't know what I would have done without that help. Marie rode to work with us as far as her transfer. And some other girls at the apartment also rode along. It's so hard without the trolleys. Thank you from all of us."

"It's my pleasure to be able to keep you happy."

"Ray, someone told me that this latest electric generating station was blown up on purpose by people who want to get rid of the streetcars, make them unreliable, so that they can sell more automotive products and make more money."

"Who told you that?"

Thinking of the surprise gold lighter for Ray Edna declined to state who. "Well, that's not important, but I heard it again after eating dinner at Sam's Chili the other night, while I was waiting for Marie. They said that the motor companies and oil companies, and rubber companies want to expand business in the Los Angeles area, and in order to sell more cars and auto products, they need to convince the public that the trolley cars are unreliable, so they can influence more people to take on the large cost of buying a car, and then, of course, sell more oil, gas, and rubber tires. This is not the first time I've heard this. I've heard it a few times and from different people, but I dismissed it as silly the first couple of times. It sounds like an unbelievable 'conspiracy.'"

"Well, who told you that, Edna?" Ray asked again in a pleasant tone.

"The sources aren't important, Ray, but do you think it's true? Why would any businessmen be so selfish? How could they put their own profits above the needs of the entire city and its population?"

"Maybe they think it will be better for people to drive cars."

"Why would it be better to have to buy a very expensive vehicle to get around, and have to pay for fuel to keep it running, and pay for oil and tires and parking, than it is to pay 5 to 10 cents a ride, with no worries about upkeep?"

"Edna, a lot of times the common folk don't really know what's best for them. They need some push to move forward in life."

Edna's temper flared. She had never heard Ray sound so haughty.

"Common folk? Common folk? Common folk have common sense, don't they? What's sensible about paying more for transportation than you can afford to pay? What's sensible about buying something you don't need? My parents were 'common folk' as you so smugly put it. I'm 'common folk' too. The common folk I know are the salt of the earth, the warmhearted souls who love this country and keep it working smoothly by doing their jobs. It sounds like you are on the side of the car and oil companies getting rid of streetcars. How blind can you be?"

"Now Edna, calm down. When we're married, you'll see how your perspective will change. With money comes power. With power and influence one's perspective tends to shift to the larger picture."

"If you're implying by a so-called 'larger picture' that I will leave behind my common sense, you are sadly mistaken. I can't think of a larger picture that does not include caring about the greater good for my fellow man or woman. There's no good I can see in getting people into debt for something they don't need."

"Why don't we talk about this some other time. You're getting too riled up. I know you're hungry and tired. Oh, there it is. I'm taking you to the Brown Derby tonight. Let's talk after you get some food into you. They have a wonderful Cobb salad here. We can have Cobb salad and your favorite, prime rib. How does that sound?"

"Fine." Edna shut down. She was feeling extremely upset. Better to be quiet until she ate and had the opportunity to relax more. She had never really lost her temper with Ray to this extent before. She was hungry and tired, but she also realized that a portion of her anger was in anticipation of having to talk to Ray about what had happened at Nation Studio. What an evening. She wished she could just leave, go back to her apartment and be alone, quiet and secure. *Oh, well. This is the man I'm going to spend my life with. If I can't trust him who can I trust?*

The limousine had stopped in front of the Brown Derby and the valet was opening her back door. He helped her out, and Ray came around and took her lightly by the elbow. "Come on, Edna. All eyes are on us. Smile for the people. Act like you're happy even if you aren't."

Edna lifted her chin high, smiled, and pretended she was having a wonderful time as she walked into the Brown Derby.

Edna could feel heads turn to look at them as they were led to a nice burgundy upholstered booth against a wall. The milieu was cozy, intimate, yet brimming with the excitement of diners involved in their animated conversations. Ray beamed as he saw that the heads were turning to look more at Edna than him, but he'd been told more than once that they did make a striking couple.

"Hello, Mr. Gibson. It's been a while. Good to see you again." The waiter set two large leather menus on the table in front of each of them.

"Thank you. A plate of those Oysters Rockefeller to start."

"Certainly, sir."

Edna left her menu in front of her. Ray could order for her. She knew that Ray always seemed to select the best dishes wherever they went.

The busboy placed some bread and butter on the table. Ray interrupted his perusing of the menu to take one roll, tear a small piece from it and place the two parts back down on his bread plate. He took the butter knife and put a pat of butter on his plate, then buttered a piece of the roll. He then exchanged butter plates with Edna.

"Eat that bread, honey. It might calm you down somewhat."

Edna ate the bread. She was hungry.

The waiter was soon back. "Your oysters will be out in a few minutes, Mr. Gibson. Did you wish to order now?"

"Alright, but please don't place our entrée orders until we've relaxed. I don't want to be rushed."

"Certainly."

"We'll share a Cobb salad, then have two prime rib dinners rare. Baked potatoes with sour cream and chives. Your grand soufflé for desert."

"Wonderful choices. I'll go see how your oysters are coming."

They both began to settle in to enjoy a leisurely dining experience. Edna grabbed her bag and pulled out a short cigarette holder that Ray had gotten for her. She placed a cigarette in it, and Ray took matches from his pocket and lit it for her. Edna took a couple of puffs, using the holder to its fullest dramatic advantage, then placed it down on the table's ashtray. She was beginning to feel a little better, more calm.

"Ray, you wanted to know about Nation Studio and what happened?"

"Yes."

"Well, suffice it to say, I doubt I'll be working for them. They're not going to want to employ me."

"Well, honey, you'll always be a star to me."

"You aren't upset that I won't be in the pictures?"

"Of course not. I'd rather not share you with the world more than I already do anyway. I'm as proud as I can be of you just as you are. You don't need to be in the motion pictures for me to love you any more than I do now."

"Oh, Ray. Thank you. I was worried about your reaction. I thought you wanted me to be in the movies."

"I want for you what you want in life, Edna. Whatever will make you happy will make me happy. If that's not for you, then so be it. I'm fine with that."

"I thought you'd be disappointed."

"No such luck. How about you? Hannity didn't hurt your feelings, did he?"

"I wouldn't exactly say that, no. No, he told me my screen test was excellent. No, he thought I was attractive and had screen appeal. We -- we -- uh -- we just didn't hit it off."

"Well, he can be an irascible guy. I can talk to him and see if I can change his mind if you want? We have some business investments in common."

"Oh, no, Ray. Please don't." *Even though Ray laughed off O'Malley's antics, this was worse with Hannity. Ray does business with Hannity. I don't need to cause Ray problems.*

"Frankly, I'll be perfectly content to have you be my wife, run the household, take care of our children."

The waiter brought the Oysters Rockefeller and set the platter down in the table's center. He served each of them the first one on a small plate and placed small fish forks down on the white tablecloth.

"Delicious," said Edna after the first bite. She thought about how Ray had already taught her so much about life. She had toured the Los Angeles area with the best possible guide.

What a fabulous life we're going to have together. I'm so incredibly lucky and grateful. Ray doesn't need to know the details about what happened with Hannity. My destiny seems to be taking me down a path that will make me perfectly content, marrying a trustworthy and respectful gentleman.

CHAPTER EIGHTEEN

THE NEWSPAPER

Since the trolley car power station explosion, many of the effected streetcar lines were still down. Additional buses had been added to help lessen the burden, but they were not as efficient, and were always packed to standing room only. The bus ride jostling was subject to the whims of each driver, some of whom liked to show their driving prowess by cutting in and out of other traffic as fast as possible.

As Edna walked out of work this evening, a newspaper boy at the corner was calling out, "Trolley car power station bodies identified. Get your paper now. Power station explosion. Buy your paper now. Bodies identified. Get your paper now. See the power station culprits. Get your paper now." His singsong selling voice was mesmerizing, and Edna decided to buy a paper.

Her ride home tonight would be crowded. She was not getting a ride from Ray's chauffeur. She might be able to read the story on her way home if she was lucky enough to be given a seat. Buying a paper was a splurge. She usually would not buy one but would read it in the break room at work, or get the news from co-workers, friends and the radio, but, in a few days she would be Mrs. Ray Gibson, so she could afford to splurge some.

As she stood with others around the paperboy, waiting to hand him her money, up walked Clark Gable. "Hello beautiful. Can I buy you a paper?" he asked her directly. Without waiting for a reply, he turned to the paperboy, "Two please."

His stature, stardom and assertiveness assured that he would be the next customer served. Edna still had not spoken. She was taken aback by seeing him in the flesh.

"Here you go," he said as he handed her one of the two papers, smiled, and started walking along Wilshire Boulevard. Edna kept her eyes on his back, as did a lot of the bystanders. He suddenly turned around and asked, "By the way, what's your name, pretty lady?"

"Edna King."

Clark Gable smiled then turned again and kept on walking. The crowd standing there kept on watching him until he turned the corner.

"That was Clark Gable," Edna stated the obvious to the people standing around the paperboy.

The paperboy interrupted his singsong sales for a moment to tell her, "Yeah, lady. He has an office up in the Taft Building. He buys a paper every evening when he's working up there."

"Well, if he ever asks about me, I work there." Edna pointed the department store out to the paperboy, in hopes she might one day get an autograph of her idol.

Edna wondered why no one at work had ever mentioned he had an office in the neighborhood Taft Building. Maybe they didn't know. *Boy, will I have something to tell the girls tomorrow.*

Edna took the paper Clark Gable had bought for her, folded it carefully in half, and started walking toward The Smoke Shop. The gold lighter she had had engraved for Ray's wedding gift must be ready by now. She would pick it up before trying to catch a crowded streetcar home.

Dinner could wait until later tonight when she would have some saltine crackers, an apple and a banana in her efficiency. She wanted to fit well into the short, white chiffon wedding dress she had put on layaway.

The Smoke Shop was not too crowded tonight and the clerk recognized her immediately. "Hi, Edna. Your lighter's ready." He went and retrieved it from a drawer behind the glass counter case. He opened the box, and showed it to Edna. "'Forever and a Day,'" just like you wanted. It turned out great; didn't it?"

Edna picked up the lighter and examined it carefully. Yes, it was just as she had envisioned. *Ray will love it.*

"Yes, it's stunning. Thanks for all your trouble, John."

"No trouble at all. It's been a pleasure doing business with you."

"And, it's all paid for now, including the engraving?"

"Yes, as of the last time you stopped by to see if it was ready. There were no additional costs.

"Say, Edna, did you hear about the two guys who were killed in that power station explosion we were talking about?"

"Not yet. I just -- I have a paper here that I'm going to read on the bus home. Clark Gable literally bought it for me. He apparently has an office in the Taft Building. Why? What did you hear?"

"Mr. Gable comes in here often. He's a terrific guy.

Well, I heard that the two guys were mobster types who apparently rigged the explosives themselves but they didn't get out in time. There were no employees there that night in the middle of the night, so at least no innocent people were hurt."

"Well, that's poetic justice, huh? Thank goodness no one else was killed."

"Yeah, I haven't seen the paper yet, but I hear they've finally printed photographs of the two gangsters who died carrying out the crime."

"Well, let's look," Edna offered. She unfolded the newspaper in her hand and handed it to him without looking at the men."

"These guys do look tough. Wonder who put them up to it? They don't look like the type to plan a generating plant explosion on their own, though. I'd bet this was a setup deal. I've told you about the conspiracy to destroy our trolley system."

"Yes," agreed Edna. Too much had come to light for her not to accept that as reality by now.

"Look, don't the two look like followers; not leaders?" He pushed the paper back to Edna with the front page spread out wide in front of her on the counter.

Edna saw the two faces looking out at the reader from much of the front page. She was stunned. There were no words.

"What do you think, huh? They look like they were told to do what they did, huh?" John persisted.

Edna found her voice, "I suppose so. They do look somewhat rough, I guess." Edna took the paper, folded it in half again with the photos folded inward, took the lighter in its box and placed it into her handbag. "Thank you, John. I better get going if I want to get a trolley. You've been terrific."

"Well, don't be a stranger. Stop by and visit even if you don't need anything from us."

"Okay. Well, thanks again."

Edna couldn't leave fast enough. She felt a panic, an anxiety. As she walked towards the trolley car stop with its line of 30 people or so, her stomach began to churn wildly. She began to feel weak, faint. *Come on, silly, you're a strong woman,* she buoyed herself. *There's a logical explanation for this.* Edna swallowed, and tried to appear normal but this was hard to brush aside. She needed to talk with Ray as soon as possible.

Edna recognized the two guys. *Those two men were two of the three men that Ray met with on board the S.S. REX. It has to be some sort of awful coincidence. What in the world could be Ray's relationship with those two? Ray had called it a "business meeting." What kind of business could Ray have been discussing with those men?*

CHAPTER NINETEEN

EDNA AND RAY

Edna had this Wednesday off, a few days before the wedding. She had been at the new house all day, arranging and rearranging furniture that she and Ray had chosen and purchased over the past few weeks. The house was looking ready for them to move into once they returned from their honeymoon. Ray had Thomas helping Edna for part of the day to shift the heavy, long mahogany dining room table and other substantial pieces that Edna wanted rearranged.

Edna loved to decorate and arrange furniture. It was something she had a natural eye for, and she was not above doing much of the manual labor herself. It was certainly nice, however, to have Thomas's help, plus she wanted to talk with him before approaching Ray.

After Edna and Thomas moved living room furniture three times into different conversational patterns, Thomas and she sat down for a break.

"You're wearing me out," Thomas stated. "You certainly are strong for a woman."

"Well, I come from hard-working, energetic stock. Guess it's just part of my nature."

"Well, your energy level exceeds mine I think," Thomas countered.

"Enough of this smalltalk, Thomas. I know you need to pick up Ray, but before you leave I need to ask you something: Did you see the paper a few days ago about the guys who blew up the power station?"

"Yes."

"Have you ever seen Ray with those two men before?" Edna asked.

Thomas averted Edna's direct gaze.

"I'd rather not get into anything that I've seen or heard with Mr. Gibson. His business stays his business and part of my job is to keep it that way. You know I respect you, but he is my boss and that is where my loyalty lies."

"Well, I understand your loyalty and that's something that I prize, however, I think your eyes told me what I needed to know. You'd better go get Mr. Gibson now. Tell him I'll have dinner waiting for him when you bring him back."

"Fine. It certainly is going to be wonderful to have you as the madam of the house. Mr. Gibson is happier recently than I've ever seen him. I'll get going now. What are you cooking for dinner?"

"It's a surprise. One of the recipes that a girl at work gave me. I think he'll like it."

"I'm sure he will. All right. See you in about an hour."

After Thomas left, Edna went to the back door and looked out at the tennis court, and at the patio table and chairs she had placed in a brick patio area at the rear of the house. It was going to be one of those lovely warm evenings that made Los Angeles sublime. She set the table for the two of them out on the patio. Candlelight and the back porch light would be fine to eat by, but if necessary, the tennis court lights could be turned on.

There was a lot to do in the next hour before Ray arrived, and she wanted to be dressed and in a relaxed mood when he arrived. She needed to have a serious conversation and did not want to approach Ray in an angry manner. It was going to be difficult and Edna needed to keep her temper tamped down while having the discussion.

She could not believe that Ray was involved in the power station explosion, but she had seen those newspaper photos of two of the men from the *S.S. REX*. *I have to know Ray's connection, if any.* Growing up, her household had been one of openness and warm cooperation between her mother and father. That was the type of relationship Edna expected with Ray. If he was keeping secrets from her, she couldn't be happy. To be cut off from the one you love, with closed doors to rooms full of secret information was not the type of life Edna wanted. She was a down-to-earth person, and up until now Ray had seemed as real as could be. But doubt had been gnawing at her ever since she saw those newspaper photos. *I have to resolve this.*

Edna was just changing into a short and svelte dinner dress as Ray arrived. She heard the car pull up, quickly zipped up the dress zipper, then took one quick look in the mirror. Yes, hair was combed, makeup freshened, and lipstick was fine. She took her two pink flower earrings and placed them both on one ear, as she walked down the hall and started down the staircase. This home was so gorgeous. She loved the feel of it.

"Hello. Where are you?" Ray walked into the living room, then looked up to see Edna walking down that spiral staircase, holding onto the railing as she maneuvered effortlessly in her high heels.

"Well, aren't you a vision," Ray offered up.

Edna reached the bottom of the stairs, walked over to Ray and gave him a light kiss on the cheek. "I hope you're hungry. I've got a good old Southern meal waiting for you." She rubbed her lipstick off his cheek.

"Great. How about a cocktail first?" Ray suggested.

"I'm ahead of you. Come with me."

Edna took Ray by the hand and started leading him through the living room towards the back porch.

"Hey, the living room looks terrific. You've done a great job of arranging the furniture."

"Thank you, sir." She didn't let him linger, but led him to the outside patio table and chairs.

"Now, this is cozy. What a beautiful scene we have here." Ray was pleased.

Edna had covered the patio table with a blue checkered tablecloth. In the center of the table was a centerpiece vase of California wildflowers: orange poppies, and yellow brown-eye daises. Two candle holders held long white candles.

"Sit down," Edna softly ordered; and, "Honey, there are some matches there. If you could light those candles for me, I'll go get you your cocktail."

"Sounds like a bargain to me," Ray responded.

Edna checked in the kitchen to make sure the pork chops were cooked and still warm. The potatoes had already been mashed, and the gravy was done, but needed reheating. The green beans were in the pan and ready to be boiled. Dinner would take all of 10 minutes when they were ready to eat. She grabbed the cocktail shaker that had already been mixed before dressing, shook it, and poured two martini glasses full of gin martinis. She dropped an olive into each, and took the glasses out to the patio.

"Here, darling," Edna set Ray's cocktail in front of him and sat down in her chair.

"Well, Edna, a toast. To our upcoming nuptials, and to your becoming Mrs. Ray Gibson."

Ray and Edna clinked their glasses together and each took a sip of their martini. Edna needed to gently ease into her conversational topic. "So how was work today, honey?" she began.

"Fine. It's certainly going to be great to be coming home to you and this home every evening. I'm just counting the days."

"Yes, I know. Did anything unusual happen at the School District today?"

"No. Not anything out of the ordinary. I was at my main headquarters office doing the usual monthly routine reports."

"Didn't make it out to do any personal business today, huh?"

"Not today."

"How's the streetcar station problem effecting the employees at the main office?"

"Oh, there are some who have been arriving late. I've sent a bulletin around to make it clear that is not acceptable. If they have to get up earlier in order to arrive on time, then that's what they need to do."

"Well, yes, but, honey --"

"Edna, let's not talk about work or business. I want to relax. Isn't that the way life should be? Your home is your refuge, and all that sort of thing. Let's make tonight relaxing and special."

"Sure, honey. Let me go check on dinner. I'll be back in a moment. Enjoy your drink and relax." Edna took her drink with her, and finished it the moment she got to the kitchen. How was she going to bring up the subject that needed addressing?

Edna turned on the burner underneath the green beans and lit it. She mixed another batch of gin martinis, placed an olive into her glass and Ray's, and put together a tiny glass bowl of a few extra mixed onion and green olive skewers to take outside for Ray's martini. She knew Ray sometimes liked extra. She filled her glass half full, and then took a tray with the silver shaker and everything else on it out to the patio.

"Here, honey. Let me fill your glass. Edna removed the lid and poured Ray another martini."

"Thank you. You're the prettiest bartender I've ever seen."

"Thank you. Drink up, so we can have dinner."

"Edna, let's not rush. It's great out here tonight. The stars are coming out in the sky, and this warm weather is perfect."

"I know, Ray, but dinner will be ready for you in ten minutes."

"We can warm it up later, can't we?"

"We'll see. Let's have another toast. To many future fun evenings." Edna clicked her glass against Ray's and they each took a sip. Ray was somewhat more relaxed now than when he first arrived. *Maybe I can ask him about the newspaper photos now.*

"Ray, remember that fun evening we spent out on the *REX*? That was such a good time."

"Yes. That was fun. You are quite the little gambler. I want to take you down to Palm Springs soon. They have a gambling club outside of town. You'll love the desert. The nights are like this. Warm, enveloping, caressing air. And the stars are as bright as they can be. The desert sky makes the stars look touchable, reachable. It's gorgeous."

"Sounds like fun. Ray, those three guys that called out to you when we first pulled up to the *S.S. REX*, how did you know them?"

"Oh, just some business. It's not important. Don't worry your pretty little head about business matters you wouldn't understand."

That does it. I wouldn't understand? He's treating me like a child; not as his partner. What lack of respect.

"Two of those guys that you met with on the *REX* at your so-called 'business meeting' were killed in the generating plant explosion that caused the trolley car lines to be put out of commission."

"I heard about that," Ray said nonchalantly and finished off his drink in one large gulp. "It's a shame," he said as he set his empty glass on the table. He reached for the shaker and poured what was left into his glass, threw in a garnish skewer and smiled at Edna.

"Good martinis, Edna."

"Yes, Ray. Gin for a change." Edna had hit another wall. He sure was smooth. She couldn't even get a rise out of him, much less any information. She stood up, grabbed the shaker and her glass, and went into the kitchen. Ray didn't want to eat yet. Maybe another drink or two would loosen his tongue. She had never seen him drunk, but she had upon occasion seen him open up to her more after a few drinks.

She would throw together some hors d'oeuvres. Edna took out of the ice box some tuna she had fixed for lunch, and took the box of Ritz Crackers she had snacked on during the day. With a knife she quickly smeared tuna on a few crackers, ate one, placed the rest on a plate, and took it out to Ray.

"Here, Ray, this will hold you for a while."

Edna went back to the kitchen, turned off all the burners, and mixed some more martinis. She was determined to resolve this issue no matter what it took.

When she went back out, half the crackers with tuna were gone, Ray's drink glass was empty on the table, and Ray was standing up with his back to her, looking at the tennis court. Edna quickly refilled his glass and sat down at the table.

"Are you surveying your territory, honey?" Edna asked.

"In a way, I suppose. Just thinking about some of the fun tennis parties we can have out there. I need to improve my game, and I know you will love it once you start playing more and perhaps take some lessons."

"We'll see," said Edna. She was willing to learn in order to play doubles with Ray. They had talked about a pro friend of Ray's giving them weekly lessons once they were married and moved into the house.

Edna was getting more and more anxious, rather than more and more relaxed. Ray, conversely, seemed to have now settled in and was perfectly at ease.

Edna concluded there was no other way except to speak directly. "Honey, there's something on my mind that I really need to resolve. It seems you don't want to talk about it, but I need to know or I'll worry constantly. I'd prefer to know the truth rather than be kept in the dark. At least then I can make my decisions based on facts and not let my imagination run wild."

"My, you sound serious. What is it, darling?"

"I need to know more about your business dealings with those two men who died in the power station explosion. We're to be married soon. Please don't keep any secrets from me."

"Well, Edna, if you are really interested --"

"I am."

"I don't like to bore you with the day-to-day details of my job as superintendent, or my other varied investments. But, since you seem so determined I'll tell you. Those two men worked with a mutual friend who is a majority stockholder through a major trust of a large oil company. You know that Los Angeles is sitting on one of the biggest oil fields in the world."

"I've sure seen a lot of oil rigs and pumps around the Los Angeles basin but I never realized that Los Angeles had so much oil. I saw a lot of oil drilling and pumping back in Texas, too."

"Sure. Texas is another big oil producer, as are Pennsylvania and Ohio. One of my largest portfolio holdings is that oil and gasoline stock, as well as many thousands of shares of a couple of automotive companies that are building factories to build cars out here in the Los Angeles area. I also own shares in some of the rubber companies that will provide tires for the burgeoning motor industry."

"Yes. But more to the point, what were those two men you met with on the *S.S. REX* doing when they died in the power station explosion?"

"Well, you can't tell anyone this information. Do you agree to keep it a secret? Between us?"

"Please just tell me what they were doing there," Edna insisted.

Now working on his fifth gin martini, Ray was ready to unburden himself. "Edna, some of the automotive interests want to get rid of the trolley car system in order to facilitate the public's desire for automobile transportation and to augment their profits. More busses and motor cars will be built and sold, which will also increase the demand for more gasoline, oil and rubber tires. It is time to replace the old with the new."

Edna was stunned. She could not believe what she was hearing. "I don't get it." She had heard the same thing from Marie, John at the Smoke Shop, and others, but she literally got chills when she heard Ray confirm it.

"Are you telling me that people you know purposefully caused the trolley car power station explosion in order to further their own financial interests?"

"Well, I wouldn't put it quite that way. In business some times strategies and tactics are like war. One must do what is necessary in order to achieve the greater goal. Business means business."

"The greater goal being what? More money?"

"Among other things, yes."

"What other things?"

"Progress. New order. Power. Success. Out with the old transportation regime and in with the new."

"You sound like a preacher in some church of religious business. What are you saying? The trolley cars in Los Angeles worked beautifully until recently, and the transportation cost is inexpensive. It's the best system in the world. Don't these business people think of anyone but themselves? How can they be so selfish? What about the greater good?"

"Well, now, honey, you're going to be the beneficiary of a lot of money being made on these stock holdings. The automobile is the future of America. We're just facilitating the Los Angeles population's inevitable move in that direction, into the future of transportation."

"But automobiles cost a lot of money. I certainly wouldn't be able to afford one on my department store salary."

"Well, as Mrs. Gibson you can have whatever car you want. And for others, payment plans will be made available. Workers can purchase a car on credit over time."

"Yes, but that huge expense could be used for a down payment on a house, or a vacation, or college education for children."

"Now, now. We know what's best. The Los Angeles workers will thank us in a few years when they are driving around in their new cars, and no trolley cars are in the middle of the streets getting in the way of their speed and progress."

"Ray, I just can't believe that you could be associated with and working with people that are trying to ruin the trolley car lines. It breaks my heart. No money in the world is worth causing thousands of workers to go through the hardship they're now going through, trying to get to work on time when the trolley car lines are down. And doing this on purpose? I'm just sick about this. I thought you were a different kind of man. I thought you cared about people. You've always been such a gentleman."

"Edna, sweetheart, I am a gentleman, a gentleman like many others who care about making money and having a nice home for his family."

"But you've always had money. You didn't need to get involved in this funny business to make more money."

"Honey, a businessman doesn't stop investing just because he's been successful in the past. There is always another deal, another goalpost to reach."

"I'm sorry, but I can't live with this. I'd heard that business interests were bribing city council members, and starting streetcar scheduling and maintenance slowdowns, and causing disrepair but -- Did you know about that also?"

"I'd heard, yes, that it was going to occur, and of course I read the papers like everyone else. And, yes, I did help somewhat by talking with some Council members I have known for years. But it's nothing that any other astute businessman wouldn't do."

"I'm sorry, Ray, but I'm just sick about all of this. I can't marry you. I can't marry someone I don't respect. As wonderful as you've been to me, I can't respect someone who puts their own personal profit motive so far above the needs of others that they'll destroy the public good to achieve their own goals.

Ray, I was brought up to be honest, to care about my neighbors, to love my neighbor as myself. If you'd been riding the trolley cars for years as I have both in Houston and here, you might think a bit differently about what you've done and are involved in doing. We can't go on, Ray. I'm sorry."

"Don't be silly, honey. You're tired and you've had too much to drink. You don't know what you're saying. Let me take my warm-hearted little communist home and you'll feel better after a good night's sleep."

Isn't that just like a man to demean a woman by telling her she doesn't know her own mind?

Edna felt sick. She slowly removed the engagement ring from her left hand and laid it down gently on the table in front of Ray.

"We're through, Ray."

CHAPTER TWENTY

MOURNING

Edna had put worse things behind her but it would take time to recover from this loss. The sorrow she felt at calling off the wedding was eating her up inside, but her work ethic kept her getting up each day and soldiering on. To Edna, though, the relationship's ending felt much like a death.

In the midst of her mourning, Broadway Hollywood bought out Dyas Department Store. She worked at the same building, but some of her friends were let go in the transition. Plus, Broadway Hollywood had a different set of rules to learn and new managers to whom Edna now must prove herself.

The Los Angeles basin had been covered for days now in that depressing morning cloud layer that sometimes formed above the ocean. It suited Edna's desolate mood.

Edna went through the motions but had lost her buoyant spark. She put one foot in front of the other, and was careful to put on a pleasant face at work. That was what was expected of Broadway employees. While working with the public, she should serve her customers in a cheerful fashion, and not wallow in her own feelings. But without her usual passion and positive outlook time passed so slowly.

At night in her tiny efficiency apartment Edna's mind repeatedly revisited her life's saddest episodes. In a scratched record fashion she replayed the days at home in Houston when her mama's open casket was displayed in their family living room, holding the little dead baby, her brother, in her mama's arms. That had been so terribly hard to take. *I remember the odd feel of Mama and the baby's skin when I kissed each of them on their foreheads before the casket was closed the last time.*

Edna thought of the well-meaning neighbors and relatives who would drop by and bring casseroles, trying to help out and cheer her father and her up.

"Oh, doesn't Katherine look peaceful."

"She's with the Lord now."

"Oh, what a precious little boy."

"Now they're in heaven together and happy."

Edna knew the people saying such things were trying to be nice, but they could not have one small inkling of how she felt. *I just wanted my mama back with her warm arms hugging me. I wanted my baby brother alive. I wanted my family together again and my life like it was.*

Friends and relatives were still living their normal lives. Expressions of sympathy could not reach Edna at the level to which her heart had sunk. Her tremendous sadness and loss had caused her to emotionally withdraw to protect herself. "Time heals all wounds," well-intentioned voices would recite. So Edna clung to reliance on time's passage to eventually restore her balance. That period in her young life had been so terribly difficult.

But I carried on because I had to be strong for my daddy. I was left the lady of the house. I had to go to school, and make sure Daddy ate and went to work. He cried and talked about missing mama for two years. He drank too much. He was so sad and sorrowful. His pain was deep.

Today was Edna's day off, and as she looked out the window at the dreary overcast sky, she felt the bluest she had in months. Life sometimes felt too cruel, too callous. It sometimes just did not seem to matter; nothing seemed to matter. Edna broke down and cried. She had to let go of some of her pain reignited by the recent loss. She had been stoic at work, but her sorrow was too much to hold in, too much to carry.

Edna replayed in her mind the day she came home from school and found her dad on top of the bedspread on his made bed, still and quiet. Napping. Edna figured he had played hooky from work. But when she tried to wake him for dinner, he did not awaken. He was not breathing.

Edna later learned he had been methodical. In advance, he had taken the day off from work and had purchased salicylic acid. As soon as she was off to school, he had neatly made his bed, laid down on top of it, and had taken the entire bottle of salicylic acid.

When Edna realized he was not breathing, she ran out of the house, down the street to Jimmy's house and had his parents call the police. After that, Edna could not make herself go back into that house again. Her Aunt Lillie and Uncle Justin had to clean out the utensils, dishes, furniture, clothing and possessions when Edna moved in with them. While cleaning out the house, they had found a note to Edna under her dad's pillow. It said, "I love you. I've gone to join your mother and brother. Be good." When Edna was given the note, she tore it into small pieces and threw it away.

I'm totally alone. I have no one who really cares about me. I have no real family. This is not the way life is meant to be.

When her father killed himself, she had been left at fourteen with the great sorrow of feeling terribly alone in the big world. And she was stuck with an unreasonable guilt that perhaps if she had just worked harder to make her father happier he would not have left her.

One self-pitying thought led to another. Edna thought about how when she learned about Jimmy's betrayal she could not walk. She basically gave up caring about life then, too. She didn't want to eat and lost a lot of weight. But that time of slow recovery taught her a lot. She learned in time to place one foot in front of the other again. And slowly, gradually, she emerged from her hysteria to join in with the flow of life. That period in Houston, living with Aunt Lillie and Uncle Justin, had built within Edna a steely resolve: She would never again let herself become destroyed by her own emotional pain and sorrow.

With Ray now out of her life, though, that pledge was becoming difficult to keep. This ending revived memories of past pain. Edna had learned to trust again and to depend on Ray. She had loved him deeply until she found out who he really was. His values were vastly different from hers.

It was outrageous how calm he was when he told me about the conspiracy to sell more autos, even glossing over the deaths involved. He can rationalize anything for the sake of business. I'll have no part of that. To be married to Ray would mean I was his knowing collaborator. I couldn't live with myself if that were the case.

Edna remembered how Ray had mentioned "the common folk" and how she had found that phrase so arrogant, as if he truly believed he was a better, more perfect human being simply because he had more money and prestige. *How absurd could Ray be? And, how would God judge Ray's behavior?*

After a few weeks of serious after-work mourning and moping, Edna's spirit slowly started reviving again. Life, like a river, continues on its relentless way with or without you. Edna realized she could no longer continue to sit on the sidelines and feel sorry for herself.

She wanted to live. There was still so much to do. She began to focus on being grateful for what she did have instead of concentrating on loss. Her health, her apartment, having a job while so many were out of work, were blessings. Feeling consciously thankful was the beginning step in making her feel better about her life in general.

This Tuesday night, Edna had been home from work for about twenty minutes when she heard a knock at her door. "Edna, it's Russ. There's a phone call for you in the lobby."

Edna answered the door to find Russ's smiling face. He was still dressed in his business suit, and had his fedora in his hand.

"Hi, Russ. Who is it? Ray again?"

"Yes."

"Tell him I'm not interested."

"Well, perhaps you could tell him yourself. He's called often. I don't think he'll stop until he speaks with you."

"Not tonight, Russ. I really have nothing to say to him. We're through and he'll just try and convince me otherwise. I'm not interested in a man who doesn't care about others, who's only interested in increasing his own wealth, no matter how he does it."

"Those are some strong words."

"Well, I know more about him than you do."

"Okay. Well, I'll go down and tell him you're unavailable, but I think one of these days you need to talk to him yourself."

"Thanks, Russ."

Edna appreciated Russ. Russ and Marie had dragged her out of her apartment to have a couple of drinks at Musso & Frank's Grill one evening, about a month ago. *Despite my mood I enjoyed his company. He's a gentleman, but also has a great sense of fun. Russ is a good listener, and when he speaks, people really pay attention since he usually has something worth saying.*

Maybe tonight she should offer Russ a drink to thank him for coming up to let her know about the call. She pulled out a bottle of bourbon she had and two glasses, and opened her apartment door to the hallway. When he came back upstairs she would ask him in for a drink. She turned her radio music on low to hear the Guy Lombardo Orchestra playing.

Edna lit her cigarette with the lighter she was going to give to Ray as a wedding present. She sat in her chair facing the hall for about fifteen minutes with her door opened a bit. Russ did not pass by, nor did anyone else. *He must have been headed out for the evening, not in.* Edna put away the bottle and glasses, and decided to go to bed early again, and listen to the radio.

CHAPTER TWENTY-ONE

SPARROWS AND SCHWAB'S

On her next day off from work, Edna awoke to a clear and sunny morning. A few sparrows she had started feeding outside her window were on the ledge, waiting for their cracker crumb breakfast. "Good morning. I'll be right back."

She went to her storage of saltines, took a package that had been accidentally crushed from being at the bottom of her purse, opened the package and took out two of the largest pieces. *I'll have those for breakfast.* She then opened her window, and poured the remaining crumbs onto her windowsill. The sparrows at first flew up in the air, but then quickly settled back to eat the meal waiting for them. She would have gotten a cat, dog or even a guinea pig if the apartment building allowed pets. But that was not permitted.

Edna felt there was some life that cared whether she lived or died. *These birds need me.* At least she felt better believing that was the case.

Edna thought about the *Bible* teaching about God knowing the feathers of each sparrow, and therefore, certainly knowing the intention and needs of people. Reckoning would come to each person after they passed from this life. No one escaped their own karma, the consequences of their own actions, whether for good or for evil.

The birds chirped as they ate, apparently happy to be getting the cracker crumbs. They looked up at Edna and stared at her, directly into her eyes. There was definitely a communication going on, and it made Edna feel somehow a part of the greater good of life.

I can't stay in my room today. It's time I start exploring life more again. I'm responsible for my own happiness; not Ray or anyone else. It would be good to get outside today and do something fun. It's been a while since I've had a chocolate soda like the ones I used to get in Houston. That would make me feel better.

She had heard from the girls at work that Schwab's Drugstore had a soda bar and that friendly people went there to eat, meet and have a soda. The drugstore also had magazines.

Perhaps I'll be a big spender today and buy my own copy of "Photoplay" or "Motion Picture" magazine. I haven't bought a magazine in ages. It would be such a splurge. I need some shampoo, also. I can find some there. I'll get dressed and go.

Edna looked out from her trolley car seat at the fashionable people walking along Hollywood Boulevard. Every time she rode the streetcar these past few weeks, she was reminded of the cold, casual way Ray had spoken about replacing trolleys with cars. *Doesn't his heart connect to the consequences of his actions?*

It was hard to fathom, and hard to let go of the gnawing irritation that some people were so blind to the results of their decisions, so dead to concern for anything but their own interests. Thank God Edna had not grown up that way.

Hollywood Boulevard this Wednesday morning was busy. Edna observed the women dressed in the latest modern styles, with their distinctive hats, gloves and heels. The men were attired smartly in their suits and hats. Hollywood was more sophisticated than Houston had been, but to this backdrop were drawn sharks, feeding off the worst of human nature, the people who callously used one another. Large cities provided a cover for those who wished to hide their true natures. All the glitter was a well-dressed front for the hearts or lack thereof that lay underneath. Life could be cruel and this city magnified that fact.

Schwab's counter was full when Edna arrived at 11:30, so she went to the magazine rack and perused the covers. *Photoplay* had another Gloria Swanson cover. Edna was not a fan of hers. She seemed unnatural, distant, phony. And, too hoity-toity. Edna liked the down-to-earth type, the stars that were warm, and comfortable being themselves. She picked up a different movie magazine and thumbed through its pages. No articles seemed to grab her attention. No magazine in the rack seemed to merit the twenty-five cents, which would mean a meal for Edna. Perhaps the shampoo department would provide better luck. *But, first things first. I'll wait until after I have my soda to shop for shampoo.*

She went over again to the counter and this time found one open counter seat. She sat down next to a lovely looking young woman who was eating a grilled cheese sandwich. The girl was eating it like she had not had a meal in days. Edna ordered a chocolate soda and waited for it to arrive.

"You're sure enjoying that grilled cheese. Is it as good as it looks?" Edna opened the conversation.

"Yes. Delicious. They make one of the best sandwiches in town. This is my main meal for the day. Watching my figure, you know."

"Yes," Edna replied.

Her soda quickly arrived and she started sipping it through its straw, slowly savoring the flavor.

"Oh, this is wonderful. They sure make a terrific chocolate soda. I'd heard about this place but this is my first time here."

"I'm at Schwab's at least once a week. It's a great place to meet other actors. They hang out here. So do writers, and some producers and directors."

"Oh, you're an actress?"

"Yes. Trying to be anyway. My name's Donna. Donna Reed."

"I'm Edna. Nice to meet you."

"Are you an actress, too?"

"No." *There's no use putting a damper on this girl's dream by telling her about my experiences.*

"Well, to be an actress I've learned one must be extremely persistent, and keep going despite rejection," Donna offered.

"That's what I understand," Edna responded. *Maybe things will be different for her.*

"I'm from Iowa. I've been here two months. Hollywood sure takes getting used to, but I'm willing to work at it. I'm taking acting classes and have had my studio stills taken. I've applied as an extra but it's tough to land even an extra's job."

"Yes. Life's hard for a lot of people these days." Edna suddenly felt blue again. They were each really thinking and talking about problems.

"Yes. But part of an actor's bag of tricks is to act like you're fine even when you're not," Donna offered.

"Yes," Edna agreed. "I suppose that's why I wouldn't be a good actress. I don't hide my true feelings. I wear my heart on my sleeve."

"Oh, but that's where you're wrong. Strong, true feelings when channeled correctly through acting techniques create some of the best acting performances. At least that's what I've learned at acting school. Great passion focused is what makes a great actor or actress. My high school drama teacher used to tell me that I was too flat, lacked strong emotion, but I'm working on that now."

I sometimes would prefer to have a little less passion. I wish I could give some of my excess emotion to this nice young lady to channel.

Edna took a sip of her chocolate soda, and was surprised by a tap on her shoulder.

"Edna King, right?"

Edna turned to find the large, tanned face of Clark Gable.

"Oh, my. The newspaper buyer."

"I've been looking for you. You have a way of sticking in a man's mind. What are you up to?"

"Having a chocolate soda. Mr. Gable, this is Donna Reed, an actress I just met. Donna, Clark Gable."

"Pleased to meet you, Mr. Gable," Donna said demurely.

"Aw, c'mon, girls. No 'Mr. Gable.' Call me 'Clark.' Say, Edna, how about giving me your telephone number. I've been speaking to some friends of mine and they may have some work for you."

"What kind of work?"

"Well, there's a movie I'm starting soon and I'd like to see how you'd do in a small walk-on role. There are a few lines and it might be a start for you."

"Clark, Donna is the actress. I work for Broadway Department Store."

"Well, you've lingered on my mind, Miss King. How about giving it a try? What do you have to lose?"

"When you put it that way, not much, I suppose, except for my job if I can't do the role on my day off."

"Well, I think that can be arranged. I have some pull at the studio, you know."

"Which studio is it?"

"Nation."

"Oh, my. Hannity there doesn't think much of me."

"Well, leave old Hannity to me. He's really a pussycat once you know how to handle him."

"Edna, you have to do this." Donna was beaming. "I've spoken with you for only a few moments but I know you could handle it."

"Well, Clark. Let me give you the number of the Marguerite Apartments where I live. If it's on a Wednesday or a Sunday, one of my days off, I'll be there."

"Fair enough."

"Hollywood 55513."

"Got it, gorgeous. You'll be hearing from me. Nice meeting you, Donna."

Clark Gable left quickly and powerfully. Every head at Schwab's counter turned to watch him walk out the door.

"Oh, my, Edna. That was incredible. Do you realize what just happened? Where did you meet him?"

"One day near Broadway Hollywood and the Taft Building he bought me a newspaper. I thanked him for the paper, gave him my name, and that was that."

"Clark Gable. He's gaining influence everywhere. Looks like you're going to have to consider the acting field. He's seriously interested in working with you."

"It sounds like fun. I'm not going to get too excited though until he telephones. If he phones. We'll see if he's on the level or just full of hot air."

Edna asked for her check and the counter guy told her it had been paid for by Mr. Gable. And so had Donna's sandwich.

"How nice," said Edna.

"Edna, let's keep in touch. I know the Marguerite Apartments. I have a friend who used to live there. Maybe we could have lunch another time and you can let me know what happened?"

"Sure, Donna. I may need information about your acting lessons."

Both women laughed as they parted ways. Donna left the counter and walked towards the drug store exit.

Edna walked over to the shampoo and cosmetics aisle and picked out a *Breck* shampoo, one of the latest and most glamorous brands. It came in a pretty bottle and Edna read on the label that this shampoo made your hair not only clean but "shiny" and "fragrant."

This is a far cry from the soap bar I used as a child in Houston.

Edna took the fancy shampoo up to the cashier. The cashier rang up the shampoo on the large cash register at the counter. "That will be fifty cents, Miss."

"Fifty cents?" Edna suddenly rethought her plan. That was a lot of money to spend from her funds. *I can get along for a while using my bath soap.* Clark Gable may have saved her some money, paying for her soda, but this shampoo splurge would have to wait. *Maybe on my birthday or a holiday.*

"I'm sorry, but I've changed my mind," Edna said. She calmly left the shampoo there and left Schwab's Drugstore. *This must be the high rent district,* Edna thought to herself. *And every penny counts.*

Edna's decision to get out of her apartment today was the right one. She had reentered the flow of life. She serendipitously met a new friend and saw Clark Gable again. One of the biggest movie stars of the day had remembered her name and offered her a part in an upcoming movie. None of this would have occurred if Edna had not dared to once again venture out beyond her self-imposed confinement.

Enough excitement for one day. I'll go home and clean the apartment and get ready for work. No telling what will happen tomorrow.

CHAPTER TWENTY-TWO

INVITATIONS

It was eight o'clock Saturday evening. Edna had just walked in the door from work. She kicked off her high heels, turned on the radio then heard a knock at the door. She put her high heels back on, and opened the door to find Russ standing there.

"Another call from Ray?" Edna asked. It had been at least a week since Ray last attempted to speak with her.

"No. Not this time. I'm driving down to the Long Beach Pike tomorrow. How about joining me?"

Edna paused while trying to decide if she really wanted to go to an amusement park. *Russ is good company. It might be fun to do something different.*

"Why not," she found herself answering. "What time are you leaving?"

"Well, I like to sleep in on Sundays. Let's take off about 11:00. We can make a day of it. Bring your bathing suit, too, in case we decide to go to the beach and do some sunbathing.

"Oh, gosh, Russ, I don't have a bathing suit right now," Edna told a small white fib. *My suit's too baggy since I've lost weight recently.*

"Well, don't worry. If we decide to sit on the sand, we can probably find something for you to wear there. Have you ever been to the Pike?"

"No, not yet. Sundays you can ride the streetcar all day long for a nickel. I took that trolley car ride out to Long Beach when I first came to town, but still haven't explored the Pike yet."

"Well, I think you'll have fun. I want to do something different and thought it might do you some good, too. We'll take my car since I'd like to drive by the South Bay and check on a little place I own by the beach. See you tomorrow at 11:00."

"Okay. Did you want to come in and have a cocktail?"

"Thank you, but I'm on my way out the door. I'll take a rain check. See you."

Edna watched Russ walk down the hall then she closed her door. *It'll be fun to spend the day with him. He was so generous to lend us his car when Marie was in trouble. And I've seen him helping other tenants in the apartment building, carrying groceries, opening doors. What should I wear to an amusement park?*

An oldie but goodie called "Floating Down the River" came on the radio and Edna began dancing by herself around her apartment. As the song was ending, there was another, more urgent knock at the door. Edna answered it to find Marie and Eric standing there.

"Edna, you won't believe who's on the phone for you. Come on. Now. You've got to come downstairs."

"Well, who?"

"Clark Gable."

"No."

"Yes. The guy says that's who he is, and his voice sounds just like him. It must be. Come on." Marie was the most excited Edna had ever seen her.

"Well, okay."

Edna followed Marie and Eric down the stairs to the lobby where they stood watching her and waiting for her to talk into the phone.

"Hello," Edna was tentative.

"Edna King?"

"Yes."

"Well, remember me? I bought you a paper and saw you again at Schwab's?"

"Oh, yes. Hello Mr. Gable."

"Clark, remember?"

"Yes. Okay. Clark."

"Say, I've talked with Hannity over at Nation and he's agreed that you can do a walk-on tomorrow in my latest. He actually remembers you fondly and apparently already has a studio screen test that a number of execs have seen, including my director."

"Tomorrow?"

"Yes. You need to be there at 6:00 a.m. We're filming on Sunday because this is an outdoor scene. Less traffic, less noise on that area of the lot and in the vicinity. You'll have about three hours for make-up, hair, costume fit, plus learning two lines. They're -- if you want to write them down --"

"Give me a moment." Edna covered the phone mouthpiece and turned to Marie and Eric. "I need pen and paper."

Marie looked into her handbag and pulled out a small black memo pad with a small yellow pencil attached to it. She handed it to Edna who thanked her and opened the pad.

"Okay, Mr. Gab -- Clark. I've got pencil and paper. Ready.

"'Sir, would y'all like some of my chitlins'" is the first line. The second is --

"Wait a minute. I'm still writing. Okay."

"Okay? The second is, 'No, sir, that's not what I meant by my chitlins.'

That's it, kiddo. Think you can handle that?"

"Sure."

"Great. A car or cab will pick you up at 5:15 a.m. See you tomorrow."

"Okay. And, thanks … Clark."

"You're quite welcome, Edna. Oh, and try and think up a marquee name. Your real name might work for this walk-on, but in the future you'll need a name that sings "star" to the public. Something more glamorous. See you tomorrow, kiddo."

"Good-night."

Edna hung up the phone and turned to Marie and Eric. "Do you believe that? Clark Gable wants me to be in his movie tomorrow."

"Tomorrow? You mean they work on Sundays?" Marie was concerned.

"I guess they work whenever they need to. I've heard it's not an easy business, but I'm not adverse to hard work."

"How well I know," Marie responded.

"Now, Edna, you be careful of those Hollywood types. Some of them have notorious reputations," Eric voiced his opinion.

"Yes, Eric, I know. I can take care of myself," Edna said, wondering if Marie had told him about the executives at Nation Studio.

"How exciting. Say, we're headed out. Why don't you join us and we can all celebrate?" Marie asked.

"No, thanks. I need to get ready for tomorrow. Oh, my, and I forgot. I told Russ I'd go with him to the Long Beach Pike."

"Oh, well, he'll understand, honey," Marie said.

"Yes. I'll leave a note under his door." Edna used Marie's pad and pencil to write Russ a short note.

"Here's your notepad back. Thanks," Edna said after she removed the note for Russ and the script lines.

Marie put the memo pad back in her purse, then turned and gave Edna a big hug. "I'm so excited for you. You knock 'em dead, or is it, 'break a leg'? Something like that. Anyway, good luck tomorrow and I want to hear every detail."

"Thanks, Marie. And Eric, you take good care of my friend here. She's something special."

"I know. Good-night, now."

Eric led Marie by the elbow towards the front door and Edna turned and walked up the stairs with new energy. *This is actually happening. I need to memorize my lines. I'm going to be in a movie with Clark Gable tomorrow. Life's amazing.*

CHAPTER TWENTY-THREE

MR. GABLE'S CHITLINS

Edna was dreaming about chitlins when her alarm woke her. It felt like only minutes since she went to sleep and it was still dark outside. She turned a light on, quickly fixed some tea and took a spitz bath. She applied her usual make-up, brushed her hair, then got dressed. *The studio will redo my makeup, but first impressions are important.*

By 5:15, Edna was standing in the downstairs lobby, watching for the car. The street lamps were still lit and the road and sidewalks were deserted.

Gee, the streets resemble a ghost town this time of morning. Edna suddenly felt extremely lonely. Then she thought about her dad who would get up at 5:00 a.m. every morning to start his iceman's route. *I must change my thinking. I can't complain. This isn't so bad. I'm going to a movie studio to be in a Clark Gable moving picture. These empty streets look like a studio set without a crew. This is an adventure. I'm lucky to have this opportunity.*

Edna saw a lone car drive past the apartment house, traveling away from the studio's direction. The driver wore a chauffeur's cap. Two minutes later, the same car pulled up right in front of her building. When the chauffeur started walking towards the apartment house, Edna went outside and met him.

"Miss King?"

"Yes."

"Great."

The chauffeur opened the back passenger side door for her and Edna climbed into the large black car.

"Thank you."

"You're welcome."

The automobile was not as impressive as Ray's limousine with its solid doors that shut with a sound of muffled strength, but this was still very nice. An isinglass tray was attached to the rear of the front passenger seating area. Edna raised the tray and was surprised to see a lighted mirror that arose from the tray once it was in place. *My gosh, is that something.* Edna quickly perused her make-up in the close-up mirror, then pushed the whole configuration back to the way she had found it.

A large glass wall separated the driver's area from where Edna was seated.

She looked out the window at the still streets, and occasionally glimpsed a newspaper boy, or another early riser signaling the day ahead.

Nation Studio's huge iron gates were shut tight this morning when the limo arrived. *Oh, oh,* thought Edna, *I hope someone hasn't changed their mind.*

Edna watched the driver get out of the car, walk to the gate appear to push some button through the black wrought-iron. A man dressed in a guard's uniform exited the guard station, carrying a cup of coffee, and did something from his side of the gate that started the gates moving open.

My, isn't that impressive. The gates were open when I was here before. That's so clever the way they move as if by magic. Open Sesame.

The driver pulled the car through the gates, gave a wave to the guard, and continued through the studio until they arrived near a bustling backlot. Edna saw people arranging cameras, lights, props, racks of costumes. The energy was like a weekday rush hour on Wilshire Boulevard.

The driver opened her door. "Here you are, Miss King. Enter that door on the left side of that building, give them your name, and they will let you know what to do next."

"Thank you."

"You're welcome."

Edna hurried to the door and entered. Just inside was a man sitting on a stool with a clipboard list.

"Name please?"

"Edna King."

"Oh, yes, Miss King. Take chair seven, and make-up and hair will be with you in the order of things." He picked up a file he had on a table near the stool, took out some pages and handed them to her.

"Here's your script. Your character is underlined in ink for you. Make sure you know those lines. You have about an hour before your shoot begins."

"Thank you." Edna took the pages and gave him her best smile.

She then went over and sat in a barber-fashioned chair facing a long line of lighted mirrors. It had a number seven on its back. She placed her purse on the floor below.

"Oh, honey, I'll put that up here." A blonde woman not much older than Edna had walked up, taken her purse and placed it on the counter in front of the mirror. "You don't want it getting all dirty, or hair all over it."

"Well, thank you."

"I'm Shirley and I'll be making you up today. You're my next assignment. Let's see, you must be the Chitlin Gal? Isn't that what the script says?"

Edna looked at the pages she had been given. "Yes, that's me." She was happy to see that her two lines were the same ones she had written down the night before.

"Great. Well, let's start by taking all your make-up off. You do a terrific job, but that store make-up won't hold up under our hot studio lights. If they do some close-ups, your make-up will start running down your face. Here, take some of this cleansing cream and these tissues and get me a clean slate."

Edna had anticipated this and did what Shirley asked.

Shirley then tried three different foundation colors on the inside of Edna's wrist.

"This color's you."

Shirley then started applying the chosen make-up base onto Edna's face. "After foundation, highlights and powder, I'll accentuate those striking blue eyes. Too bad the camera can't capture their color. Then I'll use our special studio lip cream to plump up and moisturize your lips, and finish with a bright red lipstick that looks great on film. After I'm done, the hair guy will fix your hair so you can wear the maid's white cap easily. Then you go to costume and try on your outfit. Do that as soon as you can because they might need to do some tailoring if it doesn't fit right. Got all that?"

"I think so." Edna was sleepier and quieter than usual this morning, but could feel her nerves starting to tumble her stomach. "This is all so exciting."

"I bet it is. It's not every day a girl gets to be in a movie scene with Clark Gable. He's sure a looker, isn't he?"

"Yes. And charming, too."

"He can be, sure." Shirley said that in such a tone that Edna knew there was more behind the words.

"What do you mean by 'he can be'?" Edna was curious.

"Well, I mean, he's only human. Just like everyone else he can have his down moods, and sometimes he's snarly and irritable, like a caged lion who hasn't had a good meal lately. Don't get me wrong, he's a great guy, but watch out for his anger. You don't want to be the recipient of that."

"I'll try and avoid him when he's hungry." Edna tried to lighten the news. "Or, keep a cooked steak in my pocket."

"Hey, you're a pistol. No wonder Clark liked you for this part. He likes pretty women who can give as much as they get."

"Sounds like you know him pretty well," Edna fished for more information.

"Well enough," was all that Shirley offered. "You're done now. What do you think?"

Edna looked at her image in the mirror and was pleasantly surprised. Although it had felt like inches of thick clay were being applied to her face, the final look did not appear that way. She looked fresh, pretty, yet sophisticated. It was a bright, new image.

"I don't recognize myself, but you did a fabulous job. Thank you."

"You're welcome. Hope to see more of you. Now you stay sitting here and your hair guy will be here in a few minutes." With that, Shirley left and walked over to a woman sitting in the second chair.

Edna took this time to look at the script pages she had been handed, and to make certain she had her cues memorized. She practiced line nuances in her head, giving emphasis to different words at different times. Then she studied the additional writing which explained that she was to act surprised, walk away, turn her head back over her shoulder to give Clark Gable a look of disapproval. *I wonder if I can change that? How can I give Clark Gable a look of disapproval?* Thinking about the upcoming scene, Edna was getting more and more nervous as she sat waiting for the hair guy.

"There you are. How's my Dixieland gal?"

Edna looked up from her script pages and was happy to see Maximilian standing beside her chair. "Max. It's great to see you."

"You, too, Missy King. You're finally making your big screen debut. I saw your screen test results and let me assure you that the camera loves you."

"We did have fun at that screen test, didn't we?"

"You have that right. I don't know when I've been as entertained by a newcomer interacting with a director. You've sure got guts, girl."

"Take no guff," Edna was enjoying interacting with Max again.

"Okay. Now, to work. You're serving food. We're to put your hair up so that the cap will fit nicely and your face is visible, however, I'm going to add a chignon. I have just the right one that will match your hair color. It will class up your maid act a bit."

"A hoity-toity maid, eh?"

"Well, I'm rooting for you. Just trying to help add more glamour and complexity to your character. I'd like to keep you around for awhile to entertain me. Do you have your lines memorized?"

"Yes. Clark gave them to me over the phone last night. I wrote them down and learned them before I went to sleep. And, I just memorized the cues while I was sitting here."

"Good. Then you'll have some freedom to play around with the word delivery and your action. You're starting out right, girl. I'm proud of you. When you get on the set and the director says 'action,' think 'SPARKLE'."

Edna was startled by how loudly the word sparkle came out of Max's mouth. "Think 'sparkle'?"

"Yes. Exude all the light within yourself, you know, like the brightest star in the night sky, like those klieg lights, like a fireworks finale. You naturally have that spark, that 'it factor,' but remember to remind yourself each time the director calls 'action'. That way you'll make certain that your energy is captured by the camera."

"You're giving me an awful lot to think about, Max. I'm already working on a stomach full of nerves. I'm not sure I can remember one more thing, but I'll try."

"Well, that's another thing. You must relax. All good actors let the acting flow from an energetic yet relaxed state."

"Max, I think the advice is getting overwhelming. How about if I just go and say my lines and be done with it?"

Max laughed. "Yes, well, maybe I am laying the lessons on a bit thick, but I like you and can see that you have what it takes."

"Well, thanks for your belief in me. It means a lot. Where did you learn so much about acting?"

"Years of hanging around here. And, I must confess that my first love was acting. I took many classes trying to improve my skills. I just was too stiff. I could never give up a certain reserve, could never stop my self-consciousness, thinking about what I was doing as I was doing it. That creates bad acting, the stilted, unnatural kind."

"Well, lucky for me you became a behind-the-scenes man. Look at that chignon. It's fabulous. I love it. You've transformed me into the classiest looking maid I've ever seen."

"That was the purpose, my dear. Now you go get your costume. Make certain it fits you well. If it doesn't, have them tailor it. Here's my card with my home number on it. If you need any advice or just want to talk, call me. I know you're going to knock 'em dead."

Edna got up from her chair, and gave Max a big hug. "Thanks so much. You're terrific." Edna took her purse from in front of the mirror and walked over to the wardrobe area to try on her maid's costume.

She looked sensational in the perfectly-fitted, short, black maid's costume, with the white trim, apron and hat. The black mesh stockings and three-inch heels showed off her shapely legs. She glowed with anticipation as she walked over to the set. *I'm as ready as I could ever be.*

"Hey, maid, where's my chitlins?" Edna turned around at the sound of the booming voice. Clark Gable was standing behind her, grinning.

"Well, if it isn't the devil himself," Edna played along.

"You ready for your big scene?" Clark asked.

"As ready as you are, although without your experience."

"You'll do fine. I believe in you. And, say, that outfit sure doesn't hurt your appeal any."

"Thank you. I'm lucky I'm a typical size. It didn't even need tailoring."

"Well, let's hope the camera sees what I see. If it does, your success is in the bag."

Clark took Edna by the hand and guided her to the chair where the director was seated, next to the camera.

"Here's your maid, Howard," Clark Gable said to the director.

"Nice, Clark. Are you ready, little lady?"

"Yes, sir."

"Okay. What I want you to do is carry the plate of chitlins that's sitting over on the prop table there, and take them to the three other gentlemen first. Give them each a portion on their plate, serving them from their left side. Listen carefully to the dialogue, and make sure you start at the right time. Clark will be the last one you come to. And to him you say your first line, after you hear your cue.

It's a matter of timing. You need to enter the table area at the correct moment, serve the men as they're talking, and then be around to Clark at the right time to deliver your line. Do you think you can do that?"

"I think so, yes."

"After you and Clark exchange words then you take the chitlins and leave in the same direction you entered. You enter from the left there. Stage right. Okay? Got it?"

"Yes."

"Okay. PLACES EVERYONE."

Clark Gable and three other men went and sat down at the picnic table with the blue checkered tablecloth. Edna walked over and grabbed the chitlins platter, and stood waiting off to the side.

"Ready. ACTION."

Edna listened carefully to the lines the men were speaking. When she heard her cue -- *Sparkle* -- she entered with the chitlins platter and began to serve the first man. She listened to the dialogue to pace her movement around the table. *I've got to hurry right now*, she realized at one point, and sped up a little.

As her cue was given she arrived right to Clark's left.

"Would y'all like some of my chitlins?"

Clark looked up at Edna, grinned his rogue's grin, and grabbed her behind. "Sure looks appetizing to me. Yes."

"Not those chitlins." Edna executed a graceful turn whereby her swivel removed his hand from her bottom while at the same time she flipped over a serving of chitlins right in his lap.

"Whoops. So sorry, sir." Edna smiled politely at Clark, then exited the scene.

Clark looked up surprised and after a slight pause he burst out laughing. Everyone else starting laughing, too.

"Cut, CUT," yelled the director. "Print. That scene's a wrap."

"Hey, Howard, that's not the way it was scripted. I wasn't supposed to get food in my lap. Her lines weren't right either."

"You're right, Clark. And you weren't supposed to grab her bottom either. But this business turned out better. That's that. Now go get that food off your lap and we'll continue.

Terrific, young lady. But, next time, follow the script," the director told Edna. "Now, go get changed. You'll hear from the studio."

"Thank you, sir. I enjoyed working with you. Bye Clark."

"Bye you little wildcat. You just wait. I'll get you back."

Edna walked to the wardrobe area with a huge smile on her face. She had started her career in the movies and she did it her way. *People in the movies get respect.*

CHAPTER TWENTY-FOUR

LONG BEACH PIKE

"Hey, movie star. How's it going?" Edna had opened up her door to find Russ standing there, dressed to go out.

"Russ. Hello. Another phone call?" Edna smiled.

"No. Just wanted to hear how your movie experience went."

"It was great. Haven't heard from the studio since, though, and the movie won't be out for a couple of months."

"Well, I look forward to seeing it."

"Me too, actually."

"Say, how about The Pike? You reneged on me before for Clark Gable and the movies. Somewhat understandable. But since you're not a big star yet maybe we could still have some fun this Sunday."

"You didn't make it down there without me, huh?"

"No."

"Okay. Sunday it is. That's a deal."

"Good. We'll leave here after lunch, around one."

"Great. Sounds like fun. See you then."

Edna closed the door to her apartment and began to think about what she would wear on Sunday. She could stand to be amused. Waiting to hear from the studio was painstaking. She had told all the girls at work about her bit part and they all bugged her constantly, asking her if she had heard from Clark or had signed a contract. The void was excruciating. It would be good to get away on Sunday.

Sunday was sunny. Edna and Russ took the beach drive: Santa Monica Boulevard to the ocean, then Pacific Coast Highway to Long Beach. It was a longer route, but showcased lovely scenery along the way. As they passed Manhattan Beach, Russ told Edna more about his beach house there where he stayed sometimes. He liked to keep his apartment in the city because it was more centrally located for work, but Manhattan Beach with its sandy beaches and beautiful ocean and pier was where he loved to spend time. Plus the fresh sea air was great for the lungs.

"Did you know that sand from Manhattan Beach is going to be sold and taken to the Hawaiian Islands to fill in Waikiki Beach?"

"Wow, how interesting. I thought they had enough sand of their own."

"Apparently not. Their new tourist trade needs wider beaches."

"Fascinating. How will they get it over there?"

"Huge freighters."

"Interesting."

Their conversation was comfortable and unrestrained. Edna felt relaxed with Russ.

"Where are you from originally?" she asked him. They had left the esplanade at South Torrance Beach and were now almost around the Palos Verdes Peninsula.

"I was born in Michigan but grew up in Seattle, Washington. In our youth, my brothers and I spent a lot of time boating on Lake Washington and Puget Sound. I've been down here since around 1917, after I returned from the War. The doctors suggested a warmer climate for my lungs."

"Oh, what happened to you?"

"Well, I was in the trenches in France. A whole group of us were gassed. Yellow gas. The Army shipped the survivors to a sanitarium out in the Arizona desert where we recuperated. I spent about a year out there on a paid vacation of sorts."

"Are you fine now?"

"As far as I know. I feel good anyway. Tell me more about you. I know you came from Texas, are close friends with Marie, and that you have a fun-loving nature when you're feeling good."

"Yes, well, I grew up in Houston. Dad, mom, and I had a simple life. They're gone now. I lived with my dad's brother and his wife before moving out here. My "fun-loving nature" as you say wasn't a big hit with my strict Southern Baptist Aunt.

"Well, having three brothers it's my view that everyone has their nature built into them, a bit like automobiles. Some are fast and snazzy, some are elegant and refined. Some are earthy, practical, utility focused. Humans are a bit like that in my mind. And, it's hard to make a Ford Model T into a Rolls Royce without destroying it, or vice versa. We brothers were all different."

"I guess you're right. I never really thought about people that way before. But it makes sense."

"Yes. Too many people go around judging each other yet inside we're all coming from different places, following our own unique natures. Too often we expect the other guy to act like, be like, think like us. It was Shakespeare who said, 'To thine own self be true,' and yet it seems that many people spend more time judging what the other guy is doing than trying to improve upon what is going on in their own lives."

"I do know some Baptists get so caught up in their beliefs that they think everyone else is a sinner. I guess most people, though, just want to be liked, get along and make other people feel good."

"Well, now, see, that's your nature. Not everyone thinks or acts that way. Some people could care less about being liked. One of my brothers was like that. Antisocial. Never hurt anyone. Not mean. He just didn't care about what was expected of him socially and what others thought about him. I, on the other hand, more like you, always wanted to treat other people well and be nice to them because that's the way I like to be treated."

Edna was fascinated by what Russ had to say. He was a caring individual. This trip was already a success in her mind.

"Hey, look. The Cyclone. Now there's a serious ride. That's that big roller coaster that goes out over the ocean. We're almost there."

"Russ, I have to confess. To use your expression, my 'nature' is one of being scared to death of roller coasters and amusement park rides. I'm afraid you're going to have to experience the excitement by yourself. I'll watch you and wait for you."

"Oh, I think we can find a ride you might like. The fun house? The Ferris wheel?"

"Well, we'll see. It depends on how high the Ferris wheel is."

"For a gal who I've seen so fun-loving, this surprises me."

"Well, as you said, we all have our quirks."

"Well, we do. I took you for fearless, though."

"Well, I'm pretty fearless except for, it just so happens, amusement park rides. Can't tell you why. Just my nature, I guess," Edna smiled to herself. Edna was learning more about life from Russ and liked what she heard.

By the time the lights were coming on at the amusement park, Edna had sat on a variety of benches and had enjoyed watching the crowd. Russ had ridden rides, including the Cyclone roller coaster twice. Russ brought her a pink cotton candy after one ride. And he knocked down milk bottles with a baseball and won a small stuffed dog for her. Edna, feeling guilty for not joining Russ on any ride, finally went on the Whirl-a-wind, one of the less frightening-looking structures.

"I'm never getting on another ride as long as I live," Edna confirmed as she exited the Whirl-a-wind. It frightened her much more than she had anticipated and her nervous energy was at its peak.

"How about a drink?" Russ offered. "It will calm you down. I know a place nearby where one can overlook the whole city and the Pike. We can also get a bite to eat before heading back."

"I'm usually home by this time on Sunday, getting ready for work."

"Well, we both need to eat, and I'd like to be sharp on the drive back."

"I guess I can break my usual routine. Why not? I want you thinking about your driving and not your stomach on the way home."

Edna had worn a dress that would work for dinner, but she changed from the flats she wore to some high heels she brought along for such an occasion. She freshened up her powder and lipstick in the car mirror as Russ was driving. Russ had a sports jacket and tie in the back of his car, which he put on for the restaurant.

Edna and Russ went to the top of the Breakers Hotel. The view was captivating. They could see all the lights down at the Pike, and those amusement park rides twinkled and glimmered like the enchanting playland that it was. Out on the ocean, the outlines of anchored and moving ships were lit against a blackened sky. Russ ordered Manhattans, and he lit two cigarettes and handed one to Edna. When the drinks arrived, Russ raised his glass to Edna and toasted, "To a wonderful day."

"To a wonderful day," Edna repeated as she gently clinked her glass against his.

A combo band started to play music and two couples got up and began dancing. Russ ordered some hors d'oeuvres of meatballs, and Oysters Rockefeller, plus asked for some bread and butter to be brought. They sat and talked, enjoyed their hors d'oeuvres, then Russ ordered them both a rare steak and baked potato. The food, view and music were good. They ate their fill and finished their drinks. Refreshed, they were ready to head home when the band began to play "Night and Day."

"This is one of my favorite songs," said Edna.

"Well, shall we?" asked Russ, standing up and offering his hand to Edna.

She smiled, took his hand and went with him to the dance floor. She had danced before with Russ at the Cocoanut Grove. He was a consummate dancer who moved Edna around the dance floor with the precise, gentle yet insistent push and pull a woman could easily follow. They glided around artfully, as if they had danced together for years. When the last strains of "Night and Day" faded, Russ led Edna back towards the table. It was time to start back to the apartment building. They shared one last look out the window, at the city, the amusement park, and the harbor lights. The day's excursion was coming to an end. And Edna felt oddly content.

CHAPTER TWENTY-FIVE

NIGHT ON THE TOWN

One of her friends from work, Daphne, joined Edna one evening to go see a Harlow movie at the Pantages Theatre. Otherwise life was quiet recently. Edna hadn't seen Russ in a couple of weeks. He was out of town on business.

Ray had sent her flowers at work and to her apartment, after their break-up many months ago, with notes begging her to reconsider. When the flowers didn't work he had sent a watch ring to her with a note about how she deserved the best of everything. Edna returned the ring with a note stating she was sorry but she couldn't accept it. "Please, Ray, realize that we are through." Since then, no word from Ray.

Her mind was made up. No turning back. She could not accept a life of hypocrisy and double dealing. It was not in her nature, nor how she was raised.

This Tuesday night, Edna was in her apartment after work, relaxing from a busy day. Her door was open and she was having a cocktail in her room. Since tomorrow was a day off, she hoped to see some of her neighbors pass by and perhaps invite them in. The radio was playing "Night and day, you are the one ..." when Russ walked by her open door. He was dressed in a light grey business suit, with a matching fedora still covering his head. He took off his hat and glanced in.

"Hey, movie star, isn't that our song?"

"Hi. Good to see you again. How's business?

"Oh, I was on the road for a couple of weeks, with the usual complications but everything went well. It's good to be back. How about taking you up on that raincheck for a drink you offered a while back?"

"Sure. Come on in." Edna was happy to see him.

Russ entered her apartment, stood and waited politely for her to tell him where to sit.

"Have a seat," Edna said, pointing to her other chair next to a side table with a lamp.

Russ sat down and put his hat on the table, as Edna got up, took a glass and poured Russ a bourbon.

She walked over and handed it to him, then sat back down in her chair.

"Thank you."

"You're welcome. So tell me about your travels?"

"It was a long road trip, but I love driving my car. Business took me up to Seattle. I visited with a couple of my brothers while up there. They're doing fine. We took a motor cruiser out on the Puget Sound one day and I thoroughly enjoyed it. Like old times."

"You look tan. It must have been nice up there." Edna could see freckles on the top of Russ's prematurely bald head.

"Yes, we had some rare warm weather. And, driving up there and back, even in Oregon, I was able to keep the convertible top down. Can't beat that fresh air."

"Sounds exhilarating."

"I try to make my work enjoyable. So much of life is built around working. I figure I might as well enjoy myself when possible. Otherwise, what is life about?"

"I agree. I like my job, feeling useful and the interaction with people."

"There's a Buddhist philosophy something to the effect of if you pick up garbage, you pick up the garbage in the best way you can, and that every job is as worthy as the next as long as you do it with that intention."

Edna smiled. She enjoyed Russ sharing his wisdom with her. He was a man of many facets. "Yes, I sure agree with that. My parents taught me to live like that. That's just an example of down home common sense where I come from. You always do the best you can because that's what your employer deserves, and your own self-respect requires. The added bonus is that it makes the world work and us feel better."

"Sure."

"Are you Buddhist?"

"Oh, no. I just like to read about different religions. They all have something to offer. It's the same God after all, just with many coats and colors."

Edna smiled again. "I hadn't thought about it that way. I was raised Baptist and have to confess that the strict ones seem to think they have cornered the market on God. And, not only that, they believe everything's a sin. You aren't supposed to like music. You can't dance. You shouldn't wear make-up and look pretty. You shouldn't care about this world too much. It got so silly in my mind because it seems that everything that's natural or fun in life religious fundamentalists are against."

"I know what you mean. My mother was Catholic and she tried to get us four boys to go to church every Sunday. We did when we were younger. Dad, though, wasn't very religious, and he would always stay home. As we boys grew older, it seemed ridiculous the way the system worked. We could go out and do whatever we wanted to, and as long as we confessed, and repeated the exact amount of prayers that the priest told us to say, then we were considered sin-free again.

It felt meaningless when I was asked to recite words to a God and saints who would probably be bored by listening to the same words over and over again anyway. And how are recited words really able to help you to enter heaven at some date in the future? Also, I questioned the arrogance of praying to ask God to do things for me, as if he isn't busy enough. We boys gave up going to church at some point, all except Webster, who was the closest to mother."

"I understand what you're saying. I believe in a loving God who sees everything people do and even knows what thoughts we're thinking. But in my church growing up, the congregation would first judge you and criticize you for what you weren't doing right in their minds, and as an afterthought they might get around to being loving and kind. And don't get me started on the way the women would criticize each other's outfits."

Russ and Edna started laughing. They were having fun talking about religion, the very subject most people were taught to avoid discussing.

"Say, why don't we go out and grab a bite to eat," Russ offered. I haven't been to the Cocoanut Grove for a while. How about it?"

"Well, I'd have to change. Could you give me a few minutes?"

"Sure. Let me go on down to my apartment. I just got in, and had just set my suitcase inside my door. How about if I meet you in the lobby in a half hour?"

"Sounds good," Edna said.

"Thanks for the drink," Russ said, as he left through the open door, closing it purposefully behind him.

Edna went to her closet and picked out her long blue chiffon dress with the trail down the back. *This will be nice*, Edna thought. *I haven't been to the Cocoanut Grove in awhile.*

Tonight felt like a night of possibilities. Dinner, music and dancing. Edna laughed as she thought about how some Baptist congregations would judge her wanting to enjoy herself tonight. In their minds, life on earth was a punishment, not a wonderful opportunity. *That is their choice*, thought Edna. *But I'm going to actually live my life. I'll live my life as I choose and report to my maker at the end of the journey. To each his own.*

The Cocoanut Grove was packed this evening. It was amazing how many people went out to Hollywood nightspots on weekday evenings. The whole

171

town craved adventure and fun even in this depression. Even those who couldn't afford to enter the clubs themselves would stand outside to watch for celebrities, and, just to see what everyone was wearing. It was a fashion and celebrity conscious town.

Russ and Edna were given a table over by the wall with a good view of the band. The maitre'd had recognized Edna from her evenings there with Ray and effused over her dress and how gorgeous she looked "as always."

Once they were settled and had ordered their cocktails, Edna and Russ watched some of the dancers. The orchestra was playing "All of Me." Edna spotted the pretty actress, Donna, she had met at Schwab's Drugstore. As the couple turned to the music, Edna saw that, of all people, Donna was dancing with Ray. Edna suddenly felt sick to her stomach. Donna was looking as pretty as could be and was dancing beautifully with Ray. Edna did not want to stay. The wound was more raw than she had thought.

"You took the part that once was my heart ..." The Irving Berlin lyrics and music did not help her emotional reaction.

"Russ, would you mind if we left now? I'm not feeling well. I ..."

"Well, if you wish. We haven't ..."

"I can't stay. I'm sorry." Edna quickly stood up and began moving towards the door. Russ left some bills for the drinks, and followed behind.

But it was too late. Ray spotted Edna and started on his way over, pulling Donna behind him.

"Edna. Edna," Ray was calling to her and heads were turning to look at what was happening.

She continued walking and reached the edge of the dance floor closest to the door when Ray grabbed her by the arm. "Edna, please. I have to talk with you," Ray pleaded.

"Ray, we're just leaving," Edna said. "Please let go of my arm."

"But, Edna, we have not resolved this," Ray said.

"Resolved what, Ray? There's nothing to resolve."

Edna continued walking at a quick pace and was nearing the front door, with Ray right behind her, and Russ and Donna behind them. Edna exited through the front door and kept on walking towards the parking valet, with all three now trailing behind her.

"Edna, stop. Please. Let me talk to you," Ray continued.

"There's nothing to say, Ray. I've told you we're through. When will you get it? Please leave me alone."

"Edna, don't be this way. You know how I feel."

"And, you know how I feel, Ray. It's over."

"But I love you," said Ray.

"Maybe so, Ray. But you don't care about people in general. You care more about money and power than you do about other human beings. I can't live with someone like that."

"But, Edna …"

"What you've done and been involved with is your choice, but I will not be a part of it."

Edna walked up to the parking valet and asked that Russ's car be brought around.

The four of them stood there awkwardly waiting for Russ's car.

"Hi, Ray. I'm Russ Newman." Russ broke the silence and extended a handshake. "I've spoken to you on the phone a few times, and, I think I met you once before when you were dating Edna."

"Oh, yes. Hi, Russ. How are you? How's business?"

"Business is good. Whose this lovely young lady you're with? We haven't been properly introduced."

"Oh, excuse my manners. Russ, Edna, this is Donna Reed, a budding young Hollywood starlet."

"Well, I can see why," said Russ.

"Thank you," said Donna. "Hello, Edna."

"Hello," said Edna. Her emotions were overwhelming her right now. It was difficult to be friendly with Donna, even though she held nothing against this young woman.

There was again an awkward silence until the valet finally brought Russ's Buick and opened the passenger door for Edna to enter. As she was about to get into the car, still standing, she turned and looked long and hard at Ray who was standing there next to Donna.

"Ray, please, I mean it. Never call me again." Edna slowly and carefully emphasized each word. Then she sat down in the passenger's seat of Russ's Buick and with purpose turned her head facing forward.

Russ tried to ease the tension, and pleasantly said, "Good-bye, Ray, Donna. Nice to have met you." Then he got into the driver's seat and slowly drove off.

"How about taking me to the Formosa Cafe, Russ?"

"I thought you weren't feeling well."

"He was the reason. Now that that's over, I'm still hungry, and could use a cocktail."

"Well, sure. I'm hungry, too. Let's go."

Russ didn't pry. Her tension was palpable. For a guy who had grown up without sisters, Russ still understood human nature.

The Formosa was crowded as usual, but most were at the bar. The dinner crowd was thinning, so one of the red booths was available. Edna and Russ finally got around to having a cocktail. Russ lit their cigarettes, and they both started to relax and enjoy the evening again. Russ ordered the Chinese sampler deluxe dinner for two, with extra egg rolls.

"Feeling better, now?" Russ asked.

"Yes. I knew I'd run into Ray one day. I just didn't think he would approach me in that manner. That was so out of character for him. It was embarrassing. It's tough to end a relationship, no matter what the reason is."

"Yes, it is. I was divorced a couple of years ago from my wife of thirteen years," Russ offered.

"Oh, Russ. I didn't know that. Well, then you really understand."

"Yes. It's hard, and particularly when there's a child involved."

"Oh, you have a child?"

"Well, not really mine. My ex-wife had a daughter when I married her. The girl is now about 15. I raised her as my own. It was very hard on her to see her mother and I separate. And, sometimes I go over there to visit with her because she misses me."

"Oh, of course she would. You're her father in her mind."

"Yes. Her biological father was never in the picture. He took off and never bothered to contribute to child support or be in her life."

"Some men can be so self-consumed." Edna was thinking about Ray and his know-no-boundaries philosophy of business. "They can't see beyond their own ambition nor care about how their actions might effect other people's lives."

"Yes. Growing up with my brothers, we all competed with one another, but there was still a bond that we had which kept us caring about one another. My parents were hard working people who loved one another and treated each other with respect. I think that type of influence makes a difference in the way children grow up. Although we each have different natures, role models influence manners and thoughtfulness."

"Yes. I agree. Respect is important. My parents were similar. They loved and respected each other. And, they truly cared about how others were getting along. 'Do unto others ... ' was the way they lived their lives."

"They sound terrific."

"They were. But they both passed on too soon."

"Yes. A parent's loss is difficult. My father's gone, too. Oh, here's our dinner."

"This looks delicious." Edna's appetite had returned.

Edna loved Chinese food, and the variety of plates for them to share was enticing. She was feeling good again, and was enjoying the calming influence of Russ. *Thank goodness I was with Russ the first time I ran into Ray. He defused what could have been a more difficult situation.* Although Russ didn't seem to push it the way some men do, his quiet comfortable strength got things done without the hoopla and attention that some other men sought. When she was with him Edna felt secure and respected. The world felt less difficult to maneuver.

A small combo band came back from their break and started playing background music as they were eating dinner. The music was soothing, the food was delicious. Like two old friends, their conversation was comfortable. Edna decided to tell Russ about Jimmy.

"I almost got married back in Houston, to a man I had grown up with. He had a crush on me most of his younger years."

"I can understand why."

Edna smiled at Russ, then continued.

"Then when we were about to be married he started dating another woman. I didn't find out about it for quite awhile. He would say he was working late, and friends of mine covered up for him initially. I learned he was not only out on the town with one woman but would be flirting and trying to make dates with others when he was out with her."

"That must have been a shock."

"It sure was. It destroyed my trust in others for awhile. Some of my so-called friends had known about what he was doing, had seen him out on the town with other women, but didn't tell me about it. They were afraid of how I might react. That was cowardly on their part, I think. And it took me quite some time to bounce back from that misplaced trust in Jimmy and in some so-called friends. What happened to end your marriage?"

"A combination of factors, like with many things in life. But I suppose the biggest reason was, my wife cared more about money, status, social prominence, than she did about me. Nothing was ever enough for her. She always wanted more. There came a time when we had grown too far apart in our goals to be able to remain together."

175

"Oh, that's too bad. What is it with this country nowadays? Too many people are after the almighty dollar, some to the point where they don't care who they step on to get it. It doesn't make sense to me. I'm grateful just to have enough to live on. This depression has hit so many people so hard."

"I agree. Money's important to be able to survive and thrive in life. Ambition's good. But there's a voracious greed that is too common. I discovered some of my salesmen outright lying at times in order to make sales. I've had to let some go because they just wouldn't learn that lies don't work in the long run. They couldn't be trusted to uphold the integrity of the company. It's important to make sales, but sales can be made just as easily by telling the truth."

"Yes. True. And, some people who don't even need more money are consumed by getting more. I just don't understand that way of thinking."

"Greed's not an attractive part of human nature. It's excessive desire for more than one deserves or needs. It causes too many problems. I think it occurs because people don't feel good within themselves about their own self. They feel like they need to prove themselves somehow, yet enough is never enough."

Edna took up the chorus. "Isn't greed one of the seven deadly sins? And it's similar to that sin of 'coveting' that we used to hear about in Bible school."

"Hey, you haven't rejected your church upbringing altogether. We were taught that, too. If you're greedy, you're covetous, which is a sin in any religion. Greed is selfish, hoggish, self-indulgent."

"Greed is not good." Edna thought about Ray.

"Everything in moderation." Russ repeated his mother's motto. Then couldn't help but point out, "For a couple of people who don't attend church, we're spouting platitudes like a couple of Sunday School teachers."

They both laughed.

Edna liked how Russ listened carefully to her and treated her with respect. *He understands me and thinks like I do. I could get used to relying on this man's company.*

CHAPTER TWENTY-SIX

MOVIE STAR MAKEOVER

"Edna, have you settled on your marquee name yet?" Maximilian was on the other side of the phone line.

"Hi, Max. Great to hear from you. What's up?"

"Well, m'dear, your film debut has been shown around the studio and everyone's in love with you. You jump off the screen and no one is even paying attention to Clark once you walk on. The movie's a bit of a dud, but your debut is incredible. Your chitlins line gets the biggest laugh of the whole movie."

"No. Really? Oh my gosh, Max. That's such good news. What's next?"

"Hannity knows we're simpatico and he asked me to phone you to forewarn you he wants to sign you to a five-year contract. He asked me what needs to be done, if anything, to improve your appearance. I told him you were perfect as you are, but he doesn't like your teeth in the close-ups from your original screen test, and he also says you need to learn California English."

"Getting rid of my Southern accent I can understand, but my teeth?"

"Yes. He wants you to have them all pulled and insists our studio dentist get you new uppers and lowers which will even out your smile. You'll get straight white teeth without the gap, which will photograph better in close-ups."

"Oh, my, Max. That's quite a commitment."

"I know, but anything worthwhile has a price."

"Well, I guess you're right. When do I come in to sign the contract?"

"His assistant will call you. Just a warning. You should probably get an agent or attorney to help you read and negotiate the contract. He and the studio attorneys can be terribly crafty and they will, of course, think of the studio's interests, not yours."

"Sure, Max. Do you know of anyone you can suggest?"

"I'll get a number or two for you. In the meantime, when can you make an appointment for your teeth? The sooner the better. It will take a few days to heal. I want you to be able to hit the floor running, or hit the screen smiling, so to speak."

"Max, let's get me able to eat and talk again first before running. You've really been helpful. What can I do to pay you back?"

"Remember me when you're a star. Keep that natural, fun-loving spirit of yours. The great ones stay humble and don't get big heads."

"I'll do my best, Mr. Maximilian. Oh, any ideas for a new name for me?"

"Spitfire LeMieux, Goose Creek Cathy, Chitlin' Babe?"

"Very classy, Max. I actually have a name in mind, 'Katherine King.'"

"Nice ring to it. That might do. Go get your teeth pulled."

"Okay, Max, thanks for the call."

"You're welcome, m'dear. Talk with you soon."

Edna hung up the phone and sighed. The apartment lobby was empty for a change. There was no one to share this news with. *A new name, new teeth, a new accent. How can I stay the same when so much needs to be changed already? This is almost too much, but as Max said, anything worthwhile has a price to pay. Except, not really. Many of life's best gifts are free: sunshine, air, water, the moon. Oh, well.*

I remember Hannity stating I would need to take dancing, singing and elocution lessons. Looks like my new career is beginning. There's so much to do. Better get upstairs, get a cigarette and a small bourbon. I've got a future to plan.

Edna was exuberant the next week at work. Word had spread about her upcoming movie contract and her fellow employees showered her with added respect, attention and good-natured ribbing.

"Hey, Miss Hoity-Toity, why're you still working at this joint?"

"Hey, movie star, how's it goin'?"

"Say why don't you give your job to someone who could use it."

Edna didn't reveal that she needed the money to live on, that for the Gable movie walk-on she was paid little more than a day's wages at Broadway. Until that contract was signed, Edna needed her job as much as the next person.

But the respect Edna saw in the eyes of employees that knew of her wonderful new opportunity was something she truly treasured.

Edna went to the studio dentist the next Wednesday on her day off from Broadway. He measured her mouth to prepare a new set of teeth to insert right after her natural teeth were removed. The dentist warned her that she may not feel like eating for a few days afterwards, and she should probably take at least two days off from work after her teeth were all pulled at next Wednesday's appointment.

The next day at work, Edna explained the situation and requested the following Thursday and Friday off from her usual shift. Her supervisor reluctantly agreed but with the proviso that she get him two tickets to the premiere of her upcoming movie. "You know, there are a lot of people who would love to have your job here," he told her.

Edna agreed to his demand although she wasn't even certain she would be invited to the premiere. *I'll find a way.* It was necessary to take the next step because tomorrow would only bring more obligations that would need to be fulfilled. *My life is speeding up.*

"I still like Katherine King. That has a nice ring to it."

Marie was in Edna's room helping her again brainstorm her marquee name. This time the need for a new name felt more urgent. Marie again admired the ruby red creamer with her mother's name engraved on it.

"I like it, too. And that name does sound solid, intelligent, appealing. It'll be hard at first to get used to answering to my mama's name, but, okay. That's it if the studio agrees. 'Katherine King.' That resonates with me. I could be Katie or Kate for short."

"Or Kathy."

"No, I knew a Kathy Mae back home in Texas. That's a bit too casual. Doesn't have a glamourous ring to it."

"When do you sign your contract with the studio?"

"In a couple of weeks they said, after the studio premiere. I sure wish I could get you and Eric tickets but they only gave me three and I have to give two to my boss for giving me a couple of days off for my teeth pulling."

"Oh, honey. We understand about the tickets. I sure wish I could be with you at the dentist's office, but I'll stop by after I get off of work and bring you some chicken soup. You aren't going to want much more than than I'm certain."

"Marie, the soup sounds good, but know that I'll be fine. I'm taking the streetcar there and I'm taking a cab back home afterwards."

"Good. Well, okay. Say, why don't you quit that department store job anyway? You're going to be a star, I just know it."

"Well, guess my practical nature won't let me give up a sure thing until the studio contract is signed and I'm earning a living. You know what it's like to be in fear of not having enough money to live on."

"Sure, honey. Many a time at the end of the month I've been living on free soup crackers and lemon water. You know I understand. Well, I've got to get back to my apartment. I'll see you tomorrow, Miss Katherine King."

Marie and Edna looked at each other and started to laugh.

Edna was in no condition to get back to work on Saturday. She was weak from not eating much since the dental procedure. The dentist had prescribed some pain pills but she refused to take them. She wanted to keep a clear head in case her attorney or the studio called. *If I stay home today and Sunday, I should be fine by Monday to get back to work. I'll call in sick today.*

Edna slowly walked herself downstairs to the lobby phone. Thank goodness only one tenant she hadn't seen before was in the lobby. She phoned her supervisor at Broadway and explained the situation and that she couldn't make it in today, but would be better by Monday and promised to be there.

"Sorry, Edna, but we can't have that. If you don't care about your job there are many, many people that would."

"You know I'm one of the hardest workers you have."

"I know you have been in the past, but now you're slacking off. We can't have any employee take off four days in a row no matter what the reason. Do you think you're special? How would that look to the other employees?"

"But I look and feel so terrible and haven't eaten in two days. My gums are still bleeding and there is gauze in my mouth, and --"

"That's not my problem. Either you get in here by 1:00 p.m. today when your shift starts or you're fired."

"I know I can't make it, so I guess that counts me out. But that counts you out on the premiere tickets."

"Fine. I've got my job to protect. Come in and give us the key to your locker and sign the employee termination papers within the next week. I'll have your last paycheck ready."

"Fine."

"Bye." He abruptly hung up on her.

What is his problem? Maybe I made a mistake by telling the other employees about my Gable movie role and the contract. Some people can be so darn envious sometimes.

Edna carefully climbed the stairs holding on to the handrail to steady her wobbly legs, then slowly walked down the hall to her tiny efficiency apartment. She entered and gently shut the door, then undressed and got back into bed.

CHAPTER TWENTY-SEVEN

THE LETTER AND THE MOVIE PREMIERE

By Monday morning, just as she had anticipated, Edna was beginning to feel like herself again. Marie had come by again Saturday night and Sunday and had brought her some more healing soup. Edna was regaining her strength and was now able to chew the soft vegetables and even some boiled chicken. Marie commiserated with Edna over her parting with Broadway Department Store. And, Edna at least had the luxury of now inviting Marie and Eric to the movie premiere since she now had the two extra tickets.

But Monday morning, even with her newly regained energy, Edna felt sad. She had loved working for first Dyas, then Broadway Department Store and now there was no where for her to go, no one who needed her today. But instead of wallowing in her self-pity as she had at times before, Edna consciously turned her thoughts to a more positive note. *Well, soon enough I'll be working again, after the premiere and contract's signed. I guess I can give myself a few days of rest and relaxation before starting my new career.*

In the few days before the premiere, Edna continued to heal, but she had too much time to think. She pondered and finally accepted the loss of her department store job.

With so much time for thought, one subject she hadn't completely dealt bothered her: *Ray and his cohorts' plan to destroy the streetcar system should be revealed. They shouldn't be permitted to get away with their scheme.*

One afternoon, she sat down with a pen and paper and decided to write to the Los Angeles Police Department. She knew her voice would be small against that of a big-wig like Ray, but she had to clear her conscience by doing the right thing.

She agonized over the wording for a couple of hours, until finally she completed a letter that she thought struck the right tone:

To Whom It May Concern:
I am a concerned citizen who has learned of facts
that point to a plot to destroy the Los Angeles Railway
System. The breakdowns, station explosions, and track van-

*dalism were planned by a group of highly-placed
citizens of the Los Angeles area and elsewhere in the
country. Those who have conspired to destroy the trolley
system are driven solely by a profit-motive and will stop
at nothing to achieve their end. This group wants to
increase sales of automobiles, gasoline, tires and related
products in the Los Angeles basin. They believe that the
quickest way to do so is by destroying the railway.*

*I know this sounds far-fetched, however, I have known an
individual who played a part in the recent fire at the
substation where two men died. In the past I
had conversations with that individual and others
which clearly revealed a plot to convince Los Angeles
area citizens they must buy automobiles.*

*I can not reveal the names of the people involved,
but if you look into the politicians and Railway Employees
who are driving new Cadillacs and trace where a few of
those cars came from it is my belief that you will be able
to discover the backers of the plan to destroy the Los
Angeles Railway System.*

Edna ended the letter by signing it, "Sincerely, A Concerned Citizen." She reviewed the letter carefully, and felt better after having completed it. *I can't give Ray's name. I cared too much about him. But the facts will implicate him. There's not much I can do about that. It was his choice to participate.*

Edna carefully folded the letter and placed it into an unsealed envelope. She slowly got up and walked over to the ruby red and cut-crystal creamer. She carefully placed the envelope into the one object she had remaining from her family. *I'll sleep on this, give it some time, and mail it if and when the timing feels right.*

The entire day of the movie premiere, Edna spent getting ready for that evening. She had examined her dress the day before to make certain it was completely clean, and without any hanging threads or drooping hem. She even tried it on to make certain the fit was precise. It was a sea foam green silk dress with a hand-embroidered top section, which Ray had purchased for her for one of their special evenings of dancing. The style was all the rage and would reveal her to be on the cutting edge of fashion at her first movie premiere.

By the time Marie and Eric knocked at her door at 5:00 p.m., Edna had adjusted and readjusted what she imagined to be stray hairs in her hairdo five times, and had glanced in the mirror at least ten times in the recent twenty minutes. She was more nervous than she had anticipated. Her mind realized she would be on the giant screen only briefly, no cause for worry, but her emotions were communicating separately with her stomach.

Marie, Eric and Edna arrived a block East of Grauman's Chinese Theatre at 5:45 sharp. On the side street they were to meet a valet who would drive the car in the automobile line-up to the front of the theatre and let them out on the red carpet. Since Edna was a bit player, she was to arrive at the red carpet at 6:00 p.m. even though the movie would not begin until 7:00 p.m. The crowds outside had been waiting for hours, and they would have an hour more to go before Clark Gable and his date arrived just before 7:00 p.m.

"Oh, Edna, isn't this exciting? Look at all those searchlights lighting up the sky, and the crowds." Marie was thrilled.

"I should have worn my sunglasses," Edna retorted. "It's brighter than daylight even though the sun's already set."

As their car approached the red carpet, Edna made certain she had her purse in her hand. *Now hold your chin up, stand tall, smile big, and sparkle.*

When the usher dressed in the red military jacket, black pill-box hat and black slacks opened her door, Edna emerged as gracefully and confidently as she knew how. The crowd, not knowing who she was, still let out exclamations and cheers. Their oohs and ahs were loud enough for Edna to hear over the traffic noise and the press photographers yelling, "Look this way. Over here."

She had been told by the studio that she would have a brief radio interview with Louella Parsons at the microphone. She was to tell the listening audience simply that she had a part in the movie and was thrilled to be here tonight at this wonderful premiere. Nothing more; nothing less. Then she would enter the theatre and the three tickets would be waiting for her inside.

The Photographers' flashes were blinding, but she posed and smiled as her modeling background had taught her, consciously working at acting naturally.

"What's your name"?

"Are you in the movie?"

"What's Clark Gable really like?"

Questions were shouted from the press and the public, from all sides, but after posing for a few moments as she had been instructed, she continued on to the microphone where Louella Parsons was standing.

"Hello, my dear. You are the new ingenue Katherine King; isn't that right?"

"Well, ah, yes." Edna was caught a bit off guard at the use of her new name. She had given the studio her name suggestion but hadn't been told they would use it for this movie and the publicity surrounding it.

"I hear from inside sources that you may be the new 'it' girl. What do you think about that?"

"Little old me?" Edna's fear at going off script had her reverting to her comfortable Southern roots.

"Oh, a Southern Gal. How charming." Louella Parsons was speaking directly into the microphone that Edna had been told was being broadcast not only to the crowd but to Louella Parsons' thousands of radio fans.

Edna struggled to get back on script without being rude to Miss Parsons. "I just have a little walk-in part in this movie, and I'm absolutely thrilled to be here tonight. Everyone should go see Mr. Clark Gable in this picture at their earliest convenience."

"Well, thank you, Katherine King." Louella Parsons gave Edna the cue to move on, and as Edna walked into the theater she heard Miss Parsons say into the microphone, "There my movie audience goes a young woman with charm and confidence. You'll see a lot of her in the future I wager."

Edna smiled to herself. *I passed that test.* She walked inside the lobby entrance and saw Marie and Eric standing there waiting for her.

"Edna, we told them we were with you and got the tickets already. This nice young man is going to show us to our seats. You were terrific out there. Wow, Louella Parsons. That's so exciting. I bet you'll be in her movie column now. You made quite a positive impression." Marie was more bubbly than Edna had ever seen her.

"I hope so. Let's go see where we're seated."

"Yes, ma'am," the eager young man led them forward towards the middle orchestra doors. They were placed in seats about three quarters of the way back in the center section of the orchestra, on the aisle.

"Couldn't be more perfect. Thank you," said Edna.

"You're welcome."

Edna let Eric have the aisle seat, and Marie sat in the middle. They were all settled and started to look around the audience. The orchestra section was already almost full.

"I thought we were going to be some of the first ones here, but other guests have obviously arrived before us," Edna commented to Marie and Eric.

"I guess that's how premieres work," Eric replied.

"Yes," agreed Marie.

All three of them were novices in this arena. None had attended a premiere of a major motion picture before, and particularly not in Hollywood at the Grauman's Chinese Theatre.

"This is the big time," Eric commented.

"Yes," agreed Marie.

"Look, there's Mary Pickford. I told you about the time Ray took me to her house. She was helpful in starting my career. She called the studio and their photographer on my behalf. I should tell her hello and thanks." Edna was about to get up when she noticed that Ray was sitting in the same row as Mary, only a couple of seats away from her.

"What's the matter?" Marie noticed Edna's hesitancy.

"Ray's over there sitting with her group. I won't approach her now. Maybe at the party later. I do want to thank her, but just don't want to deal with Ray tonight."

"Are you hungry? Shall I go get us some snacks, ladies?" Eric was offering.

"Not for me, Eric. Thanks." Edna didn't want to mess up her make-up and was willing to wait until the after-movie party. "I ate a late lunch. Besides my stomach is just too nervous to eat anything right now."

"I'm fine, too, honey," Marie told Eric. "Thanks. But you go if you want something."

"No, that's okay." Eric stayed seated.

Edna, Marie and Eric exchanged nervous small talk along with the rest of the audience. Edna felt the same palpable excitement in the theater tonight that she had felt when she saw *The Jazz Singer* in Houston. But, as Edna looked around the audience, she noticed how different this Hollywood premiere audience was. Everyone was dressed like a movie star. The women all wore beautiful gowns or dresses, and the men wore dressy suits or tuxedos. It was an astounding congregation of attractive people. And yet they also were exuding excitement and anticipation.

Sophisticated Hollywood people feel the same emotions as the average Joe, Edna thought to herself. *But these types don't always show it.* Edna had never thought quite in those terms before. *This premiere is exciting for them, too.*

"What an evening this is, Edna. I'll remember this for the rest of my life," Marie had leaned over to tell Edna. Just then the crowd's sound decibels increased. Edna and Marie looked in the direction of where faces had focused.

"It's Clark. Here he comes," said Edna as she watched the three ushers guiding the tall handsome tuxedoed man and his entourage to their roped-off section close to the front.

As Clark Gable and his beautiful platinum blonde date passed by their row, Clark leaned over to Edna and said, "Hey, Gorgeous. Good to see ya."

"Hi, Clark," was all Edna could muster before he passed by.

She looked for Hannity in the group following Clark but figured he must already be seated. Or, perhaps the studio head didn't take time off from business to attend these types of functions.

Edna hadn't seen Maximilian tonight either and wondered if she would see him at the after party. They hadn't talked in a week or so.

At exactly seven o'clock, the house lights lowered, the beautiful brocade gold curtain opened and the audience began to applaud. *This is it*, thought Edna. *My movie debut.*

CHAPTER TWENTY-EIGHT

A FALLING STAR

When Edna first walked across that huge screen there were whistles from men in the Grauman's audience. Her gigantic screen size she found shocking and embarrassing. *It's hard to see yourself that large. It's not real.* But she found herself fascinated by what looked to be a huge, vibrant, glamorous young woman in a maid's costume.

As she said her line about "Not those ...", dumped the chitlins in Gable's lap, and turned to walk away from a surprised Clark Gable, the audience burst out in loud laughter, followed by "you tell him" and other comments from the audience.

The audience gave Edna the biggest laugh of the entire movie, which, unfortunately was not as good overall as the rest of Clark's earlier films. Yet, Edna felt satisfied, her heart filled with a warm, loving feeling towards the audience and life in general. How could a first performance be appreciated any more?

At the party across the street at the Hotel Roosevelt, Edna, Eric and Marie had a nice table. When Clark and his gang walked by, Clark leaned over to Edna, kissed her on the cheek and whispered "You're going to be a star, young lady." During dinner, attendees continued to interrupt their meal by coming over and complimenting her on her performance. It was a heady experience.

"May I have your autograph" was asked multiple times during dinner. Edna spontaneously smiled at each request, and conscientiously signed "Katherine King" in her best penmanship across the pages of the various autograph albums, menus, napkins, and other items that were presented to her.

Marie at one point leaned over and kidded her, "Oh, Miss King, I think you're fabulous. Please, could I inconvenience you by asking you to sign my glove?"

Eric, Marie and Edna all laughed.

When the band began to play, Edna asked Eric and Marie if it would be okay with them if they left. "It's been a long day, and after all the excitement of planning for this evening, I'd really like to get a good night's sleep. Do you mind?"

"Of course not," Marie agreed.

"Eric, why don't you go get your car and Edna and I will meet you out in front of the hotel in fifteen minutes?"

"Sure." Eric went off to get the automobile in response to Marie's request, and the two women sat there talking.

Marie and Edna were still talking ten minutes later but about to leave when Ray walked up to their table. Edna did not see him coming.

"Katherine King, may I have your autograph?" Ray began.

Edna looked up to see him standing, hovering above her. She felt her stomach get queasy. "Ray, hello. You caught me off guard."

"Well, you don't have to be on guard against me, do you?"

"Ray, you know how I feel. I'm sorry." Edna tried to sound as casual and light as possible. *No use causing unnecessary drama.*

"You were wonderful in the movie. The highlight." Ray took another step closer.

"Well, thank you, Ray," Edna said, politely fighting her instinct to get up and leave.

"Edna, I'd like to --"

Edna turned to Marie and with urgency stated, "Eric will be waiting for us."

"Yes," Marie agreed.

The two women stood up to leave, and as they did, Ray's large right hand grabbed Edna by her left forearm. "Don't go. Let me have one dance with you before you leave."

"I'm sorry, Ray, but Eric will be waiting. Thank you for asking." Edna tried to say the words lightly and politely but noticed the curtness in her own voice.

"Oh, come on, sweetheart. You owe me a dance." Ray was persistent and did not let go of her forearm.

"Ray, I don't believe I owe you one single solitary thing. Good night."

Edna, surprised by her own forcefulness, abruptly yanked her elbow back, away from his grasp, took Marie by the hand and walked quickly towards the door. Edna did not think Ray would start a scene in front of tonight's crowd, with Edna the hit of the night. His reputation was too important to him. She was right. He remained standing there as the two ladies left the ballroom and walked out to the front of the hotel.

"That was close," said Edna as they stood just a minute waiting for Eric's car to pull up.

"It was."

"I thought he might start something right there."

"Me too. Well, some people find it very hard to let go when a relationship ends. Plus you're quite the catch now, Edna -- or should I start calling you Katherine?"

"Might as well. I should get used to the new name otherwise people will be calling me and I'll ignore them thinking they've got the wrong person."

The two ladies laughed and climbed into Eric's car. All in all, it had been a glorious evening in Hollywood.

Edna was thrilled to see language in movie reviews and Hollywood columns over the next few days stating that her appearance was the "best and brightest moment" in an otherwise "pedestrian movie." They also carved out an exception for Clark in various glowing phrases to the effect that "all women love to gaze at Mr. Gable even if the words he's scripted to say are dull and pedantic."

Even Louella Parsons had backhanded praise for Edna's performance: "Once she weasels out of that 'lil 'ole Southern accent, Miss Katherine King will be one of the hottest new stars in Hollywood. Mark my words."

Edna had made an impression on the viewing audience, one that would help her with her contract negotiations and signing. She spent some time cutting out all the newspaper and magazine articles she had either bought or been given by friends from the department store or the apartment building.

One late afternoon as she was pasting some articles into the new scrapbook that Marie and Eric had given her as a thank-you gift for the premiere evening, she heard a knock at the door. When she opened it she saw Russ standing there, obviously in a hurry.

"Hey, movie star, you've got a phone call from a fan, says his name is Maximilian."

"Oh, thanks, Russ."

"Hurry up. I'll walk you down there. I was just leaving. I'm late for an appointment."

Edna quickly closed her door and walked with Russ down the hall and steps.

"I haven't seen you in a while."

"Well, I've been out of town. How about you. Life treating you well?"

"Too well. Can't believe my good luck recently."

"I know. I've heard. Say how about Friday night? Dinner? We can catch up."

"Sounds good, Russ. I'd like that."

"Okay. I'll be at your door at seven. See you then," Russ said as he continued past the phone, through the lobby and out the front door.

Edna gathered her thoughts and picked up the dangling receiver. "You still there, Max?"

"Edna, darling. I missed you at the premiere. Saw you in the audience and at the party from afar, but every time I wanted to come talk with you a crowd of ardent fans was seeking your ink scribble on paper."

"That was something, wasn't it? I've never had so much attention. I didn't spot you in the crowd."

"Well, we makeover artists are relegated to side and back tables. In the studio executives' eyes we just aren't worth much. From their perspective, it's all about them and their ideas, and we only carry out what they say."

"Max, you're sounding like a bit of a victim. You're not usually so down. Why the gloom?"

"My Southern Belle, I'm the messenger of bad news. Now don't kill the messenger."

"Maximilian, just spill it. What?"

"I've heard from a few horses' mouths that you're not coming to work for us or any studio. Your contact negotiations have been killed, as well as any opportunity at any other studios."

"Oh, c'mon, Max. What's the punch line?"

"Sweetheart, I'm serious." Max paused and let the silence linger in the air until he could stand it no longer.

"Are you still there?"

"Yes. Yes, I am." Edna's voice was lower, slower, weaker, as if she did not have enough air to breathe.

"Honey, I wanted to let you know before someone else dealt the blow. It's hard for me to do this, but, please, I want you to know I'm on your side."

Edna regathered her thoughts. "Well, what does the rumor mill say is the reason for this about face?"

"The rumor is that Ray Gibson and Hannity are in business together. Your old beau told Hannity in no uncertain terms that he doesn't want you to be made a star or even to have a contract. If he can't have you, then neither can the public."

"Oh, Max, no." Edna was again without words. It was hard for her to get a breath. *I can't believe this is happening.*

"I'm so sorry, dear. You have what it takes, but once you're black-balled in this town, you can never get into the country club. It's some unwritten law of the tribe. Don't quite understand it but I've seen it happen on a couple of occasions before. It's not your fault. It's the way things are done in Hollywood. It's just business."

Edna felt suddenly sick to her stomach. *There's that phrase again, 'It's just business.'*

"Max, I have to go. Sorry. Talk with you soon. Thanks for the information."

"Okay, darling. Well --"

Edna hung up the phone quickly before he got out another ridiculous phrase. She looked around and saw no one in the lobby. Just as well. She slowly walked up the stairs and down the hall, noting how ragged the carpet was looking in certain spots.

She opened her door, walked into her apartment, went over and sat in her chair. *I have to think. Oh, God, give me strength.*

CHAPTER TWENTY-NINE

FIRE AND DESIRE

Ray called Friday afternoon. Edna refused to take the call, but a tenant took the time to write the message from Ray down precisely as he asked. The tenant slipped the piece of paper under Edna's door.

"I can make your happiness happen. If you want to be a star, give me a chance. Yours always, Ray."

After Edna read the note, she tore it into the smallest pieces she could manage then precisely and methodically placed the scraps of paper into an ashtray forming a tiny pyramid shape. She then took the gold lighter that she had bought for Ray and looked intently at the engraving, "Forever and a Day." Then she flicked the lighter lid open, and carefully lit the tiny bonfire.

Edna watched as sparks flew from the small fire. It was a hypnotic site. When the last of the burning embers converted from a reddish orange to black soot, she slowly stood up, picked up the ashtray, and took it over to the wastebasket where she carefully emptied its contents.

She then walked to her ruby red creamer and took the envelope from there. She removed the letter she had written to the authorities from the envelope, and carefully re-read it, examining each word for ambiguity or misconstrued content. She finally determined it said exactly what she wanted it to say. Then she double-checked to confirm the address she had obtained for the Los Angeles Police Department was written correctly on the front of the envelope. The letter was then very gently refolded and placed back into the envelope.

Edna went to her small side-table drawer, took out one first class postage stamp, licked it and placed it straight and even with the upper right hand corner of the envelope. Then she licked the envelope and sealed it, careful to smooth out the envelope's back seal so that no ripples remained.

Edna then took the stamped envelope and walked down to the corner mailbox where she placed the envelope into the box.

Edna again spent hours for a few days feeling somewhat helpless and victimized. Marie tried to convince her to try for a movie career at another studio, but Hannity and Ray had even gotten to Edna's attorney, and Edna was told by him that other studios would be ordered to one by one figuratively slam the door in her face.

"Well, why don't you get Clark Gable to help you," Marie had suggested. But Edna knew that even Clark's charm and influence could not persuade the movie studio bosses to do something they thought was bad for their business interests.

Ray had told her months ago he counseled Hannity to sell Los Angeles Railway stock and buy Standard Motors and related companies to bolster the studio financials. If Ray prospered, so would Hannity and Nation Studio.

Edna had learned some hard lessons. The world valued and supported the strong and the capable. The survival of the fittest created a society where the weak and the useless were passed by, or worse, trampled upon. Edna had relearned that lesson again and again, and this time she was determined to not stay down for long.

Poor me. Feeling sorry for myself because I won't be a movie star. How can I complain about that? I have food, and I have a roof over my head. There's a couple months of rent money left. I'm being silly. I can't change others, only myself. Get up and dust yourself off.

What worried her most was obtaining a new job in this economy. But with her renewed attitude the ideas started to come. *I was good at math in school; maybe I can apply as a bank teller. I like people; I could be a hostess in a restaurant. I worked in a slaughterhouse; if I have to, I could do that again.*

She could have the life she wanted. *I guess I've been looking in the wrong direction. It's not the respect of others I really want, it's my own respect and I've never lost that. I've always done the best I could. I have self respect, and the rest is just a matter of action and time.*

This Friday night, Earl Carroll's was buzzing. Russ and Edna had one of the best tables in the house. The waiter had just brought them their third martini, and they were fully enjoying the evening. Marvelous how a martini could blot out depressing thoughts. Earl Carroll's production had revolving stages that floated in water. The stages would turn 180 degrees periodically, and then turn back to reveal the beautiful showgirls in another spectacular change of costume.

"I saw your movie. Quite a stunning impression you make on that big screen."

"Thanks. My career is short-lived. That's my last hurrah in the movie business."

"Why's that? You're a natural."

"Oh, I don't know. It just isn't my idea of a good life." Edna could not bear to get into the heaviness of what had happened when she was finally really enjoying herself again.

"You know, I tried my hand in the movies once, too." Russ calmly told her.

"Oh?"

"Yes. It was in a silent film, a crowd scene. I was an extra in a group that threw oranges at some keystone-type cops. Boy, all that sitting and waiting and sitting and waiting sure got to me. Plus another extra with bum aim hit me hard in the back of the head. Not the easiest of jobs."

"Well, then you understand. Movie work isn't as glamorous as the audience fantasizes."

"Right. It's darn hard work. Heck, I can have as much fun as any movie star can in my time off of work. But I can sure do without those tedious hours, the 5:00 a.m. rising and all the waiting. And, even worse, the public thinking they know you and own a piece of you just because they've seen your picture enlarged, moving up there on that big screen."

"Yes, bugging you for autographs, tearing at your clothes because they think they'll somehow get a bit of fame themselves if they touch you." Edna and Russ both started laughing. They thought alike. Fame was not important to either one of them. They were both more concerned with the real, the true, the values that most people lived by.

"Well, Miss retired movie starlet, I guess you're the most important woman in my life right now," Russ said out of the blue.

The remark surprised Edna, but she was also excited by it. *He really does care about me. I'm glad. I really like him, too.*

The nightclub was dark except for the brightly lit stage performance, and the tips of patrons' cigarettes glowing like fireflies throughout the large room. Edna rested her cigarette holder and cigarette on the ashtray, then absentmindedly pulled her toothpick of olives out of the martini and began to eat them. Something sharp hit her teeth. *Oh, oh. That's all I need.* This was not the moment to break one of her new studio teeth. She carefully removed the olive toothpick from her mouth and held it close to her eyes. Around one of the olives was a diamond ring with four large diamonds in a row.

"A ring in a cocktail. Does that make it a cocktail ring?" Edna looked over at Russ who was calmly smiling at her.

"How about a wedding ring? Shall we tie the knot?" Russ asked casually.

Edna took the diamond band and placed it on her left ring finger. "It fits perfectly. How did you know my size?"

"I asked Marie."

This is so sudden, but I would be a fool to turn down this terrific man.

"We can drive to Vegas after the show, get married, and be back for my work on Monday. What do you say?"

"Well, I don't have any extra clothes or ..."

"We can buy what you need in Vegas."

Edna drank half of her third martini in one large sip. It was all happening so fast, but she had liked and trusted Russ from the very beginning. "Well, I guess I'm game if you are. Okay. Why not. Let's do it." She turned and gave Russ a big hug and a quick kiss. *What would be gained by waiting?*

The couple ate some of their dinner entrees, but Edna was too excited to eat much. She hadn't anticipated Russ proposing although the possibility of their eventually marrying had not completely escaped her. They got along so well.

Russ was honest, and was not the type of man to put power or money ahead of people. Yet he made a good living. He owned a beach house in Manhattan Beach and was financially comfortable. Edna felt emotionally at ease with him. She genuinely liked and respected him. *I won't have to face life's struggles by myself anymore. I'm marrying this wonderful man who shares my values.*

As Edna admired the diamond ring in the car on the way to Vegas, she wished she could freeze in time the sense of anticipation, love and happiness she felt right then. Moments like this were meant to be memorized, to be savored, and treasured. *Good things come to us each in their own time. This is what life is about, belonging, caring, mutual respect. I'm at home once more.*

PART III

MANHATTAN BEACH,
CALIFORNIA 1943

CHAPTER THIRTY

LIFE'S A BEACH

World War II compelled a redirection of American business. Large corporations worked to capacity fulfilling vital government contracts. As profits grew, the auto industry scheme to replace trolley car systems with automobiles moved from short to long-term priority.

Attrition would now suffice. Don't repair or renew the trolley cars. Let service slack. Don't insist upon good management yet continue to raise fares.

Russ was still working for the rubber company out of New Jersey, but the United States rubber "Czar," had usurped the industry. Now rubber supply was directed first towards production of war-time vehicle tires.

Edna never told Russ what she knew about Ray and his business manipulations. She had never received a reply from the police, nor had she read about the scandal in the news. The past was best kept in the past.

In the security of her marriage with Russ, Edna felt safe to fully express and deal with her feelings, then quickly get over them and move forward. Being happy with her present life, she more easily ignored painful past events.

Edna loved married life. Russ asked her to be a full-time housewife like most American women, and she was happy to comply. They hoped to have a child but that had not yet occurred. Recently she and Russ had been discussing the possibility of adoption.

They moved down to the Manhattan Beach house soon after marriage and Russ commuted to work downtown. Their house was a block from the beach and the property covered half a city block. There was a large front yard where they entertained. The beach cities were full of open, fun-loving people who enjoyed having a good time. Couples would come over and play cards, have a few drinks, listen to music and dance. It was quite a social atmosphere.

Edna loved decorating the house. She and Russ had put together a tropical room that contained a bamboo bar, with a dried frond roof overhang. On the many nights when all the blinds had to be drawn for wartime safety, that room downstairs was where everyone congregated. It was situated so that the lights could be left on without fear of Japanese submarines or planes spotting light.

Edna enjoyed cooking dinner for Russ when he came home from work. She would fix martinis and have a glass chilled for him, awaiting his arrival. They would sit and discuss the day, and Russ would relax before dinnertime. After they caught up, he would sit in his easy chair and read the evening newspaper to keep up with the current events of the day, and the war campaigns.

This sunny Wednesday, all of Edna's household chores had been completed early, and she was feeling restless. She decided to walk over to the soda shop and grab an ice cream soda, and talk with Bill, the soda jerk.

It was such a beautiful Manhattan Beach day. Edna enjoyed the fresh air and sunshine as she walked the few steps up to the brick soda shop on Highland Avenue. When she entered, Bill greeted her with, "Hi, Edna. A chocolate soda for you?"

As she sat down at an empty counter stool, she answered, "Yes, Bill. Sounds good."

A young, sandy-blonde woman seated two stools away was eating what looked to be a bacon, lettuce and tomato sandwich. She started a conversation. "You must come here a lot. He knows your name."

"Yes. I'm here whenever I get the chance, and crave something sweet."

"That's what I should have had, a chocolate soda. I didn't think of that." Edna looked closer at the young woman who appeared to be somewhere between 16 and 25. It was difficult to decipher her age. Edna thought she seemed sweet. She was somewhat soft-spoken, maybe shy.

"Back home in Houston when I was a child we had a wonderful soda shop, and I've loved chocolate sodas since then. They make darn good sodas here, too."

"Oh, you're from Texas. I thought I heard a slight Southern twang, but I wasn't sure."

"A few years back, I took a night school course to try and tone down the drawl. People used to laugh at the way I'd say certain words like 'co-in' and 'y'all.' But whenever I get excited or tired, the 'y'alls' and 'co-ins' reappear."

"I know how that is. I'm trying to learn to speak well. When I concentrate, I can do it just fine, but, the minute I let down my guard, my focus, I fall into my old patterns and habits of speaking. Voice pitch and tone are very important according to my vocal coach."

"Oh, you're studying voice?"

"Well, some times. When I get some extra money. I'm doing some modeling. I'd like to take acting lessons. My boyfriend doesn't like me modeling and doesn't like me taking voice or acting lessons. He says I'm putting on airs and thinks I'm too full of myself when I practice voice."

Bill brought over the chocolate soda. "Here you go, Edna."

"Thanks, Bill."

"Enjoy," said Bill, and went off to help a new customer.

"Your name is Edna? I'm Norma, Norma Jeane."

"Nice to meet you, Norma Jeane. Do you live around here?"

"No. Well, in the Los Angeles area, yes. I was born and raised in the Los Angeles area. But, mainly inland. I like to come down to the beach when I can. It makes me feel so free. This is a day off. I needed to get away and think some, plan what to do. I live in Hawthorne now, a few miles from here."

"Oh, yes. That's close. Just inland."

"Yes."

"My husband, Russ, and I live nearby, on 4th."

"Oh, how nice. I just love it down here. The people are so friendly and you can't beat these beautiful, sunny beach days."

"Yes. It's a lot of fun. A terrific group lives down here by the beach. I lived some time in downtown Los Angeles, and this area is so much less formal and class conscious than in the city."

"Yes," Norma agreed. "I'd sure love to live down here. The air's so fresh from that ocean breeze. And, walking on the beach makes me feel like my soul can take off flying."

Edna kept her thoughts to herself. *This young woman's attractive, interesting, quite creative in an odd, artistic way.*

"Say, we're having people over this weekend for a get-together. Russ loves to barbecue. Why don't you and your boyfriend join us? The more the merrier. It will be Sunday afternoon. People just do what they want. We have a few cocktails, play cards, sunbathe, listen to music."

"Oh, how nice of you. I don't drink, though, but it would be fun to get together and meet some other couples, especially if they're as nice as you."

"Well, some of our friends are a little older. But, I get along with and like people of all ages. I think you and your boyfriend would have a nice time."

"Well, I'll ask Jimmy and see what he says. I'd sure like to come. He's sometimes a bit anti-social. Is there a telephone number where I can call you and let you know?"

"Sure." Edna took out a pad of paper and pencil from her purse and wrote down the number for Norma. "Why don't you write down where you can be reached, too, just in case."

"Oh, I'll call you," Norma offered. "I promise. One way or the other. The people I live with, I don't always want them knowing my business."

"I understand. Back in Houston I used to live with my dad's brother and his wife. My aunt wanted to know every place I went and every person I saw. Then she'd accuse me of doing all sorts of things I'd never even think of doing. Sometimes it's smarter to keep your business to yourself."

"Yes," offered Norma. "It's just that certain people can be so controlling and want to know where you are at any given second. It's hard to live like that. It makes me feel like a caged animal. I need to be free, to feel free to be me."

"Yes, I can sure understand." Edna decided to change the subject as she continued to sip on her chocolate soda.

"What kind of modeling have you done?"

"Oh, so far, I've done mostly photographic modeling. I did some photo shoots on the beach in Malibu the other day. And, I've done some poses for calendars and for advertising."

"Oh, how fun. When I used to work for Dyas, then Broadway Department Store, I did runway modeling for the fashion shows. I enjoyed it and sure learned about fashion. In fact, one of the gals I modeled with there will be at the house this weekend. You'd like her. Real nice woman. Very exotic looking. She was in a pin-up calendar for service men."

"Oh, yes. That's what I want to do."

"Her coloring is the exact opposite of yours, dark black hair, dark brown eyes."

"Oh. One of the photographers I've worked with said I would look better as a platinum blond, and so did one of my girlfriends. What do you think?" Norma asked.

"You'd look wonderful as a platinum blond. I've changed my hair color a few times, but haven't tried that yet. I love Harlow's hair color. Did you see her in the movie, 'Platinum Blond'?"

"Oh, yes. I loved that movie. And did you see Harlow in 'Hold Your Man' with Clark Gable? She's terrific. And I love Clark Gable. He's so strong. So masculine."

"Yes, I saw that movie. I love Gable, too. He's got a terrific smile, and those dimples. I've met him. He's even more handsome in person. Tall, manly, charming."

"I think I've seen almost every movie he's made. I sometimes pretend he's my father," Norma offered.

Guess she missed the one movie I was in. Good.

"Well, don't tell my husband, but I sometimes fantasize about Clark Gable, too, but not that he's my father. He's quite the man. I loved him in 'Gone With The Wind.' It's no wonder so many women adore him."

"Yes," Norma agreed.

Both women grew quiet in their thoughts about Gable. Edna thought about how Clark Gable had stepped up and tried to get her a movie contract with another studio when Nation Studio wouldn't sign her. *He tried but I was black-balled.*

"Well, my soda's gone," said Edna. "I'd better get walking home and finish preparing for dinner. It's been nice talking with you, honey. Now, don't forget, I want you to come over and spend an afternoon with us. You'll enjoy it. Give me a call and let me know." Edna got up and started to leave.

"Yes, Edna. I'll call after I talk with Jimmy. It was nice meeting you," Norma said.

"Nice to have met you. Bye, Bill. Thanks."

"Bye, Edna."

Edna left the soda shop and headed towards home. The sunlight glistened and bounced on the ocean surface. *Norma is sure a sweet young girl*, thought Edna. *I hope she calls. It would be nice to have her over.*

Edna loved to meet new people and expand their social circle. Russ so often invited people over for business purposes, but Edna liked to have a variety of people over. Every person had a story, and most people were fascinating in one way or another once you got beneath the surface.

It was three weeks before Edna received a telephone call from Norma. She had almost given up on the young woman.

"Hello, Edna?"

"Yes."

"This is Norma, the girl you met at the soda shop in Manhattan Beach about three weeks ago," Norma offered.

"Oh, yes. How are you?" Edna responded. "I thought you'd lost my number."

"Well, it's not that. It's just that it was hard to get around to talking to Jimmy about coming to visit you. He has been busy and so have I. Is the offer still open to come over some time?"

"Well, sure. Actually this weekend we're having another get-together. My model friend I told you about will be over again, and so will my dear friend, Marie. Also, the Berkeys, who live near us. How about Sunday at 1:00? We're going to barbecue again. You and your boyfriend are welcome to join us."

"Oh, gosh, thank you. Yes, I would like that very much. Can we bring anything?"

"Just yourselves, and a bathing suit if you want to sunbathe. We all dress in casual beachwear."

"Sounds good. What's your address?"

Edna gave Norma the address, they said their goodbyes, and Edna hung up the telephone. *That was a surprise. Great. The more the merrier.*

Sunday was another one of those gloriously perfect beach days. Anne and Chuck Davis, a couple that managed the Manhattan Beach Hotel on Marine Avenue, came over at 11:00 a.m. Anne would help Edna get the hors d'oeuvres and side dishes ready, while Chuck helped Russ set up the bar area and the barbecue.

Anne and Chuck were from New Orleans where Anne had been a jazz singer in a band in which Chuck played the drums. They had lived in California about five years and had recently been spending a lot of time with Edna and Russ. Anne was exuberant and creative, and had nicknamed Edna "Rusty," because of Edna's red hair; plus she liked the combo of "Russ and Rusty." Edna kind of liked the sound of it, too, and did not discourage the nickname. The moniker stuck with their beach friends.

Today, after Anne had a few drinks, maybe Edna could coax her to sing. Anne and Chuck were staunch Catholics and had already been to mass this morning before coming over. They never missed Sunday mass and never ate meat on Fridays.

By one o'clock, everything was prepared and ready as the other guests started arriving. Daphne, the model friend of Edna's, was the first to arrive. Although in the past she had arrived with a date, today she had arrived alone. She wore her bathing suit under a sun dress and planned to sunbathe, to achieve that healthy, "lady of leisure" look that all Southern Californian's strove to maintain.

Edna showed Daphne where the chaise lounges were placed today, and had Russ make her a cocktail.

Next to arrive were the Berkeys who owned a large two-story house down the street that covered a full city block. They were an older distinguished couple, and Edna just adored them. Jessie Berkey had helped Edna learn to make certain casserole dishes that Russ liked. Milt, her husband, was a retired CEO but still enjoyed conversing with Russ about the business world and real estate matters. The two couples got together often, and played cards, gin rummy, canasta, or poker. The Berkeys wanted Edna to learn bridge, but she had not yet taken up that gauntlet. Edna loved gin rummy and dominos, so she tried to keep the games steered in that direction. She was good at both.

Today the Berkeys brought over a bottle of expensive Scotch for Russ' bar, and Russ opened it and poured them each a glass of their scotch, over ice.

By 1:15, all invited guests but Norma and her boyfriend were there. The conversation was lively as everyone was greeting each other and having their first cocktail. It was a larger group than usual today. Marie had arrived with Eric, who was still her finance after many, many years of dating. Edna was convinced he needed some persuasion to finally tie the knot after all these years, and asked Russ to talk with him at some point in the afternoon about marriage. Russ, although reluctant to get involved in other's personal lives, finally agreed with Edna -- she could be very persuasive -- that he would do so.

Around 2:00 Edna answered the door to find a platinum blonde Norma and her boyfriend. Edna almost didn't recognize her.

"Oh, look at you. I love your hair. So glad you could make it." Edna had given up on them as a no show.

"Come on in. The others are already a couple of cocktails ahead of you. Grab a drink, have some hors d'oeuvres. The barbecue will be served at 3:00."

"Thank you. Edna, this is Jim Dougherty. We just got married about a week ago."

"Well, how wonderful for you. Mr. and Mrs. Dougherty, it is a pleasure to have you both over. Glad you could make it today. Norma, let me introduce you to Daphne, my friend from Broadway Hollywood I told you about. Jim, why don't you go grab your drinks from my husband, Russ, the tanned gentleman over behind the bar, wearing that yacht captain's hat."

"Sure," said Jim, and headed over to where Russ was.

Edna took Norma by the hand and took her over to the shaded table where Daphne was now seated. "Daphne, this is Norma Jeane Dougherty. She's done some modeling also, photographic. She's interested in doing a calendar."

"A pleasure to meet you," said Daphne. "Here, dear, sit down and talk with me for a while."

"Oh, but my husband, Jim, is over there." Norma offered somewhat shyly.

"He'll find you. Tell me about your modeling assignments. I'm interested in what you've done."

Edna left the two women to get acquainted and walked over to where Ann was sitting quietly with her head tilted upwards and her eyes closed, getting some sun on her face.

"Hey, brownie, you're getting awfully dark. How about singing us a tune?"

"Oh, Rusty. Not yet. I'm soaking in these healthy rays that we can't get over at our place. The hotel patrons don't like to see the managers lounging around in the sun. Let me take advantage of this marvelous weather a little bit longer."

"Okay. I want you to enjoy yourself."

Edna walked off, satisfied that Ann was doing just what Ann wanted to do. The radio could provide background music for now. She went over and turned the radio up a little. Some upbeat music was playing. Berl Olswanger and his orchestra were playing a catchy arrangement. Edna went over to the bar where Russ, Chuck and Milt Berkey were heatedly discussing baseball. Edna took Russ's hand and pulled him towards her. "Excuse me, gentlemen, but I need to borrow Russ for a moment."

"Dance with me, honey," Edna said to Russ as she pulled him away. The two started dancing right there on the brick patio by the side of the bar. "How is everything going, sweetheart?" Edna inquired as Russ gracefully maneuvered her around.

"Great. Having a lot of fun. How about you?" Russ inquired.

"Same thing. Did you meet the young girl and her husband I told you about?"

"Yes, I met Jim. He got a beer, and he took her -- what's her name --"

"Norma --"

"He took Norma over a seltzer water with ice. Who wouldn't notice that beautiful platinum blond hair. She's gorgeous. Introduce me."

"Oh, Russ. She's just a child."

"I know. Her husband told me she's not even old enough to drink. But, such a pretty young woman."

"Oh, you. Concentrate on this dance with me right now, if you would, please. I could use some of your attention if just for this moment. I'll introduce you later."

"Sure, honey." Russ loved teasing Edna. She always took the bait. It was fun to see how she would get her ire up over the smallest things. He could get a rise out of her without even trying hard.

"Russ, why is that tiki over there? I put it in the other corner." Edna suddenly asked. The song was ending and they were both walking back towards the outside bar.

"You each owe me a quarter, Chuck and Milt." Russ said.

Then to Edna, "Honey, tell them what you just said."

"I just asked Russ why the tiki was over in the right corner when I had put it over in the left."

Chuck, Milt and Russ all burst out laughing. "See, guys, I told you she notices every little thing. Sometimes I'll change the angle of one of the knick-knacks we have on the shelf in the inside bar area. She'll notice it immediately and demand it be put back like it was. This woman has an uncanny ability to remember where objects are and exactly how they're placed."

"Gee, I'm glad Ann doesn't have that sort of eagle eye, Edna. I'd be in big trouble the way I knock things around and get things disorganized in our small unit."

"Okay, Russ. Here's your quarter," Milt handed over his part of the bet, and Chuck reached into his pocket and then contributed his.

"See, honey, you're a winner. You're making me money just by being yourself."

Edna smiled, gave Russ a kiss on the cheek, and left saying, "Guys, don't let him take you for any more money. He's got a bunch of sure bets he can make. He knows me all too well."

Edna decided to go talk with Marie for a while and see how she was doing.

"Honey, how are things going?" Edna asked Marie, who was now stretched out sunbathing on one of the chaise lounges.

"Just great, Edna. This is a terrific weekend, isn't it?"

"Yes. Say, I wanted to let you know that I asked Russ to talk with Eric about marriage and how wonderful it is. Doesn't hurt to gently push the issue. You two have been dating for too many years now."

"I know, Edna. I don't know why he won't agree to set a date. I really love him and know he loves me. I'm past ready to become his wife."

"Well, honey, have you suggested a wedding date; or better yet, have you brought up the subject with him directly?"

"Well, we've discussed our future at times during our long engagement. We both talk about 'when we are married,' but he just has not taken that last step of asking me to marry him. I want children before I feel like their grandmother."

"I know how you feel. Russ and I have been trying to have children since we first got married. He's promised me though, that if we don't have a child in the next year that we can adopt one. I want a child no matter what."

"I know how you feel. You've been saying you wanted a family ever since I've known you. Me too. Eric just seems reluctant to make that final commitment. I still haven't met his family. They're back in the midwest. I've spoken with his mother once on the telephone when I was over at Eric's place, and she seems very nice. I really don't know why he's so hesitant."

"Marie, honey. It's been my experience that sometimes you need to steer a man in the direction you want him to go. If subtle hints don't do the trick, then a direct question, or ultimatum is the next step. Don't let him stay so safe. Let him know you won't always be there unless he sets a date to get married. If he can't step up to the plate, then it's time for you to move on with your life."

"Oh, honey, I can't. I love him."

"Marie, I know you do. But, you'd be surprised at how many people you can love in your life. Love comes from you, not from the other person. If you decide to love someone you pretty much can."

"Well, it's easy for you to say, Edna, because the men have always flocked to you. With me, I'm more reserved and frankly don't attract men the way you do. I've found in Eric a man with the temperament, looks, and values that I am completely compatible with. He's the one for me."

"Well, honey. As I said, I've asked Russ to talk with him about marriage. Let's see how that turns out. You two need to tie the knot. Where is Eric anyway? I haven't seen much of him today."

"You know how he doesn't like to sit in the sun. His skin won't take it. He's in the tropical room, probably playing solitaire or darts and having a cocktail. I think Russ was in there talking with him for a while, and I saw Milt go in for awhile."

"Oh, okay. Well, I'd better mingle with some of the others. I'll talk with you later, honey."

"Okay, Edna." Marie took a sip of her vodka tonic, and laid back in the chaise lounge to do some more serious sunbathing.

Edna walked over to where Norma and Jim were now sitting alone under a table with umbrella. The young couple appeared somewhat uncomfortable. Edna wanted everyone to have a good time at her house. "How are you two enjoying yourselves?"

"Oh, just fine, Edna. Thank you," said Norma. "Sit down and join us for a minute."

"Okay. Did you and Daphne have a nice talk comparing notes about modeling?"

"Oh, yes. She's a terrific woman. I'm going to stop by and see her at the department store one day and maybe go to lunch or get a cup of coffee. She has a lot of experience in the modeling field."

"Yes. She's sharp. I thought you two would get along. She has some experience and contacts in modeling that might be helpful to you." Then Edna turned her attention to Jim.

"Jim, how are you enjoying your day?"

"Fine."

"Did you want another cocktail?"

"No, thank you."

"How about you, Norma?"

"Oh, no, Edna, my seltzer's fine. I'm not old enough to drink —— not legally anyway."

"Would you like a tour of the house?"

"Oh, yes. I'd love that. Jimmy, come with us?"

"No, Norma. I'll relax out here if you don't mind."

"Okay. Let's go, Norma. I'll show you our place."

Edna took Norma Jeane on a full tour of the house. They entered the downstairs patio doors and started into the bamboo room area. Eric was standing playing the nickel slot machine.

"Oh, this is so adorable, Edna," Norma Jeane gushed. "I feel like I'm on vacation in this room, far away from the Los Angeles area. I love that bamboo bar. It's like what I imagine Hawaii or Tahiti to be like. Did you have an interior decorator decorate it?"

"No. Russ and I did it together. He's real handy with a hammer, and I love to decorate. We came up with the ideas together. Living by the beach, we thought the bamboo and rattan, easy-living style was appropriate."

"It's perfect."

"Eric, are you winning?"

"Not yet, Edna, but I'm working at breaking the bank."

"Eric, this is Norma."

"Hi, Norma," said Eric, barely glancing at her.

"Nice to meet you, Eric," said Norma.

Edna then took Norma upstairs to see the main living room and dining room area, again, both done in a rattan and bamboo theme.

"I love your furniture. Your house is so warm and cozy. I sure could live in a place like this."

"Well, we sure like it. It's not huge, but it suits our purposes. It's plenty for the two of us. But, with children, I don't know if this place will be large enough."

"Oh, I love children. Do you have one or two bedrooms?"

"Let me show you." Edna took Norma through the two bedrooms, one of which was converted into a combination home office and den. Both rooms were neat as a pin. Spotless.

"Oh, this is so cute." Norma pointed to a knickknack of a little girl figurine that Edna had on top of her bedroom dresser. "I want a baby soon, too. In my dresser at home, one drawer is already full of baby clothes. I take them out sometimes and look at them, then refold them. I so want a child to call my own, to be my family." Norma seemed suddenly sad.

"Well, honey, you and Jimmy just got married. And, you're both young. Give it some time. You'll get your wish."

"I hope so. I've never had a real family to call my own that I could depend on. It's my dream to have my own family."

"I know how you feel, Norma. I was lucky enough to have a wonderful family for a few years until both my parents and a little brother passed. But, having a child to complete our family is what I dream of now. It means a lot to me. So, I sure understand your longing."

"Yes." Norma still looked sad and changed the subject. "Your house is so charming. Thanks for showing it to me. It gives Jimmy and me something to strive for."

"Well, you're just starting out. You'll have a home of your own that you like one day."

"I sure hope so. It would mean so much to me. I've never had a place that felt like mine. I'm ready for that."

"Sure, honey. Well, let's go back and join the gang, huh? They'll be wondering what we're up to."

"Sure, Edna. And, thanks again for the tour and for inviting us over."

"Sure, honey."

The two women went back outside to find Jim still sitting under the umbrella, but he was now talking with Chuck. Norma joined them. Russ and Ann were dancing in a playful way to some Spanish song, and Russ had switched from his Captain's hat to his Spanish bolero hat with the black dangling round baubles.

"Russ, I leave you for five minutes and you hog the limelight," Edna kidded him.

"Ann's the entertainer, sweetheart, not me. But, life is for the living. Enjoy yourself. Here, you dance with Ann while I make you another cocktail. You need to get with the spirit of the party."

"Rusty, we're having fun, pretending we're in Spain celebrating after a bullfight," Ann offered. "Let's dance while Russ gets you a picker-upper."

Ann and Edna danced to the Spanish dance, suddenly becoming very flamboyant and entertaining everyone with their antics. All eyes were on them.

As the dance was ending, Edna whispered into Ann's ear, then took the lead by taking her in her arms and holding her backwards over one arm in a grand finale. Everyone laughed and applauded.

"Now who's hogging the attention? Here's your drink, honey. Drink up. Enjoy yourself," Russ then grabbed Ann's hand again to dance the next number.

The afternoon was another fun Sunday, and the group stayed on until around six, when it finally began to break up. It had been a full, busy day, and Edna was happy to collapse for a few minutes into the living room chair before starting the cleanup. "Honey, we're so lucky," Edna said to Russ as he joined her in the living room.

"We sure are, baby. Life could not be better."

"No," responded Edna. *Unless we had a child.*

The radio began to play "My Baby Just Cares for Me," and Russ got up and held out his hand to Edna. "Come on, my baby, one last dance before I help you clean up."

CHAPTER THIRTY-ONE

PALM SPRINGS AND THE RUSSELL CLUB

Poolside at the Mirador Hotel, it was 100 degrees in the shade. Edna, Russ, Norma Jeane, and Daphne were in Palm Springs for the weekend. Norma's husband Jim was off on Catalina Island in Coast Guard training, so Russ and Edna had been spending some time with the young woman. Norma had stayed over in Catalina with Jim for a while but had now come back home to stay with his parents and work some.

Russ and Edna often spent time with Daphne. All three of them bet over their gin rummy games. Daphne and Norma Jeane had struck up a friendship since the barbecue. Daphne had shared with Norma her modeling agencies contacts and had guided her with information about her calendar shoot.

"Come on, Norma, let's cool off in the pool," Daphne egged the younger woman on. "Put on that new bathing cap you bought this morning."

Norma Jeane and Daphne had gone shopping this morning while Russ and Edna slept late in the adjoining room. After awakening, Russ and Edna ate a leisurely room service breakfast and read the Sunday paper.

"Okay, Daphne." Norma Jeane reached into her bag and took out her new bathing cap. It still had a price tag on it, which she removed, being careful not to tear the cap which was made out of a new type of thin clear plastic combined with a soft rubber. When she placed it on her head, her platinum hair shown through. It was the first time any of them had seen a see-through bathing cap.

"Norma, your hair looks gorgeous in that cap. Your blond hair is accentuated more than ever. That is the prettiest bathing cap I think I've ever seen." Russ was the first to compliment the new-style bathing cap.

"Yes," Edna agreed. "It's striking."

"Like I told her," Daphne said, "one should always try and be unique. Don't be the same as everyone else. Make yourself different. Don't follow the crowd because then you remain ordinary. Be special. Isn't that cap just the most perfect for her hair?" Daphne was preaching on her high horse again, but Daphne lived what she said. She was stunningly individual, and often dramatic in her pronouncements.

"Yes. Great choice. Your hair shimmers. That cap is so attractive on you, Norma Jeane," Russ responded again.

"Not everyone's hair would look pretty flattened into a cap like that. I suppose the hair coloring is what makes it particularly striking," Edna said.

"Edna and Russ, come swimming with us," said Norma Jeane.

"I'd like to relax and just enjoy watching you two for now," said Russ, with a large smile and gleam in his eye.

"I'm not a swimmer, honey," said Edna. "I'm enjoying myself just lying on this chaise and relaxing with Russ."

"Okay. Well, here we go," said Norma Jeane.

Daphne also had a beautiful swim cap on, black background like her hair, with large pink plastic flowers on one side. Her bathing suit was black, and she looked to Edna much too well-groomed and sophisticated to get wet. As she entered the water, however, it was clear that she was a terrific swimmer. She did the breast stroke the length of the pool, turned and then swam back very easily and gracefully while keeping her head above the water and her make-up dry. Edna admired Daphne. The woman was smart as a whip and as talented and confident as they came.

Norma Jeane, on the other hand, sat on the top step of the pool and left her feet dangling in the water for a while, getting used to the water temperature which, although warm, was cooler than the outside air. She was tentative, and posed languidly by the poolside before entering the water.

Edna noticed how Russ kept his eyes glued on the sensual young woman and for the first time in their marriage she felt jealousy. Norma Jeane was indeed sensuous and her hair color was gorgeous, but Russ didn't have to stare. That was so unlike him.

"Russ, would you order me a bourbon and coke, honey?" Edna needed to redirect his attention.

"Sure. I could use a Bloody Mary myself." Russ looked around and did not see the poolside waiter, so he got up from his chaise lounge and walked over to the poolside bar. He ordered their drinks.

The bartender was also captivated by Norma Jeane. She was now in the water up to her waist but was more gently splashing with and in the water rather than swimming.

"That's one good-looking woman," the bartender offered.

"Yes. She sure is. She's still a teenager, though. And, married," Russ offered.

"Well, I can enjoy looking, can't I?" the bartender said as he tried to pay attention to making the two drinks.

"Doesn't cost a thing," Russ said and winked. "I'm trying to keep my watching to a minimum because I can feel my wife getting upset. I've never seen her jealous of any female before, but that young woman just exudes something different from most women."

"That's for sure. She's walking sexuality. I watched her walk to the pool and I wanted to jump over the bar and help her into the pool. She's the type a guy wants to rescue, to protect."

"Whoa, down boy. Although I know what you mean. She makes a man feel like a man without even trying. It's nice to have her around. My wife has taken her under her wing, but if I show too much interest I'm afraid that she may not be part of our crowd much longer."

"How long are you here for?"

"We're going home this evening. We drove up from Manhattan Beach Friday night after work, but this is our first day in the sun. We showed Norma Jeane around the town and the gals went shopping. Today's our day in the sun before back to work for me tomorrow."

"Well, here are your drinks. Do me a favor, would you? If the waiter isn't around, call me over when that young blondie wants a drink. I'll help her out."

"Sure." Russ signed his room number and name to the check, included a nice tip, and returned to Edna and the chaise lounge with the two cool drinks.

"Here, honey," Russ set the drinks down on the small table between their two chaise lounges. "Some refreshment for you."

"Thanks." Edna's tone lacked its usual warmth.

"I'm going to move my chaise to follow the sun, honey," Russ said, "to keep my tan even. Did you want yours moved?"

"No, thanks. You know how I freckle. This is fine." Edna took a sip of her drink, and then leaned back in her chaise again. Russ moved his out from under the shady overhang to get more sun on his face and chest area, rather than just on his legs.

Through her sunglasses Edna could see Norma Jeane talking with a little girl about seven years of age in the shallow end of the pool. As she watched them interacting, Edna thought about the fact that Norma was just barely out of childhood herself. How silly for Edna to be jealous of her. Edna suddenly felt foolish and resolved to change her perception about Russ, Norma Jeane, the bathing cap, the hair. Besides, the little girl in the pool revived Edna's maternal instincts again. It was time to complete her own family.

The following Friday night, Edna and Russ had made a date to meet for a drink, then dinner, at the Russell Club in downtown Los Angeles after Russ got off of work. Edna took a cab to meet him since there was no longer a train or streetcar from the beach to downtown. The driver let Edna off in front of the Russell Club around 5:15 p.m. Edna entered and saw that the place was dark, and still fairly empty. Russ was to meet her there at 5:30.

The Russell Club was one of the few clubs that permitted women to sit at the bar. After all, it was wartime, and women were doing the jobs of men in the factories and elsewhere. Edna took a seat at the empty bar and asked the bartender for a gin martini, up.

"Sure, ma'am."

"Please, Edna's my name. 'Ma'am' makes me feel so old. Or, my nickname is Rusty. Take your pick."

"I'm Gary."

"Well, Gary, my husband, Russell Newman is meeting me here in about ten minutes. Help me play a joke on him. I'm going to pretend that I don't know who he is, and let him try and flirt with me. I want to see if he notices my new hairdo."

"Well, your own husband should recognize you."

"We'll see."

Edna nursed her drink for a few minutes and sat anxiously awaiting Russ's arrival. She puffed on her cigarette to try and calm her nerves. She looked in the mirror behind the bar periodically to make certain her hairdo was all in place.

Around 5:35, the door opened, and Russ entered, took off his hat, and sat down at the bar about four seats away from her.

"Gary, I'll take a gin martini, up."

"Sure thing, Russ." Gary went to make the drink, and Edna silently sipped her cocktail.

It was obvious to Edna that Russ was still preoccupied from his day at work, but she was becoming somewhat upset that he did not even look her way. She pulled out a new cigarette, placed it to her mouth and asked Russ if she could have a light. He politely said, "sure," got up from his stool, walked over and lit her cigarette. Then he returned to his seat.

After Russ took a couple of sips from his drink he asked Gary, "I'm supposed to meet my wife here. Has anyone called for me, or been in and left?"

"No, Russ."

"She's usually early. She was taking a cab here from the beach. Well, maybe she's caught in traffic."

"Yes. Could be." Gary played along.

Edna sat and fumed and then took a large sip of her cocktail. Her own husband didn't know her. *Maybe he's getting tired of me. Is our romance over?*

Russ, relaxing now, took a look down the bar to his right and noticed Edna's dwindling drink.

"Gary, will you buy that gorgeous blonde a drink on me," said Russ loud enough for Edna to hear him.

"It's me, Russ. Don't you recognize me?" Edna couldn't stand it any longer.

With that, both Russ and Gary burst out laughing. "I knew it was you the whole time. I wanted to see what you would do. I called earlier and told Gary you were going to meet me here and would probably be early as usual, and that he should treat you right."

Russ and Gary exchanged looks and started laughing again. Edna fumed for a couple of seconds, then started laughing with them. Her joke had backfired. They had put one over on her.

Russ moved down the barstools and sat next to his platinum blonde wife.

"You've been busy today I see," he said.

"How do you like it?" Edna asked.

"Lovely. Do you think it goes with your freckles, though?"

"Russ." Edna gave him a gentle slap against his arm. "Quit teasing me. I did this because --"

"I know why you did it. You couldn't stand the way I was complimenting Norma Jeane last weekend. It was actually that see-through bathing cap I was admiring."

"Oh, I really believe that. You are a cad. Here I try and do something different for you to reignite our romance and you turn the joke on me. I don't know what I'm going to do with you."

"Keep loving me, I hope."

"Well, that's a given. So do you really like it?"

"Sure, but we can't call you Rusty anymore. Do you think I should dye the few locks I have left platinum to match your hairdo? Then we can be Goldie and Goldilocks, or Frick and Frack?"

"Very funny. I just thought this would be fun for a change. I'm a new woman, your blond bombshell."

"You are a bombshell, honey. That's for certain, no matter what color your hair is. You keep me entertained. I never know what you're going to do next."

"Good. I like to keep you guessing."

Russ started to tease her again.

216

"How about a bite to eat, gorgeous? My wife won't have to know."

"Sure, handsome. I'm game." Edna played along.

"In fact, you're such a looker, I might have to take you out to a fancy club like Mocambo or Ciro's, and show you off. It's not often I'm escorting a beautiful platinum blonde."

Russ and Edna got off their respective stools, and Russ left the drink money and a big tip for Gary on the bar. "Adios, Gary. We're off to paint the town. See you soon."

As they walked towards the door, a framed movie poster on the wall caught Edna's eye. "Oh, look, Russ. That's the movie I was in. And, look at the tiny print at the bottom, 'introducing Miss Katherine King.' What do you know?"

"That's terrific, sweetheart. We'll have to get one of those for our tropical game room."

For a moment Edna thought about what it would have been like to have become famous in the movies, to have had the adulation and respect of thousands of fans. *No. I have my self-respect, and the respect of the man I love. That's enough for me.*

Edna put her arm through Russ's and the couple walked out of the Russell Club for an evening of dinner and dancing. "Look at that moon tonight, Russ. It's beautiful." Edna started singing, "The moon belongs to ev'ryone. The best things in life are free ..."

THE END

EPILOGUE

On April 9, 1947, criminal conspiracy indictments were handed down in the case of "The United States of America v. National City Lines, Inc., American City Lines, Inc., Pacific City Lines, Inc., Firestone Tire & Rubber Company, General Motors Corporation, Phillips Petroleum Company, Mack Manufacturing Corporation, Standard Oil Company of California and its subsidiary Federal Engineering Corporation, et al."

On March 12, 1949, the jury found the well-defended defendants guilty of "conspiracy to monopolize the transit business" in order to sell their own oil, tires, and motor vehicles. The streetcar conspiracy affected sixteen states, forty-two cities, and millions of Americans.

The judge sentenced each defendant corporation a fine of $5,000.00; except for Standard Oil, whose fine was $1,000.00. Some individual executives were given fines of one dollar each.

Today in Los Angeles, many of the old trolley car routes that had for years fallen by the wayside from intentional disrepair are once again being utilized for public transportation. At great expense to the taxpayers, new electric railways and new subways have been resurrected on those old rights-of-way. The automobile overcrowding on the streets and freeways was one of the primary justifications given to the citizens of Los Angeles to encourage their support for the tremendous expense entailed in the construction of an entirely new public transportation system.

BIBLIOGRAPHY

Allen, Frederick Lewis, *Since Yesterday, The 1930s in America, September 3, 1929 - September 3, 1939*. Perennial Library ed., Harper & Row, Publishers, Inc., New York,

Beauchamp, Cari, *Without Lying Down, Frances Marion and the Powerful Women of Early Hollywood*. A Lisa Drew Book/ Scribner, Simon & Schuster, Inc., New York, 1997. *Joseph P. Kennedy Presents: His Hollywood Years*. Knopf, New York, 2009. *Adventures of a Hollywood Secretary, Her Private Letters from Inside the Studios of the 1920s, Letters of Valeria Belletti*. University of California Press, Berkeley and Los Angeles, 2006.

Bengtson, John. *Silent Traces, Discovering Early Hollywood Through the Films of Charlie Chaplin*. Santa Monica Press, Santa Monica, 2006.

Black, Edwin. *Internal Combustion: How Corporations and Governments Addicted the World to Oil and Derailed the Alternatives*. St. Martin's Press, New York, 2006.

Diehl, Digby. *Front Page: 100 Years of the "Los Angeles Times" 1881-1981."* Harry N. Abrams, Inc., New York, 1981.

Dreiser, Theodore. *The Titan*. John Lane Company, New York, 1914.

Freeth, Nick. *Remembering the '40s: Decade in Words and Pictures*. Barnes & Noble Books, New York, 2002.

Goddard, Stephen B. *Getting There: The Epic Struggle between Road and Rail in the American Century*. University of Chicago Press, 1996.

Griffith, Richard and Arthur Mayer. *The Movies*. Simon and Schuster, New York, 1970.

Kyvig, David E. *Daily Life in the United States 1920-1940: How Americans Lived Through the Roaring Twenties and the Great Depression.* Ivan R. Dee, Chicago, 2004.

Lord, Rosemary. *Hollywood Then and Now.* Thunder Bay Press, San Diego, California, 2003.

McCutcheon, Marc. *The Writer's Guide to Everyday Life from Prohibition through World War II.* Writer's Digest Books, an imprint of F&W Publications, Inc., Cincinnati, Ohio, 1995.

Parker, Robert Miles. *L.A.* Harcourt Brace Jovanovich, Publishers, San Diego, New York, London, 1984.

Phillips, Kevin. *American Dynasty.* Viking Penguin, New York, 2004.

Quinby, Cdr. E.J. *Interurban Interlude.* Model Craftsman Publishing Corp., Ramsey, N.J., 1968.

Sinclair, Upton. *Oil!* Penguin Books, New York, 2007.

Walker, Jim. *Los Angeles Railway Yellow Cars.* Arcadia Publishing, 2007.

Walker, Jim. *Pacific Electric Red Cars.* Arcadia Publishing, 2006.

Williams, Gregory Paul. *The Story of Hollywood, An Illustrated History.* BL Press LLC, 2011.

Wolfe, Donald H. *The Last Days of Marilyn Monroe.* William Morrow and Company, Inc., New York, 1998.

PERIODICALS

Mencken, H.L., ed. "Strolling Along the Boulevard," in "Americana." *The American Mercury.* Alfred A. Knopf Publisher, New York, 1928. Vol. 14, No. 55, July 1928, p. 312.

Quirk, James R., ed. *Photoplay Magazine.* Photoplay Publishing Company, New York, Chicago, Vol. 32, No. 5, October 1927. *Photoplay Magazine.* Photoplay Publishing Company, New York, Chicago, Vol. 34, No. 5, October 1928.

Photoplay. Photoplay Publishing Company, New York, Chicago. October 1931.

DOCUMENTARIES

Who Killed the Electric Car? A Sony Classics Release, Electric Entertainment. Dean Devlin/Punyminor Production; a film by Chris Paine. 2006 EV Confidential LLC.

This Was Pacific Electric. Six City Productions, Inc. Christine Vasquez, producer; Thom Eberhardt, writer and director.

MOVIES

There are too many movies to list. Every popular movie from the 1920s, 1930s and 1940s has been viewed in gathering background information for this book. However, two more recent classics should be mentioned: *Who Framed Roger Rabbit,* and *Chinatown.* And, although *Hollywood Heyday* was conceptualized more than ten years ago, and the first draft was finished before *The Artist* was released, kudos must be given to that Academy-Award winning motion picture which beautifully captured the tone, era and history of early Hollywood.

MISCELLANEOUS
ACKNOWLEDGEMENTS

Thanks must be given to the Orange Empire Railway Museum and its devoted staff who showed me around the park with its wonderful old red cars and yellow cars one very hot day in Perris, California. An intelligent, long-time volunteer at Orange Empire told me he does not believe that there was ever a conspiracy to get rid of the wonderful Los Angeles area trolley cars. I would surmise there are those at certain corporations who would say the same. Even the truth can be approached from more than one perspective, and many near-truths, half-truths, and non-truths proliferate.

Thanks is also due to Anna Olswanger whose encouragement helped to move this book forward when at times the muse was dormant. She instilled in me the concept I fought, i.e., that writing is rewriting; and, by stating she wanted others to "love the book as much as I do," she inspired me to propel the rewrites beyond each doldrum. Grateful acknowledgement also for the use of her brilliantly talented father's name, Berl Olswanger.

Acknowledgement is also given to the late Helen Thomas who thought 1930s Hollywood to be the most exciting of Hollywood's periods, and encouraged me to "write … write" this book about those times.

Grateful acknowledgement is made for the fictional use of the names and likeness of Mary Pickford, Clark Gable, Donna Reed, Ozzie Nelson, Norma Jeane and Jim Dougherty. Also thanks is due for the fictional use of the image and likeness of the great Al Jolson and the historic movie *The Jazz Singer*.

Credit must be given for the use of lyrics from "The Best Things in Life are Free," the 1927 song written by Buddy DeSylva, Lew Brown, and Ray Henderson. The lyrics still have universal appeal which time has not diminished.

I'd like to address a reader who found the heroine too earnest. Sincerity and integrity were exactly the intention. In this era of edge, dark subject matter, greed and blustering narcissism, we could use more sincerity.

Loving gratitude must go to my mother whose many oral stories of her days spent in Texas, and in Hollywood of the early 30s and 40s, find their expression in the pages of this book. Hopefully the words herein captured some of her vivid description. And, yes, her sincerity, values and heartfelt warmth formed the basis for the heroine of this book.